IN A GILDED CAGE

IN A GILDED CAGE

RHYS BOWEN

WHEELER
CHIVERS

This Large Print edition is published by Wheeler Publishing, Waterville, Maine, USA and by BBC Audiobooks Ltd, Bath, England.
Wheeler Publishing, a part of Gale, Cengage Learning.
A Molly Murphy Mystery.

The text of this Large Print edition is unabridged.
Other aspects of the book may vary from the original edition.
Set in 16 pt. Plantin.
Printed on permanent paper.

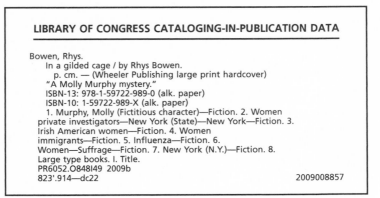

LIBRARY OF CONGRESS CATALOGING-IN-PUBLICATION DATA

Bowen, Rhys.
    In a gilded cage / by Rhys Bowen.
        p. cm. — (Wheeler Publishing large print hardcover)
    "A Molly Murphy mystery."
    ISBN-13: 978-1-59722-989-0 (alk. paper)
    ISBN-10: 1-59722-989-X (alk. paper)
        1. Murphy, Molly (Fictitious character)—Fiction. 2. Women private investigators—New York (State)—New York—Fiction. 3. Irish American women—Fiction. 4. Women immigrants—Fiction. 5. Influenza—Fiction. 6. Women—Suffrage—Fiction. 7. New York (N.Y.)—Fiction. 8. Large type books. I. Title.
    PR6052.O848I49 2009b
    823'.914—dc22   2009008857

BRITISH LIBRARY CATALOGUING-IN-PUBLICATION DATA AVAILABLE

Published in 2009 in the U.S. by arrangement with St. Martin's Press, LLC.
Published in 2009 in the U.K. by arrangement with the author.

U.K. Hardcover: 978 1 408 44205 0 (Chivers Large Print)
U.K. Softcover: 978 1 408 44206 7 (Camden Large Print)

Printed in the United States of America
1 2 3 4 5 6 7 13 12 11 10 09

ACKNOWLEDGMENTS

Grateful thanks to Doris Ann Norris for sending me a book called *Lee's Priceless Recipes,* published 1895, containing, among other things, the secrets to patent medicines, cosmetics, and other glorious ways to poison people without really trying.

As always thanks to my home-based editing team: Clare, Jane, and John for their insights, as well as my New York team, Kelley Ragland and Meg Ruley.

ONE

It is a well-known fact that we Irish are prone to bouts of melancholy, even without the help of the bottle. I suppose it goes along with the Celtic temperament and long, wet winters. Anyway, I was experiencing such a bout myself as I trudged home through a rainstorm that was wetter and colder than anything I had experienced at home in Ireland. March winds and April showers bring forth May flowers — that was how I learned it at school in Ballykillin. Well, it was now the middle of April and the gale that was accompanying the rain was worse than anything we'd experienced in March. I would never understand the New York weather! One minute it could be sunny and springlike and suddenly the temperature would plunge thirty degrees and we'd be back in winter again.

We had endured a particularly long, cold winter, with snow well into March. The bleak conditions had produced all kinds of sicknesses and people had been dropping like flies as influenza of the nastiest kind had turned to pneumonia. Even I, usually known for my robust constitution, had succumbed and spent over a week with a raging fever that finally subsided, leaving me feeling weak and drained. It had been almost three weeks now and I had hardly left the house until my small detective agency, P. Riley and Associates (I now being sole proprietor and associate rolled into one), received a job offer I simply couldn't turn down. It was from Macy's new department store, at Thirty-fourth Street and Herald Square. They wanted me to look into a case of shoplifting that even their own store detectives had not managed to stop. Naturally I was thrilled and flattered, and I accepted immediately. I would have crawled from my deathbed for such an assignment. If I was successful, who knew where it might lead?

The weather had finally been springlike when I set off for work that morning, which was why I'd worn my light business two-piece and not thought to take a top-coat or a brolly. Both of which I was now regretting as I came out of Macy's to find that the temperature had plunged again and it was blowing a gale. Within seconds I was soaked to the skin, freezing cold, and thoroughly miserable.

I should have been feeling on top of the world. I'd just concluded another successful case. In the guise of a new counter assistant I had spotted the pilfered goods being smuggled out in the trash by one of Macy's own employees and then retrieved from the big trash bins by an accomplice. I had been handsomely rewarded for my services and was glowing with pride, dying to share my news with somebody when I stepped out of Macy's back door and into the gale.

I had hopped on a passing Broadway trolley and later regretted this move as well, as I had to walk home from Broadway with the rain driving straight into my face and one hand jamming my charming spring hat onto my head. By the time I was halfway home I was well and truly sorry for myself. I was still weak, of course. I was not usually the kind of person who wallowed in self-pity or thought of herself as a helpless female. But as I trudged onward I was overwhelmed with gloomy thoughts. I longed for home and family and someone to take care of me.

I suppose this wave of blackness and insecurity had something to do with my intended, Daniel Sullivan. We weren't officially betrothed yet, but we had definitely reached the stage of an understanding. And it was this that was making me unsettled and jittery.

Had my mother still been alive, she would have relished telling me that I was never satisfied. I suppose she was right — when Daniel had been in disgrace and on suspension from his position as captain of police, he had shown up on my doorstep every single day, and I had found myself wishing he'd be reinstated quickly, not just for his sake but for mine too. I found myself seriously wondering whether marriage and domestic bliss were what I wanted for myself.

But recently he had been reinstated under the new commissioner of police and since then I had scarcely seen him. He had popped in once while I was at the height of my sickness, expressed concern, and then fled, not to be seen again. So now I was filled with doubts: did this lack of attention mean that he had tired of me, or was he merely taking me for granted now that he had more interesting ways to spend his time? If I married him I'd have to come to terms with the fact that this was what life as a policeman's wife would be like. And how would I take to being the good little woman, sitting at home with my darning, waiting for him and worrying about him? Plenty of food for thought there. Never satisfied, I chided myself. Wants security but doesn't want to be tied down. Wants love but wants freedom. Wants . . .

I never did get to the third want, as a great gust of wind swept off the Hudson and snatched my hat from my head. I gave a scream of despair and leaped after it. It was a new hat, my first extravagant purchase since my detective agency started to make money, and I wasn't about to see it disappear under the wheels of a passing wagon or hansom cab. I lifted my skirts and chased it in most undignified fashion to Fifth Avenue. Then a particularly violent gust caught it again and swept it out into the street just as I was about to pick it up. I didn't think twice as I ran after it. There was an angry honking and I was conscious of a low black shape hurtling toward me.

"Holy mother of God," I gasped as I flung myself to one side. The automobile screeched to a halt inches in front of my hat, which now lay in the mud.

"What the devil do you think you're doing," shouted an angry voice. "You could have gotten yourself killed."

"I'm sorry," I began, then my mouth dropped open as the gentleman removed his driving goggles and I recognized him at the same moment he recognized me. "Daniel!" I exclaimed.

"Molly, what a damned stupid thing to do," he snapped. "These machines go fast, you know. And they don't stop on a dime. They're not like horses."

"I said I was sorry," I snapped back, feeling foolish now as a crowd gathered. "The wind took my hat and I wasn't about to lose it." As I said this I stepped gingerly into the mud and retrieved the hat, which was rain-soaked and definitely the worse for wear.

"Climb up," Daniel reached across to open the door for me, "and I'll drive you home. You look as if you've been dragged through a hedge backward."

"Thank you for the compliment, kind sir," I retorted, and was about to say I'd rather walk. But common sense won out, of course, and I dutifully climbed up to sit beside Daniel in the automobile.

"What were you doing out in this rain without an umbrella?" Daniel said, still glaring at me angrily. "You have no business being out at all on a day like this. You've been seriously ill, Molly."

"I was feeling better and, anyway, I had

12

an assignment," I said. "It was too good to turn down. And if you want to know, when I left home at seven this morning the sky was blue. And believe me, I've regretted the decision to wear my spring clothes every moment of the last half hour."

Daniel looked at my angry face, with my hair plastered to my cheeks and drops running freely down my nose, and started to laugh. "I shouldn't laugh, I know." He attempted to stop smiling. "But you really do look like the orphan of the storm. Come here. Let me kiss that little wet nose."

He pulled me toward him and kissed the tip of my nose, then put his hand under my chin and repeated the process on my lips. His mouth was warm against mine and I found myself climbing down just a little from my high horse.

"Right, let's get you home and out of those wet clothes before you catch pneumonia," Daniel said. "I have to be back at headquarters within the hour, though."

He released the brake and put his foot on the accelerator pedal. The machine responded by coughing, bucking like a wild bronco, and then dying. Daniel muttered a curse under his breath and stepped down into the storm. "Now I've got to start the blasted thing again," he said. I watched while he took out the crank, went around to the front of the vehicle, and cranked several times before the contraption coughed and sprang to life. Daniel hopped in smartly before it could stall again and we were off. I glanced at him and started to laugh. "Now who looks like the orphan of the storm?" I said triumphantly.

In a minute or so we had pulled up outside my little house in Patchin Place. It is a street some might describe as an alley, but I think of it as a charming backwater in Greenwich Village. Miraculously the rain chose the same moment to stop, and a patch of blue appeared between the dark storm clouds. Daniel climbed down and came around to assist me. I opened the door, put on the kettle, and went to change out of my wet clothes. There wasn't much to be done about my sodden hair but at least the rest of me looked dry and respectable as I came downstairs again.

"Sometimes I despair of you," Daniel said. "Sit down. I'll make the tea."

He took the kettle from the hob and filled the teapot. "You don't have any brandy or rum to put into it, I suppose?"

"I don't," I said. "I live a very frugal life, as you well know."

He smiled. "Pity. Well, at least this will be

14

hot and sweet. Better than nothing." He poured me a cup. "Get that down you, woman." He looked at me with fond exasperation. "You haven't an ounce of common sense in your body, have you? When you're not risking your life by chasing murderers you're risking it by not taking care of your health. This is not an ordinary influenza, you know. I can't tell you how many funeral processions I've witnessed in the past weeks. One of our own men, a strapping lad of twenty-five, went down with it and was dead within three days. And yet you go running around in a storm when you should still be in bed."

"I couldn't turn it down, Daniel," I said. "It was Macy's department store. They were offering a handsome fee and it was a case their own store detective hadn't managed to crack."

"And were you successful?"

"I was. They thought they had a clever shoplifter, but it turned out to be a conspiracy of their own employees — a counter assistant who dropped small items into a passing trash bin and another accomplice who retrieved the items from the trash. I was lucky enough to spot a bottle of perfume disappearing from a counter."

"Good for you," Daniel said. "Now let's

hope you live to enjoy the spoils."

"I'm feeling much better," I said. "Or at least I was when I set out this morning. And I can't say you've seemed overly concerned about the state of my health until now. You took one look at my fevered brow and beat a hasty retreat, never to be seen again."

Daniel grimaced. "Yes, I know. I'm sorry about that."

"I understand that gentlemen have an aversion to being around sickness."

"No, it wasn't that, I assure you. I was most concerned about you."

"So concerned that I've not seen you in two weeks and had to throw myself in front of your automobile to get your attention."

He managed a grin. "Actually I've been on a case that has kept me busy day and night. I've hardly even had a chance to sleep."

"What kind of case is it?" I took a long swig of hot tea and felt the warmth going through my body. "Let me know if I can be of help."

Daniel smiled in a way that I took as patronizing. "My dear girl, you know I can't discuss a criminal case with you, and I certainly wouldn't let you help me."

"You don't think I'm any good as a detective?" I asked.

"I think you're very competent in your own way," he said cautiously, "but I have to play by the rules, and besides, I try to keep you well away from murders of any sort. So you stick to your kind of investigations and I'll stick to mine."

"Don't be so damned patronizing." I flung the tea towel in his direction.

"My, we are testy, aren't we?" He laughed. "And I wasn't intending to be patronizing. I'm glad that your business is going well, but you know my feelings. I'd be much happier if you didn't have to work and especially if you didn't have to put yourself in harm's way. Now that I'm back on the job, we can make proper plans for the future. I'm saving up for a house, Molly."

"You haven't asked me to marry you yet," I reminded him.

"I intend to do it properly, at the right moment," he said.

"And you don't know that I'll say yes."

Those alarming blue eyes flashed. "No, I don't know that, but I'm hopeful. At least you're now seeing the reality of what life with me will be like. Odd hours. Coming and going. Calls in the middle of the night, and times when you'll see nothing of me for days on end."

"You make it sound so delightful. It's a

wonder I don't accept you on the spot," I retorted, and he chuckled.

"I know I've been neglecting you recently," he said. "I'll make it up to you when this case is successfully concluded, I promise."

"You must get Easter off, surely? Why don't we walk in the Easter Parade? I've always wanted to do that."

"The Easter Parade? Oh come, Molly. That is for the nouveaux riches wanting to show off their expensive hats, and I'm afraid that sodden chapeau of yours wouldn't be able to compete."

"I don't wish to compete. I just want to experience things that New Yorkers do," I said. "And I'd like a chance to stroll up the avenue with my beau on my arm for once."

"I wish we could, but the answer is no, I don't get Easter off. Not while people are killing each other all over the lower portion of Manhattan." He drained his teacup and stood up. "Speaking of which, I have to go, I'm afraid. I'm expected at headquarters. Good-bye, my sweet. Take care of yourself, please. No more walking out in the rain until you are completely recovered." He came over to me, kissed me on the forehead, and was out of the front door before I could even respond. I went to the door after him and watched him working furiously to crank that machine to life.

"You should stick to horses, they're easier to start," I called after him.

He looked up and grinned. "This is an experiment. The commissioner of police wants to find out if automobiles might be useful in police work. So far I'm not impressed." He gave another mighty jerk as he said this and the machine sputtered into action. With that he leaped onto the seat, waved, and reversed down Patchin Place.

Two

As the automobile chugged away from Patchin Place, the front door opposite me opened and my neighbor Sid's face peered out. "Hello, Molly. What was that infernal noise we just heard?"

"Daniel driving an automobile," I said. "He rescued me from the rain and drove me home."

"Come on over and have a glass of wine," Sid said. "We've got exciting news to share."

I needed no second urging to join her. My neighbors Elena Goldfarb and Augusta Walcott, usually known by their irreverent nicknames Sid and Gus, never failed to bring joy into my life. They were generous to a fault and always experimenting with new foods and cultural experiences, making each visit to their home an adventure. The fact that their own choice of lifestyle was not a universally accepted one was neither here nor there.

Sid ushered me into the drawing room with a flourish.

Gus was sitting in one of the armchairs beside a roaring fire, a glass of red wine in her hand and a black lace shawl, hung with jet beads, around her shoulders. In contrast Sid was wearing baggy trousers that looked as if they'd come from a Turkish harem. I scarcely noticed their strange manner of dress any longer, although I could see that it might appear startling to strangers.

Gus looked up. "Why, you've found Molly. How clever of you, just when we needed her. And did you discover what the infernal noise was?" she asked.

"It was Molly's Captain Sullivan, driving an automobile. But he delivered Molly from the rain so is to be pardoned on this occasion, one feels."

"What were you doing out in the rain to start with?" Gus frowned at me. "You are supposed to be staying in bed and recuperating. You've been quite ill, you know."

"I know, and I would have been much worse if you two hadn't looked after me so well. But I had a job to do at Macy's department store and the weather this morning seemed quite balmy, so off I went without an umbrella or top-coat. Luckily the wind blew my hat in front of Daniel's automobile,

21

so he motored me home."

"Horrid contraptions, automobiles," Gus said. "They'll never catch on, you mark my words. Think how noisy the city would become if everyone owned one. Sid and I think that flight is the transportation of the future. We should all have personal hot air balloons and drift serenely through the clouds."

"Rather inconvenient, don't you think?" I said. "We'd all be bumping into each other and if a strong wind came up we'd wind up in Boston when we wanted to go to Philadelphia."

Gus chuckled. "Ah, but think of the romance of flight. Why would one care about the destination? Sid, we have to find someone with a hot air balloon and cross the country in it. Think of sailing over the Rockies."

"Think of making a hard landing on a mountain peak," I said.

"Molly, you are entirely too practical. For heaven's sake, pour the girl a glass of wine and tell her about our grand outing."

Red wine was poured from a crystal decanter. I took a sip, savoring the smooth warmth as it went down my throat. I was still such a newcomer to luxuries like wine that each new tasting was a delightful experience.

"It's Hungarian," Sid said proudly. "We've never tried Hungarian wine before and this one is called Bull's Blood so of course we had to try it. It's divine, isn't it? Gus is now quite determined to go to Hungary and see the bulls for herself."

Gus chuckled. "You also expressed a desire to sail down the Danube from its source to the Black Sea."

Sid perched on the arm of Gus's chair and sighed. "There are too many choices in life. Too many places to go and things to do. And then one feels that one's life has become too frivolous and selfish and resolves to do something for the good of humanity."

"And if one is smart, one combines the two — adventure and philanthropy," Gus said. "Such will be our outing on Sunday, I hope."

"Sunday? Where will you be going on Sunday?"

"The Easter Parade. Where else?"

I registered surprise. "I should have thought that you two were the last people on earth to want to parade in your finery."

"We are," Sid answered, "unless it's for a good cause. We plan to march as part of the

VWVW brigade."

"The what?"

"It's an acronym for Vassar Wants Votes for Women," Gus explained. "We'll be part of a contingent of Vassar alums, bringing our cause before the populace of New York and, we hope, making more women conscious of the basic civil right still denied them."

I nodded approval. "I wish I'd been to Vassar so that I could join you."

"We'd love you to join us, Molly," Sid said. "But we felt that you would not be strong enough to walk the length of Fifth Avenue so soon after your sickness."

"I've a good Irish peasant constitution," I said, "and I was used to walking miles a day at home. I'm sure I'd be able to do it."

"Then I say the more the merrier." Sid raised her glass to me. "Nobody need know that you are not a Vassar girl. As it happens we haven't had the response we hoped for and will be low on numbers, so you'd truly be helping the cause."

"In that case I gladly accept. I suggested to Daniel that we take part in the parade and he was most scathing about it. He said it was only for the newly rich to show off."

"That is, of course, true," Sid agreed.

"Some of the Four Hundred also participate every year," Gus said. "I have relatives who always take part."

"Gus has relatives in every city, I swear," Sid commented, looking fondly at Gus.

"Will we be expected to dress up and wear fancy hats?" I said, beginning to have doubts as I realized that Vassar girls tended to be wealthy. "Because you've seen the extent of my wardrobe."

"Absolutely not. Your business costume will be ideal. We aim to look like responsible members of the community, not pampered darlings full of frippery. And they'll give us a sash to wear and a banner to carry, stating our purpose. So wear comfortable shoes. It's a long march."

"It's not that long," Gus interjected. "Only ten blocks. And I'm sure there will be a carriage available should one of the young ladies need to ride."

"I'll not need to ride and I'll come prepared," I said. "In fact I'm willing to do my share to help the cause. It is ridiculous that a businesswoman like myself should not have a say in the government."

"Well said, Molly. I can see you'll be a regular firebrand."

"Let us just hope that Sunday is fine and dry," Gus said. "It would be too bad if it rained as it did today."

"Will it be called off if it rains?" I asked.

"It's never been called off, has it, Gus?" Sid asked.

"Not that I can remember," Gus agreed. "The smart set don't care, of course. They simply raise the hood of their carriages and proceed from church as usual. But there would be a dearth of spectators if it rained like today."

"So most people ride in carriages, not walk?"

"Almost everyone does. We are walking so that we stand out and exhibit our solidarity with the masses," Sid said. "The parade starts at ten o'clock, so we'll leave here in time to muster at nine forty-five."

"Muster? You make it sound like a war." I laughed.

"It is," Sid said soberly. "An out-and-out war that must be won, Molly. We have lived as poor, dependent creatures for too long, at the mercy of our lords and masters. Now it is time we took control of our own destiny."

Inspired and inflamed, warmed by red wine and rhetoric, I went back to my own house.

THREE

Fortunately, Sunday dawned bright and clear. A cold wind was blowing, sending cotton-wool clouds racing across the sky, but there was no hint of rain as we left Patchin Place and caught the trolley to Forty-seventh Street, then walked to Fifth Avenue, where the parade would begin. A crowd had already formed along both sides of the avenue, starting at St. Nicholas Church, and some rather elegant carriages were lined up, in the starting gate, so to speak. Even a rapid glance showed some startling Easter bonnets that were not bonnets at all but hats adorned with every kind of fruit, flower, feather, and even bird known to creation.

In contrast, the Vassar girls were easy to pick out, standing together around the corner on Forty-seventh, and dressed so simply that I looked right at home in my business suit. To my amazement, Sid and

Gus were dressed in uncharacteristic fashion, like prim and sober young women in two-piece costumes not dissimilar to my own. Sid's was dove-gray; Gus's, dark-green pinwale. They were warmly welcomed by the Vassar contingent. I was introduced and received one or two inquisitive stares as well as some friendly smiles. Someone handed me a sash to wear over one shoulder: "VWVW. Votes for Women." The banner proclaimed, more fully, "Vassar graduates demand their rights. Votes for women now." Other banners read, "We can do anything a man can, except vote. Half the population has no voice. Women, demand to be heard! Take your rightful place in society."

I felt rather pleased and excited as I took the pole of the banner I was to carry with one of the Vassar girls. The young woman who was holding the other pole smiled at me. "Hello," she said. "I don't believe we've met before, I'm Emily Boswell. What year were you?"

"I'm afraid I'm an impostor," I said. "My name's Molly Murphy and I'm only here because my neighbors dragged me along to boost numbers. And because I feel strongly about the cause."

She was tall, with a thin, sallow face, serious brown eyes, and black hair severely drawn back into a bun beneath a plain bonnet. One would never call her a beauty, but there was something vaguely exotic about her, and her face lit up in a lovely smile as I indicated Sid and Gus. "Why, it is you, Augusta," she said. "I was hoping you'd be here."

"Emily, dear. How good to see you again," Gus said, and they embraced. "Sid, look, it's Emily." As Sid greeted the newcomer, Gus turned to me. "I was Emily's mentor during my senior year. She is quite the brightest girl I have ever encountered."

"You exaggerate, Augusta." Emily blushed. "But I will admit to having a thirst for knowledge."

"Sid and I were quite devastated when we didn't see you at the reunion earlier this year," Gus said. "It was marvelous fun seeing the old crowd again, and you were sorely missed."

Emily's smile faded. "I really wanted to attend, but my employer would not hear of my taking time off work. He's a disagreeable old man, someone akin to Mr. Scrooge, and would probably not even grant me the day off for the death of my mother. Since my mother is already dead, I've yet to test that theory."

"You have a real job? How wonderful."

"I wouldn't describe it as wonderful. More necessity than anything," Emily said. "I am alone in the world and need to support myself. I balked at being a governess so I'm working at a pharmacy."

"How perfect for you," Gus said. "You were always interested in chemistry, I remember."

"I was and still am, but my employer resists letting me do anything more than work at the counter, taking the money and wrapping up the prescriptions. I have tried to persuade him to give me a chance to be his apprentice, but he thinks that such work is beyond any woman, even a Vassar graduate."

"How typical," Sid said. "What will it take for men to see that we are as capable as they are of rational thought?"

"Let us hope that demonstrations such as this one will begin to change their minds," Emily said.

"I had hoped for a bigger turnout," Sid said, looking at the group, which numbered less than twenty. "Frankly, this is a disappointment."

Emily nodded. "I contacted several friends but they declined. Some thought it was a lost cause. Some thought this was neither the time nor the place for this kind of

30

demonstration, and some husbands or fathers forbade them."

"Forbade them? Then why did they bother to educate us if they didn't want us to think for ourselves," Sid said angrily. "Never mind, we'll wave our banners proudly and maybe we'll open a few minds today."

"I see we are starting to line up," Emily said. "We had better take our places."

Emily and I unfurled our banner and held it aloft. She gave me an encouraging smile. "So where were you educated, Miss Murphy?"

"In Ireland. But I wasn't fortunate enough to go to college like you and your friends. And please call me Molly."

"Gladly, if you'll call me Emily. So you've recently come from Ireland, have you? With your family?"

"Two years ago and quite alone."

"And you've managed to make your way in New York City? I admire you for that. New York is not a city that is kind to immigrants, so I've heard."

"No, it's been a struggle at times, but I've managed to keep my head above water, with the help of Sid and Gus, who have been so good to me."

"You are also employed then?"

"I run my own business. A small detective

agency."

Those brown eyes shot open. "A detective agency? How thrilling. But can you actually make a go of it? Do men entrust their secrets to a woman?"

"Sometimes they do. I have just this week concluded an assignment for Mr. Macy."

"Of department store fame?"

"The very same. And earlier this year I went abroad for Tommy Burke, the theater impresario."

"Mercy me," she said. "How I envy you such an exciting life."

"Sometimes it's a little too exciting," I confessed. "I try to take only simple cases but they've landed me in hot water more than once. My young man tells me that I've used up most of my nine lives."

"You have a sweetheart too? You are indeed fortunate."

"Sometimes I dispute that claim as well." I grinned. "He's a policeman."

"Then you can be of assistance to each other in your work. That is ideal, isn't it, when a couple can share interests and talk as intellectual equals."

"It is indeed," I said, deciding to keep quiet about Daniel's tendency toward chauvinist ideas. "Do you have a young man yourself?"

She blushed prettily. "I do. He works at the same drugstore as I, but he's studying hard. He's a real apprentice and Mr. McPherson is teaching him the art of compounding medicines. He's very good at it too. He has a brilliant brain. It's a pity his family has no money and that he didn't have a chance to further his education at a university."

"You said you are also having to make your own way in the world," I said. "How did you manage to go to Vassar?"

"Relatives paid for me," she said, and I saw a trace of annoyance cross her face. "But look, the parade is starting ahead of us. See those carriages moving off?"

We started to walk. The wind tugged at our banners and the effort of holding them aloft made conversation impossible. As we entered Fifth Avenue the crowd became aware of us. I heard some shouts of encouragement as well as some wolf whistles and improper suggestions. "Show us a bit of leg, girlies. You'll never find yourself a husband dressed like that. Where are your Easter bonnets?"

Among these was a buzz of genuine disapproval. "Women will never get the vote," one man shouted, stepping out to wave a fist at us. "Over my dead body."

"That's what comes of educating women," another man yelled. "Keep 'em home having babies. That's their rightful place."

"Can you imagine what a mess of silliness there would be if women had a say in running the country?" the first man countered. "Why, they might even try to elect a woman president."

There was a roar of laughter at this suggestion.

"Go home, girls. Go back where you belong and stop making fools of yourselves."

"You seem to be the one making a fool of yourself at the moment, sir," one of the young women ahead of us said calmly. "Now please stand back and let us proceed."

Emily and I glanced at each other. I had never considered that our little demonstration would turn ugly. Or that people would react so violently. I noticed that there were women among those shouting abuse at us. Some looked sorry for us. The term *bluestocking* was repeated as we processed up the avenue.

"I think we shall not have an easy fight on our hands," I said to Emily, as the parade ahead of us halted for a moment.

"No, it certainly won't be easy. Most women are content with their lot and have no wish to worry about politics."

"But it's not just politics, is it?" I said. "It's about having a say in the running of a community."

"Of course it is. Local measures regarding water and transportation. School bonds. Women have no voice in things that are important to them — their health, their safety, and their children. This is what we have to get across to the women of America. But they don't want to listen."

The parade moved on again. Since we were following a considerable number of horse-drawn carriages, we had to walk carefully and watch where we put our feet. As I looked down something struck me on the shoulder. I reacted with alarm and saw that my costume was now caked with mud. Another clod of mud struck the hat of the woman in front of me. A roar of laughter went up from the crowd.

"Pay no attention to them," Emily said. "It's just urchins amusing themselves."

"Go home!" The chant rose again.

We marched on, chins held high as mud spattered our banners.

Suddenly a man darted out from the crowd. "Lucinda. What do you think you are doing!" he shouted, grabbing the arm of one of the young women at the head of our procession. "Leave this absurd farce at once.

You are embarrassing yourself and your family."

He was a young man with an impressive mustache and he carried a silver-tipped cane.

"Go away, Laurence," the girl said, shaking him off. "It's none of your business what I choose to do. And it is you who are embarrassing me."

"I will not allow you to make a fool of yourself like this. You are coming with me." He started to drag her out of the line.

"Let go of me. I'm not leaving my friends. This is a free country. I've a right to express my opinion." The girl was shouting now.

"Leave her alone!" the girl behind her joined in the fray.

More men from the crowd dashed out and soon there was an out-and-out fracas. Whistles were blown and policemen appeared.

"All right. Enough of this," one of them said sternly. "Step aside. Move out of the way and let the parade proceed."

"But we're part of the parade," Sid said.

"Not anymore, miss. You're causing a right disturbance but I'm letting you off with a warning. Disperse now and go home or I'll have to arrest you for disturbing the peace."

"We were doing nothing but marching

peacefully," Sid said. "It was that man who attacked a member of our group."

"Only trying to protect my sister, Officer," the man said. "I'm Laurence Patterson the Third and I believe you know my father, Justice Laurence Patterson."

"Know the gentleman well, sir." The sergeant touched his cap. "I suggest you take the young lady home before any harm comes to her. Off you go, miss."

Lucinda shot us a furious look as she was led away.

"This isn't fair, Sergeant," Sid said. "We have the same right as any citizen of New York to march in the parade."

"Not if your presence causes a disruption, which it clearly was. It's my job to make sure the parade goes nice and smoothly. So this is my final warning. Go home or get arrested."

"We choose to get arrested," Sid said. "Are you with me, sisters?"

The policeman sighed. "Very well, if you insist. Take 'em away, men. There's a Black Maria waiting around the corner on Fiftieth."

"This is outrageous!" Sid exclaimed.

"My father will hear of this," another woman shouted.

"Your father will thank me, miss, for keeping you safe," the sergeant called after us.

"Why, it's Miss Murphy, isn't it?" said a voice in my ear, and I looked into the face of a young constable I recognized. He was one of the few who had been loyal to Daniel during his time of disgrace.

"Hello, Constable Byrne," I said, giving him a weak smile.

"What are you doing mixed up with this lot?" he said.

"Campaigning for the vote for women, like the others."

"Listen," he said quietly, "why don't I just escort you through the crowd and let you make your own way home. No need for you to go through the unpleasantness of jail. I'm sure Captain Sullivan wouldn't want it."

I must admit I was sorely tempted, having experienced jail on more than one occasion. But then I saw Sid and Gus and Emily being marched down the street like common criminals.

"I'm sorry," I said, "but I can't abandon my friends now. I know where my duty lies. Take me to the Black Maria with them."

"Very well, if you insist." He looked most worried. "But Captain Sullivan won't like it."

"You could do me one favor, please, Constable. Could you get word of this to

38

Captain Sullivan? I've no wish for my friends and me to spend longer in jail than necessary."

"I'll do my best, Miss Murphy," he said, and helped me up into the back of the police wagon.

FOUR

"Isn't this exciting," said a voice from the darkness as the Black Maria took off, lurching from side to side.

"Absolutely ripping," another voice agreed.

"I'm going to contact our friend Nellie Bly and make sure it gets into all the papers," a voice that sounded like Sid's said. "This will give us better publicity than we had hoped for. And maybe stir up sympathy among other women when they see how we've been treated."

"I hope they don't actually treat us badly," a small voice said with a tremor of alarm. "I've no wish to be locked up in a dismal cell with only bread and water."

"They'll fine us and let us go with a warning," Sid said. "Besides, we must be prepared to suffer for the cause. You saw how those men in the crowd behaved. We don't have an easy task ahead of us, that's for sure."

"Oh dear, my father's going to be furious," another voice whispered. "You saw how Lucinda's brother behaved. My father will be ten times worse."

"Stick to your guns, Matilda," Gus said. "You are over twenty-one and able to make up your own mind."

"Yes, but I'm still living under his roof. I've no profession and no marriage prospects. What will I do if he throws me out?"

"Come and live with us," Gus said. "We've a spare room and Molly's just across the street with spare rooms too. We'll start a little colony of Vassar girls suffering for the cause!"

This caused merriment and the black mood was broken. All the same, I could understand that it was terrifying for these young women to be lurching along in pitch darkness, not knowing where they were headed. I knew, and I wasn't looking forward to it, I can tell you. I just prayed that these delicate flowers were not shoved into cells with female pickpockets and prostitutes to teach them a lesson. In fact I prayed that the constable would be able to find Daniel and deliver my message.

After what seemed like an eternity the

wagon came to a halt. The doors were flung open and a rough voice said, "All right, you girls. Out you get. No dillydallying. Come on. Move it."

One by one we climbed down, blinking in the bright sunlight. It took me a moment or two before I saw that we were, as I feared, at the courthouse. So we were to spend a night in the underground cells and then come before the magistrate in the morning. Not a happy thought. The rest of the women were now rather subdued. They walked close together, some holding hands for mutual support, darting nervous glances around them as we were driven like sheep into the side entrance of the building. We were halted in front of a sergeant sitting at a tall desk and had to give our names and addresses. Our accompanying policeman then informed him that we were being booked on the charge of disturbing the peace. The sergeant nodded. "Take 'em down, then," he said, and we were escorted down a flight of steps. It was dark down there and didn't smell too appetizing. Memories of similar experiences in cells came back to me. I remembered the bucket in the corner. Surely these girls would be even more sensitive than I and refuse to use it. I just hoped we weren't held for too long.

"In here," one of our attendants barked, and opened a cell door with a giant key. He pushed six of the women inside, then stopped the seventh from entering. That door clanged shut and he repeated the process in the next two cells. I was among the last group. Sid and Gus were not with me. Emily was. Apart from her, the girls in my cell looked as if they were about to expire from fright.

"Don't worry," I said, sounding braver than I felt. "I have experienced this before and lived to tell the tale."

"You've been in jail?" They were looking at me as if I were a different species of animal.

"Unfortunately yes. I work as a private detective and I've been arrested for what the police considered loitering, when I was, in fact, observing a house. Had I been a man they would never have thought twice about me. But a woman standing alone on a sidewalk at ten o'clock at night has to have evil intentions."

"That is so unfair," one of the girls said.

"Have you not noticed everything about our lives is unfair?" a tall fair girl demanded. "We are at the mercy of our fathers and then our husbands. If a woman tries to make her own way in the world she is judged as odd and a troublemaker."

"Nellie Bly seems to have managed that hurdle," I pointed out. "Nobody could have behaved more outrageously than she and yet she is happily married and accepted in society."

"But look at what she has achieved," the fair girl said. "How many of us would be prepared to put our lives on the line in a mental institution or expose corruption in the women's prisons?"

I didn't like to say that I had done both. "Her actions should be a beacon of hope to the rest of us," I said. "And it won't hurt when we come before the magistrate tomorrow to mention that we know her."

"How long will they keep us here, do you think?" the frail one with the trembling voice asked.

"Overnight probably. Courts are not in session on Sundays."

"Overnight? What will my family think when I do not return home? They will be so worried."

"We'll try to get word to your families," I said. "We can at least hope that we will be rescued before too long."

"Rescued? By whom?"

I didn't want to raise any false hopes. "They may have noticed that some of you

44

have influential names and not wish to embarrass your families," I said.

"It's a pity there are no really important names among us," Emily said. "I tried to persuade Fanny Poindexter to join us, but she was afraid of upsetting her husband."

"Her father's name would certainly have caused them to think twice about arresting us," the tall, fair one said, "but I found it was impossible to recruit married women to our cause. They are all under their husbands' thumbs."

Our conversation lapsed into silence. There wasn't enough room on the wooden plank bench for us all to sit comfortably but it was cold and damp down there and we were glad to huddle together for warmth. I realized that I was feeling rather frail myself at this point. I had only had a piece of bread for breakfast and the clammy dizziness of my illness had returned.

"I wonder what time it is," I said.

"The time? It is one-thirty." To my absolute envy one of our group unbuttoned her jacket and revealed a dinky little cloisonné watch pinned to her blouse. I hoped to own such a thing myself someday. If I received more commissions like the Macy's one — a sobering thought came to me. If this incident was reported in the papers and my name was mentioned, it could possibly harm my business prospects. Oh dear. Lack of forward thinking has once again gotten you into hot water, Molly Murphy.

I was just in the midst of this thought when an angry male voice echoed down the hallway.

"Holding them in the cells? On what grounds? Are you out of your mind, man? Where are they?"

The voice came nearer, along with rapidly advancing footsteps, and to my delight Daniel's face appeared outside my cell. "Molly, what the devil?" he exclaimed. "Can I not leave you alone for two seconds without your needing to be rescued from some predicament?"

He made an impatient gesture to the sergeant, who was now looking subdued. "Go on, let them out."

"They were disturbing the peace, sir," the sergeant complained, as he put the key into our door.

"Young ladies? Disturbing the peace? What were they doing? Dancing the Viennese waltz in public?"

"Carrying banners, sir. Votes for women and all that nonsense. A scuffle broke out and we had to arrest them for their own good."

"I should have thought your boys had enough to do with keeping pickpockets and genuine criminals at bay," Daniel snapped.

"Only obeying orders, sir," the sergeant muttered. "The commissioner himself said to pounce at any sign of trouble and we pounced."

"A little too enthusiastically, it would seem," Daniel said. "These young ladies come from the Four Hundred, surely you must realize that. When their fathers come to us to complain, your name will be mentioned . . ."

"Only doing my job, sir," the sergeant mumbled, his large, whiskered face now beet-red.

One by one we came out of our cells.

"And you young ladies ought to thank your lucky stars that I happened to hear of this," Daniel said, still glaring. "A night in the cells is not an experience you'd wish to repeat. By nightfall you'd have been joined by the least savory women in the city. What on earth were you thinking?"

"We were using our constitutional right to assemble and to protest," Sid said. "We were marching in the parade, in orderly fashion, when we were set upon."

"I have to say you brought it upon yourselves, Miss Goldfarb. You know how most

47

men feel about giving women the vote. A holiday parade was neither the time nor the place for such sentiments."

"Then where do you suggest we make our message known, Captain Sullivan?" Sid demanded. "At the weekly sewing circle?"

"Your behavior certainly has done little to win you support, Miss Goldfarb," Daniel said, as he ushered us up the stairs. "Men who believed women to be too irresponsible to be involved in public life will now be even more convinced they are right." He turned to the group of us. "Now, ladies, I suggest that you go home as swiftly as possible and stay there."

"Thank you, Captain," the trembly one said. "Thank you for saving us."

Daniel tipped his hat. "My pleasure, miss."

"Will you take a cab with us, Molly dear?" Gus asked.

I glanced at Daniel.

"I will be taking Molly home," he said. "She has been sick and should never have been allowed to undertake something like this in the first place. Let us pray she doesn't have a relapse and come down with pneumonia. Come, Molly."

"Oh, but I could easily ride with Sid and Gus," I said. "I know how busy you are."

"I said I was driving you home," he said

firmly. "I still have the automobile and can have you home in no time at all. Good day to you, ladies. I hope you will exercise more prudence in your future decisions." He tipped his hat, then grasped me firmly by the arm and propelled me across the grass to where the automobile was waiting.

I was seething with anger. The moment we were out of earshot of the other women, I exploded. "How dare you drag me away like a naughty child," I said. "You embarrassed me in front of my friends."

"I can't believe you would act so foolishly," he said, looking equally angry. "Risking your health for this harebrained notion."

"What is harebrained about women having the right to vote?" I demanded. "Why should half the population have no say in the running of the country?"

"Because the running of the country is best left to those who were raised to do it. Men have always been the leaders, women the nurturers."

"What about Queen Victoria?" I said. "Queen Elizabeth? Boadicea? Cleopatra? Joan of Arc?"

"All women who behaved like men," he replied. "How can a woman be a good wife and mother if she is concerned with affairs outside the home?"

"Maybe not every woman wants to be a good wife and mother," I said. "I'm not sure that I do."

"Oh, come, Molly. Don't tell me you've been influenced by those pathetic bluestockings. You want to have children someday, don't you?"

"Yes, I suppose so," I said at last. "But I also want the freedom to think and act for myself. If we marry, Daniel, you are not going to lay down the law. It is not going to be your household. It will be our household, our family. We will run it jointly or not at all. You will never walk all over me."

We faced each other like a pair of fighting dogs, me with hands firmly on my hips. Finally a smile twitched at his lips. "No, I can't ever see myself walking all over you."

"You'd better drive me home. I'm keeping you from your work," I said.

Daniel helped me climb up to the automobile seat. "I suppose it's those neighbors of yours," he said as the car started and we drove away. "They persuaded you to join this stupidity."

"Nobody persuaded me. I thought their cause was just and wanted to be part of it. And I'll thank you not to continually run down my two dear friends. They have been most kind to me. In fact, without their help

50

I probably would not have survived in this city."

"They care about you so much that they show no concern for your delicate state of health," Daniel said.

"They also expressed concern that the parade might be too much for me, but I asked to join them."

"I suppose they have as much trouble trying to control your actions as I do," Daniel said at last, "but please think twice in the future before embarking on such a venture. Think of the harm something like this could do to your own career prospects, as well as to my reputation. You are now known to be my future bride, even if it is not official yet. And how do you think Mr. Macy would react next time he wanted to hire a female detective?"

"You do have a point there," I admitted.

"Amazing. We actually agree on something." He turned to me with a quizzical smile. "We may yet have a future together, Miss Headstrong."

"Only if you stop behaving like a typical male and trying to order me around."

"But I am a typical male, Molly. I can't help the way I was raised. I can't help the society I was raised in. And I only act this way because I love you and want to protect you."

I opened my mouth to say that I didn't need to be loved and protected, but then of course I realized that I did. Daniel noted my silence, then reached across and covered my hand with his, giving my fingers a fond squeeze.

FIVE

By that evening I found, to my annoyance, that Daniel had been right. I felt tired, achy, and feverish and went to bed with a cup of hot broth. The next morning it hurt me to breathe and I became seriously alarmed. I remembered Daniel's story of the young constable whose influenza turned to pneumonia and who was dead within three days.

"This will never do," I said. I got up, dressed, and went to the nearest dispensary, where I was given a bottle of tonic. I was told that it contained both iron and brewer's yeast and that it was what I needed to build me up. It looked and tasted like tar, so I suppose it had to be doing me some good.

I crawled home and went back to bed, wondering exactly what pneumonia felt like and what I should do about it. My own mother had died of pneumonia and I could still remember her rasping breath and her skin, which felt burning to the touch. What

I really wanted was Sid and Gus to come over and take care of me, so when I was awakened by knocking I made it rapidly down the stairs and opened the front door. Only when I realized that the person standing there was neither Sid nor Gus did I remember that I was in my nightgown, with my hair wild and unbrushed.

"Miss Murphy — Molly," the person said. "It's Emily. Emily Boswell. We met yesterday."

"Forgive me," I stammered. "I've not been feeling well and I thought it was Sid or Gus come to visit."

"I'm sorry to hear you are unwell. I'll go away and come back on another occasion then, shall I? Or is there something I could do for you? Let me at least help you back to bed."

She came in. The house was in no state to admit strangers but I was beyond caring. She took me upstairs and tucked me back in my bed. "You're feverish," she said, feeling my brow.

"Yes, I had almost recovered from a nasty bout of influenza and I'm afraid that yesterday's little antics have brought a relapse."

"Dear me. Are you taking anything to bring down that fever?"

"I went to the dispensary and they gave

me a tonic."

"Tonic?" she said scornfully. "A lot of good that will do."

"They said it contained iron and would be good to strengthen my blood."

"To build you up, yes, although there are plenty of quack tonics circulating at the moment that do nothing for you. But you should have been given aspirin. It does wonders in bringing down a fever. It's only available with a doctor's prescription, but I can go and bring you some from our pharmacy."

"Really, that's too much trouble," I protested, but she ignored me. "I'll be back shortly," she said, and she was. What's more, she had brought chicken soup from the Jewish delicatessen as well as the aspirin. She mixed the powder with water and handed it to me. "Drink it right down," she said. "It tastes horribly bitter but it really is a wonder drug."

I did as I was told, then sat up and sipped the chicken soup. It was delicious. "You are extremely good to go to all this trouble," I said.

"No trouble. We women must help each other whenever we can," she said. "The Lord knows that any man will flee from you as fast as he can at the least hint of sickness. I notice that even my own Ned will take a couple of steps away from the counter when a sick person comes into our drugstore, or find some excuse to be busy so that I have to wait on that particular customer." She laughed merrily.

"I'm sorry, I never did find out why you came to see me in the first place," I said. "Was it to bring me more information on our cause?"

"No, it was more personal than that, I'm afraid," she said. "I want to engage your services."

"Holy mother of God!" I couldn't have been more surprised. "As a detective, you mean?"

She nodded. "Look, if you don't feel up to discussing it this evening, I quite understand. I should leave you to sleep and come back when you are well."

"Certainly not," I said. "Now I'm intrigued. You should know that I was born curious and won't rest until I know all the details."

"Very well." She smiled. "But first I should say that I work for my living. I have saved a little but my funds are limited. I don't know what your fees might be, but I fear I might not be able to pay them."

"My fees can be discussed when I hear

the nature of your case and decide whether it is something within the scope of my agency," I said. "I'm sure we can reach some kind of agreement that will not bankrupt you and will satisfy me."

"Very well." She perched at the bottom of my bed, her hands folded primly on her lap. "Let me first give you my background. My parents were missionaries in China. They died in a cholera epidemic when I was a baby. I was miraculously spared and brought back to America, where I was raised by a couple called Lynch. One of them was a distant relative of my mother — a second cousin, I believe. Anyway, they were good enough to raise me, and I called them 'Aunt' and 'Uncle.' "

She paused and fiddled with the ribbon on her hat. "Aunt Lydia died when I was five. I remember her as pretty and gentle. She was much younger than Uncle Horace and was always of a sickly constitution. My image of her is lying in bed, propped up among pillows, her face as white as the pillows around her. After she died my uncle hired a series of governesses for me. He showed me no love or affection and actually went out of his way to avoid contact with me. Whether he blamed me in some way for his wife's death, or whether his grief at her

57

passing made him bitter, I can't say. As I said, I was very young when she died.

"When I was about sixteen he called me into his study and said that he was going to do his duty and abide by my parents' wishes that I go to Vassar, but I was to understand that this concluded his obligation to me. When I graduated it was up to me to make my own way in the world and I could no longer consider his residence as my home, nor expect any future financial assistance."

"I suppose that seems fair enough," I said.

She nodded. "Although he is a rich man and a small allowance would hardly make a dent in his cigar budget, and one might have thought that he would welcome some companionship in that big, empty house. He has a mansion on Seventy-ninth Street, just off Fifth Avenue, you know."

"My, then he is wealthy."

"Oh, indeed. He owns mills in Massachusetts as well as various other commercial enterprises."

"I am told that it is not uncommon for rich men to have become rich because they don't like to part with their money."

"That's true enough." She laughed. "My uncle is a regular penny-pincher. I remember getting a severe dressing-down as a small child because I had scuffed the toes of my shoes by dragging my feet on a swing. 'Do you think shoes grow on trees?' he demanded. And I am stuck with Mr. McPherson at the drugstore — another skinflint. It is lucky that Ned is employed there too, or I'd never have been able to obtain the aspirin for you. Old McPherson would never give anything away."

"Really, I have no wish to get you into trouble at work," I said, attempting to sit up.

"Honestly, Molly. A packet of aspirin powder costs pennies. And Mr. McPherson can dock it from my wages if he so chooses. God knows he pays me little enough. If I had been a male assistant, he would have had to cough up at least five more dollars a week."

"To continue with your story," I reminded her. "You have told me that you are an orphan and have been raised by distant relatives who felt they were doing their duty but showed you little affection."

She nodded. "So now I am alone in the world. I had accepted that and was prepared to make the best of my situation when a strange thing happened. A few weeks ago I served a couple at the drugstore. The wife's face was badly scarred, poor thing, and she wondered if there was some kind of cream or preparation that would make the scars fade. Well, it happens that Ned has been experimenting with ladies' cosmetics. He's been copying some of the recipes from Paris and he's actually getting rather good at it. In fact he plans to open his own business someday, if he can save up enough money for capital."

"An ambitious young man then," I commented.

She nodded. "He is. Very ambitious. Anyway, I called Ned out of the dispensary and while we were chatting it transpired that the cause of the wife's disfiguration was smallpox that she had contracted while they were serving as missionaries in China. They had only recently returned home." She looked up at me. "Of course, when I heard that, I asked them immediately if they had been in China long and had known my parents. They had, indeed, been in China for twenty years but could not recall meeting a Mr. and Mrs. Boswell."

She paused, studying her hands for a moment before continuing, "Naturally I was disappointed at the time, but China is a big country and I expect that missionaries work in comparative isolation. So I thought no more about it. Afterward, however, I began to wonder: had I been told the truth about my parents? I recalled that even my sweet Aunt Lydia had changed the subject when I wanted to know details about my mother and father. And why had there been no photographs, no mementos, even from frugal missionaries? Was there in fact some kind of scandal about them — had they somehow disgraced the family name, which was why Uncle Horace wanted nothing to do with me? And then an even more disturbing thought crept into my mind — was it possible that I had been left money and Uncle Horace had cheated me out of my inheritance?" She looked up at me with that keen, fierce gaze. "So you see Miss Murphy, Molly, I have to know the truth, however unpleasant it is."

"Could you not approach your uncle and demand to be told?"

"My uncle refuses to see me again. I have been to the house a couple of times but on each occasion I was informed that he was away from home, seeing to his business affairs. I left him notes on both occasions but received no reply."

"Which only reinforced your suspicions that all was not right," I suggested.

She nodded vehemently. "So now I have to know. Can you help me, Molly? Can you tell me who I am?"

"I'll do my best," I said. "Although I have to say that I don't have the resources to go to China on your behalf."

"I wouldn't expect you to," she said. "But there are missionary societies headquartered here in the United States."

"Of course," I said. "I will certainly approach them. I know little of Protestants or missionaries but I am willing to learn."

"Thank you. Thank you." She reached forward and clasped my hands in hers. "I can't tell you what this will mean to me to finally know the truth."

"I can't guarantee that I will come to the truth," I said, "and I can't guarantee that you will be happy with the news."

"I understand that. But I have to know. It is even more important right now. If Ned asks me to marry him, as I suspect he soon will, then I need to accept with no reservations. I can't have him marrying someone whose parent committed some kind of crime, for example."

"Oh come on, Emily," I said. "I'm sure Ned loves you for yourself, and you are not responsible for the behavior of your parents."

"But what about the sins of the fathers being visited on the children? If, for example, I had a murderer for a father? Would that trait not have a chance of coming out in me someday?"

"Then perhaps I should have tested the chicken soup first," I said, and we both laughed.

"Really, Emily, I think you are worrying too much about this," I said. "I'm sure the explanation will be a simple one — most likely your Uncle Horace taking your inheritance for himself, by the sound of it."

Emily got to her feet. "I should leave you now. I have taken too much of your time when you should be resting. Let us talk again when you are fully recovered."

"Where can I contact you?" I asked.

"Here is my address." She handed me a card on which her name and address were written in a neat, sloping hand, as well as the name and address of her drugstore.

"My room is on West Seventy-seventh," she said, as I examined it. "It is around the corner from my place of employment on Columbus Avenue. Highly convenient, as Mr. McPherson can't abide tardiness. He docks money from our pay packets if we are but one minute late."

"He sounds like a regular old tartar," I said. "Why don't you leave and find employment somewhere else?"

She blushed. "Because of Ned, of course.

And one day if we are married, then I won't have to work."

"You want to stop working when you marry?" I asked in surprise.

"I have no wish to go on working behind a counter," she said. "My dream, before I knew of my situation, was to go to medical school and become a physician. Of course, that is no longer possible. However, if our plans come to fruition, then Ned will have his own cosmetics and perfume company and I can help him in his laboratory."

"I hope it all works out for you," I said.

She patted my hand. "And I hope you recover swiftly. I look forward to your visit. Come to the store at one o'clock. I am given half an hour for lunch. I am only here this morning because Mr. McPherson did grudgingly admit that we could come in late on the day after Easter. Or you could come to my lodgings if you like, although I have to admit it's a rather dreary little room, not fit for entertaining. I am usually home in the evenings by seven-thirty. Now sleep. Doctor's orders. I can let myself out."

With that she tiptoed down the stairs and I fell asleep, clutching her card.

Six

The chicken soup and the aspirin together must have worked wonders because I awoke in the morning feeling more like my old self. I placed Emily's card on the table as I had breakfast and jotted down thoughts as they came to me. Obviously the place to start would be her birth certificate. Then the various missionary societies and maybe even the state department. Would an entry permit of some kind be needed for a closed and dangerous country like China? And then Vassar, of course. Her personal details would have been recorded on her admission form.

I bathed, dressed, and tried to tame my hair into submission under a hat. It needed washing badly but I'd have to wait until the weather was warm enough so that I didn't risk catching another chill. It looked like the proverbial haystack. I needed a barrage of hat pins to hold the hat in place but at last I was ready to go out and face the world.

I opened my front door and found a scene of commotion going on outside. A window cleaner was on his ladder, cleaning the top-floor windows at number 9, and Sid was standing outside, hands on hips, giving him directions. "You've missed that corner again," I heard her saying. "There. To the right." She saw me and sighed. "It's no use. The wretched man doesn't speak English and my Italian is limited to chianti and gorgonzola. Our experiences on Sunday have inspired Gus to paint again and the windows of her studio were positively filthy. Sì. Bene." She nodded violently as the man slopped water on the window. "Much better. Molto better. Benissimo. Bravo." She turned back to me. "At least my visits to the opera have proved useful," she said. "Where are you off to?"

"I'm going to visit a client," I said.

"My, aren't we all little busy bees today?" Sid smiled. "Gus painting away feverishly, you with your client, and I am writing an article on our experiences for a rather radical magazine. And most men think that we women languish at home sipping tea and playing patience."

"That isn't true for most women," I said. "They spend their days cooking, cleaning, beating carpets, scrubbing floors with a brood of children under their feet."

"You're right," Sid agreed. "Do you see that as your lot when you marry the famous Captain Sullivan?"

"Most certainly not. For one thing, I'll not be marrying him if he can't furnish me with a servant. And I don't know about the brood of children, either."

"You stick to your guns with him, Molly," Sid said, "or he will bully you into submission. And saddle you with children, too. We saw his true colors on Sunday. Determined to keep us helpless females in our place. I hope you will consider carefully before agreeing to marry him."

"He hasn't yet asked me officially." I knew I was skirting the subject. "And I am quite aware than we will have to reach an understanding about my role in a marriage before I take that plunge."

"It's just that I've seen so many of our Vassar friends — bright girls with good brains and bright futures ahead of them — turn into traditional simpering females the moment they marry, because this is what their husbands want."

I laughed. "Can you ever see me simpering?"

She laughed too. "Frankly, no. I think

Daniel Sullivan has met his match in you."
With that she happened to glance up at the
ladder again as drops of water splashed
down on her. "Watch what you're doing,
Mario. Attenzione!"

I left them to it and walked to the Sixth
Street El station, where I took the train all
the way to Seventy-third. This neighborhood on the Upper West Side gave the feel
of being part of a small town, not a giant
city. Gardeners were tending early blooms
in the strip of land between Broadway and
Columbus Avenue. The small shops along
Broadway had that Main Street feel. This
wouldn't last, however, as some impressive
new apartment buildings were going up,
complete with marble façades and turrets.
The Dakota, which towered over everything
like a great fortress on the park, had started
a trend, and this would soon be a fashionable place to live.

At the moment it was one of the few
neighborhoods I had been in that hadn't
obviously been settled by a single ethnic
group. I saw Irish faces, and fair-haired
northern Europeans and dark-haired Italians and Jews. I also, to my interest, saw a
Negro woman, holding a delightful little girl
with neatly braided hair by the hand as she
emerged from the baker's shop. Having

68

grown up on the remote west coast of Ireland, Negroes and Chinese were still a novelty to me. Not here, however. Nobody gave her a second glance as she disappeared down Broadway.

I made my way up Columbus looking for the drugstore. Drugstores were a new experience for me. I had come to associate the word with that delightful invention, the soda fountain, where I had had my first taste of milkshakes and sundaes. But McPherson's Dispensatory was not like this: it was clearly an old-fashioned apothecary, what we in Ireland would call a chemist's shop. In the window hung several large glass globes filled with colored liquid. Below them were displays of various patent remedies: Draper's Toothache Remedy, Lydia Pinkham's Vegetable Compound, and Wampole's Preparation Tonic and Stimulant. In one corner was a small display of ladies' face preparations, as used in Paris. A bell jangled as I pushed open the door. Inside was a high counter and behind it shelves containing an assortment of jars and bottles. In the middle of this wall was an opening through which I could see into a back room. Its walls were lined with cupboards, some glass-fronted, others tiny wooden squares. I caught sight of two men in white coats at work at a table, their backs to me.

At the sound of the bell, the older one looked up, saw me, and barked, "Counter, Ned."

"Where's Emily?" Ned asked.

"Off delivering a package for me. She should have been back by now. Dawdling to look in shop windows, I shouldn't wonder," the older one snapped. The owner, Mr. McPherson, obviously.

Ned pushed open a swing door and came through to the shop front, wiping his hands on his coat as he came toward me. "Can I help you, miss?" he asked.

For once I was speechless. This was Emily's young man and he was a veritable Adonis. She hadn't mentioned his good looks and yet he would have been any girl's dream. He was slim, with wavy black hair, dark flashing eyes, and a pencil mustache. I immediately thought of Mr. Darcy or Heathcliff, one of those brooding heroes in the romantic novels I had so loved as a young girl.

"Uh — I came to meet Emily," I stammered. "She told me she has her lunch break at one. I hope I haven't missed her."

"No, she should be back any second now. She was sent out on a delivery."

"You must be Ned," I said, although I

knew quite well who he was. "Emily's told me about you."

"You're a friend of hers then?" he asked, eyeing me with interest. "From Vassar?"

"No such luck. I met her through mutual friends. She's a grand girl, isn't she?"

"Oh yes," he said. "A grand girl. Very smart."

"She's very proud of you. She tells me you've a promising career ahead of you."

He made a face and I couldn't tell whether it was one of embarrassment or annoyance. "Someday, maybe. Right now I'm only an apprentice." He glanced over his shoulder and lowered his voice. "And the old man doesn't let me do much more than make up liniments for old men's rheumatics. But I'm studying in my spare time and I hope to make something of myself someday."

"Ned — I don't pay you to gossip," came the sharp voice from the back room. "If the young lady hasn't come to purchase some-thing then I suggest she wait outside."

"You see what it's like," Ned muttered to me. "Never a moment to myself. Ah, here's Emily now."

Emily burst in through the front door, her cheeks glowing from having hurried. "Sorry I'm late," she gasped, "but I decided to stop in on Mrs. Hartmann, since she lives just across the street from the delivery."

"I don't pay you to dillydally and gossip," Mr. McPherson snapped. "Next time you want to go visiting, do it during your lunch break."

"Oh, but Mr. McPherson, she's your own valued employee. I'd have thought you'd want an update on her condition," Emily said.

Mr. McPherson merely grunted.

"Well, how is she?" Ned asked.

"A little better," Emily said. "Starting to sit up and take solid food again."

"Well, that's good news. I must go and see her myself," Ned said. "In my own time, of course," he added, glancing back at his boss, then touched Emily's arm. "And you have a visitor."

Her face lit up. "Molly. You're better. How splendid."

"Your ministrations obviously did the trick," I said. "I woke this morning feeling my old self again. So I'm anxious to get to work."

"Work? What work?" Ned asked.

"Molly is a real live detective," Emily said. "Have you two been introduced?"

"Not exactly," I said. "Being a detective, I deduced that this young man might be Ned but he doesn't know my name."

"Oh, then let me introduce you now. Molly Murphy, this is Ned Tate."

We shook hands. His hand was slim and elegant, with well-manicured fingernails. Obviously a young man who thought a lot of himself, I decided.

"Are you lunching with any of your other friends?" Ned asked. "Or is Molly not part of your rich socialite set?"

Emily laughed. "My rich socialite set? Just because some of my Vassar friends have married well doesn't mean that I'm part of any rich set."

"I only thought that your bosom pal Fanny whatever-her-name-is lived nearby and that you saw her frequently."

"Fanny does live in the Dakota," Emily said, "but I hardly see her frequently anymore. Our lives are so different now. She has all the time in the world and I have none. Speaking of which, my precious half hour is rapidly disappearing. Come, Molly, we must away. If you'll excuse us, Ned."

"I'll leave you ladies to your luncheon then," he said, with a polite bow. "I have to get back to work," he added loudly for Mr. McPherson's benefit.

"Too right you do," Mr. McPherson said, looking up from his table. "Does Mrs. Hartmann require any more of the stomach powders?"

"No, she said she didn't need anything," Emily said. "She said she was on the mend."

"Well, let's hope she'll be back at work soon. You young slackers don't know the meaning of work."

I followed Emily out of the shop.

"So what did you think of Ned?" Emily asked. Her eyes were shining.

"He is very handsome," I said.

"Isn't he just? And so smart too. It was my lucky day when I answered that advertisement in McPherson's window."

I couldn't help wondering what it was about Emily that had caught Ned's eye. Maybe I had misjudged him and he was more impressed with her intellect than her looks. He had certainly given me a once-over all right.

"I usually just go to the café across the street," Emily said. "They have a ten-cent daily special that is sometimes quite good. And I only have one gas ring in my room so it's hard to cook at home."

"Fine with me," I said. "As long as it's quiet enough to talk."

We dodged the traffic and went inside a pleasant little tea room called the Black Cat. I could see why Emily came here. The other occupants were women and the tables had white cloths on them — overall an air of gentility. The waitress greeted Emily and two plates of the special were brought. It was some kind of meat pie and cabbage, mainly hot and filling but with little flavor. Maybe I had become used to good meals with Sid and Gus.

After we had satisfied our immediate hunger I took out my little notebook. "So I'm anxious to get started on your case," I said. "Let us begin with your parents' full names."

"I believe they were William and Mary," she said. "I think that's what Aunt Lydia told me."

"And where in China were you born?"

"I have no idea. In the interior, that's all I know."

"What about your birth certificate? Doesn't that give all those details?"

"I have no birth certificate," she said. "That's the problem. As I understand it, a cholera epidemic was raging when I was born. My parents died when I was only a few days old and a devoted servant whisked me away to safety. I was deposited at the nearest mission and eventually brought back to America."

"What a romantic story," I said. "Tragic,

75

of course, but the fact that you survived against all odds is amazing."

She nodded. "I know, isn't it?"

"So where did your parents come from?"

"Massachusetts, I believe. As I said, Aunt Lydia, who could have told me these things, died when I was too young to ask the right questions, and Uncle Horace showed no interest in me whatever."

"Your parents were your aunt's relatives, then?"

"I believe my mother and Aunt Lydia were second cousins, or second cousins once removed. Not close relatives, at any rate."

"And what was your aunt's maiden name?"

"I'm afraid I don't even know that."

"That should be easy enough to discover. She died when you were five. There will be a death certificate."

"Of course."

"So I could go to her birthplace and check for other relatives."

"I understood that there were none. They took me in because they were my only surviving kin. At least that's what Uncle Horace said once." She saw my look and gave me a sympathetic smile. "I'm sorry. I knew this was not going to be easy."

"I love a good challenge," I said. "And it

can't be that hard. After all, how many missionaries could there be in China at one time? Maybe twenty or thirty at the most. I know," I perked up as a bright idea hit me, "we could start with that couple who came into your shop. You said they didn't know your parents, but you also mentioned that they had been in China for twenty years. I presume you are older than twenty —"

"Yes, I'm twenty-five."

"So it's quite possible that they didn't arrive until after your parents had died."

"That's quite possible," Emily bucked up at this.

"At any rate, they could give us details of the various denominations of missionaries who were working in China twenty years ago, then all I'd have to do is contact their headquarters."

"Molly, you're a genius." Emily beamed at me. "I'm so glad I came to you. But as to your fees . . ."

I hesitated. Part of me wanted to say that I'd work for nothing, but the other, more practical part reminded me that I had to eat and that this case would be occupying my time as well as costing me money in transportation and stamps. "How about we start with twenty dollars," I said, "and if I find that I need to travel or take considerably more time, then we can decide how far you wish to proceed."

"Oh, that sounds wonderful," Emily said. "But twenty dollars — I'm sure you usually charge much more."

"We working women have to stick together." I smiled at her. "So what information do you have on the couple who came into your shop?"

"It was about three weeks ago. They were called Hinchley and they were only passing through New York. They were staying at a hotel."

"Do you know which one?"

"We filled out a prescription for them, so it will be on file at the shop."

"Then we can look it up after lunch."

"It will have to be surreptitiously," Emily said. "Mr. McPherson is sure to make a fuss if he sees me nosing through his prescription files."

"Then I had better not accompany you. He was clearly annoyed by my presence the first time," I said. "Drop me a note with the name of the hotel and then I can go to work."

"Of course. I'll send it out in the afternoon post, with Old McPherson's stamp on it too." She laughed. "Dear me, that doesn't sound like the child of dead missionaries,

78

does it? But he really doesn't have to be so unpleasant."

"Is he equally nasty to Ned?"

"Marginally less so, I'd say. But Ned sticks it out because he is learning a lot. Whatever his temperament, Mr. McPherson certainly knows his stuff. He is a whiz at compounding."

"Compounding?"

"Mixing the various remedies to exactly the right proportions. It's a delicate business, as you can well imagine. Some of our cures contain deadly elements that can kill in larger doses. A druggist has to be extremely precise."

The waitress came to take our plates and I insisted on paying the bill.

"But I'm the one who is hiring you," Emily protested.

"You've already hired me and now we're on my time." I laughed. "So when should we arrange to meet again? Do you have free time at the weekend? I should have something to report by then."

"Usually I have alternate Saturday afternoons free," Emily said. "But Mrs. Hartmann, the other counter assistant, who has been with the firm for years, is out sick with some kind of grippe, so I will be doing her

Saturday duty. But Sunday afternoon I'll be free."

"What about Ned? Doesn't he have priority over your free time?"

"He goes to see his mother on Sundays. She lives in Brooklyn and is not in the best of health. He's a most devoted son. He gives her a generous portion of his earnings."

"So will you be required to have her in your home when you marry?" I asked.

She blushed again. "He hasn't yet officially proposed to me. He wants to establish himself in his career first, so I know we may have a long wait. Oh, but he is worth it, Molly. I know he's bound for great things."

"And in the meantime," I said, "what about you? I understand from Gus that you were one of the most gifted students in your class. Can you also not further your education in some way like Ned?"

"There is little point if Mr. McPherson won't even let me into the dispensatory room. One cannot learn pharmacy skills by reading and observing. Ned provides me with books to read and notes from his lectures, so I am quite well informed, but there it must probably rest."

"That's a shame," I said.

"Life is unfair, I've come to accept it," she said.

With that we parted company.

SEVEN

Emily's note arrived for me in the mail the next morning. The hotel was on Broadway, not too far from McPherson's. I took the El again, noting as the train made its way north that spring had indeed finally come to New York City. Windows on the second floor, beside the track, were open, and bedding was laid out to air. Some windows even sported window boxes with a bright splash of daffodils or tulips. Women below were beating rags, scrubbing steps. It was spring cleaning time. Which reminded me that I should be doing a little of the same myself. I put that thought aside. I had done enough housekeeping during my formative years to cure me of any desire for extra tasks. My mother had died when I was fourteen and I had taken care of three untidy brothers and an equally untidy, ungrateful father. I resolved to ask Sid about her Italian window washer.

The train stopped at Seventy-third and I alighted. The hotel was a block to the north on Broadway. As I reached the corner, I paused to admire the imposing new building called the Ansonia, now almost complete. In fact, I stood like the little country bumpkin that I still was, staring up as its amazing seventeen floors rose up into the sky, all richly decorated in carved stone and tipped with turrets like a French chateau. I understood that it was to be an apartment hotel, a temporary home for the very well-to-do. If all the hotels around here were of that class, then my missionary couple were not the humble Christian folk I had taken them for.

Of course, when I located the Park View hotel, not a stone's throw from the glorious Ansonia building, I had to take back my uncharitable thoughts. It was a severely simple establishment with a plain brick façade and only a sign over the front door advertising its presence. And "Park View" was definitely a misnomer. It was, at most, five stories high, and could only have a glimpse of the park from its roof.

I opened the door and found myself in a dreary lounge with a couple of faded armchairs, a brass spittoon, and a tired aspidistra. The woman who appeared at the sound of my feet was the sort of harridan who seems to flourish as a landlady.

"Yes?" she said, with little warmth in her voice. "Can I help you?"

"You had a couple to stay here a few weeks ago. A Mr. and Mrs. Hinchley. They were missionaries from China."

Her face softened just a little. "Ah, yes. Lovely, refined Christian people they were, too. They held a prayer service after dinner one night."

"I need to contact them rather urgently," I said. "I wondered if they gave you their home address."

"And what would this be about, miss?" she asked.

"I'm here on behalf of a dear friend," I said. "Her parents were missionaries in China at the same time as the Hinchleys. She has questions she needs to ask them."

"Fellow missionaries from China, were they?" I had clearly won her over. "I'd really like to help you, miss, but I'm afraid I can't. When they left this establishment they were going to take the train clear across the country, prior to sailing for China again out of Vancouver."

"Oh, I see."

"I'm sorry, miss. And sorry for your friend, too."

"Would you happen to know which of the missionary societies they were with?"

"I'm afraid not. In this line of work you don't get a lot of time for idle chatter. They were honest, sober folks and they paid their bill. That's usually good enough for me."

I bade her good day and came out of the hotel feeling distinctly annoyed. Back to square one. I had hoped to show up on Emily's doorstep on Sunday with her whole case solved. She had been so impressed with my profession that I wanted to live up to her expectations. I had to admit now that I was being unrealistic. My experience as a detective has always been one step forward and two back, mostly paths that lead nowhere, and failure always a possibility.

So what was my next line of inquiry? Find out the names of all the missionary societies and get in touch with them. I wasn't sure how to do this, having never been inside a Protestant church in my life. Would their pastors know of such things? At least it would be a place to start. I walked down Broadway looking for a church. It had always struck me that there was a church on every street corner in New York, but of course when I wanted one, I walked several blocks without seeing a spire.

I was becoming increasingly irritable when

I passed a bookshop and paused to look in its window, I have always had a love of books. In fact if I ever came into money, the first thing I'd buy would be a grand library for myself. I gazed with envy at the rich leather covers and wondered if I dared go inside and treat myself. Then I decided that maybe those serving as missionaries in China might sometimes write their memoirs. At least it would be a start. I went inside, savoring that wonderful dusty, leathery smell that lingers around good books.

"May I help you, miss?" an elderly gentleman asked, appearing from behind a counter at the back of the store.

"I was wondering about missionaries in China," I said. "Do you know if any accounts have been written of their lives there?"

"Of course there is the new book about the massacre," he said. "We received the first copies only a few weeks ago and it's been flying off the shelves ever since."

"Massacre?"

"The Boxer Rebellion. You didn't hear about it? Shocking it was. They were all killed. Every one of them. Men, women, children. The whole city was abuzz about it. It can't have been much more than two years ago."

"I'm afraid I was in Ireland two years ago and the only shocking events I heard about were the battles in the Boer War in South Africa where our own boys were fighting," I said.

"Well, it was a terrible tragedy and it's all documented here in this little book." He went to a shelf and brought down a slim volume with a red paper cover. "I only hope the brutal events described therein won't be too much for your delicate sensibilities."

I was tempted to say that I didn't possess any delicate sensibilities that I knew of. Instead I thanked him kindly, parted with twenty cents, and refused his offer to wrap the book in brown paper. I carried it out into the light and studied the cover. *The Tragedy of Paotingfu,* by Isaac C. Ketler. *An authentic story of the Life, Services and Sacrifices of the Presbyterian, Congregational and China Inland Missionaries who Suffered Martyrdom at Paotingfu, China, June 30 and July 1, 1900.* So now I knew that these particular missionaries were Presbyterian and I had an author's name — presumably one of the party had survived to write the tale. What's more, the publisher was one Fleming H. Revell, of New York, Chicago, and Toronto. After an hour or so's diligent sleuthing, I had located their New York office and came away with an address in Pennsylvania for the author. I wrote to him and explained my plight — not mentioning I was a detective, of course. In fact my letter leaned toward the sentimental — my poor dear friend, orphaned at birth, raised knowing nothing of her parents, no mementos, no photographs, etcetera. Any help he could give me would be greatly appreciated — headquarters of missionary societies, other missionaries who might have been in China twenty-five years ago. I sealed the envelope and mailed the letter, feeling rather proud of myself.

My next task should be to find her Aunt Lydia's maiden name. I was tempted to pay a visit to the mansion on East Seventy-ninth where Horace Lynch still lived and see if the direct approach might work. Perhaps one simple question and answer would reveal the truth about Emily's background. But then I dismissed this idea. If there were any kind of underhand business, if he had indeed stolen her inheritance, then I should tread very carefully. Best to thoroughly check the Chinese connection first. It was just possible that everything Emily had been told was true but not completely accurate — maybe her parents had been in another Asian country rather than China. Maybe they had died before the Hinchleys arrived. And maybe Horace Lynch was so unpleasant to her simply because he objected to spending his precious money on someone who wasn't a close relative, or on the education of a female.

Lots of things to think about, then. I went to City Hall, where they produced Lydia Lynch's death certificate. From this I found that her maiden name was Johnson and that she had been born in Williamstown, Massachusetts. So a train ride to New England might be in my future. For the present, all I could do was wait for an answer to my letter from Isaac C. Ketler.

Unfortunately it is not within my temperament to wait patiently; nor can I sit idly. I had mailed the letter on Wednesday, and it should have arrived in Pennsylvania the next morning, and if Mr. Ketler had been at all diligent, I should have expected a response by Friday. When none had come with the morning post, I decided I should at least let Emily know that I had been working on her behalf. So I presented myself at the pharmacy and waited for Emily to emerge for her lunch hour. When she hadn't appeared by ten minutes past one, I dared to enter that establishment to find out what was keeping her. At the sound of the bell jangling she appeared in person from the back room, tying the ribbons on a severe black bonnet of the type often worn by the women in the Salvation Army.

"Holy mother of God, you're not thinking of following your parents into good works, are you?" I said jovially. "You look like a Salvation Army lass."

She didn't smile, making me realize that I had spoken rather too hastily to someone with whom I had such recent acquaintanceship.

"Oh, Molly." She sounded flustered. "I'm afraid you've caught us at a bad moment. We're just about to shut up shop and go to a funeral."

"A funeral. I'm sorry. Was it a friend who passed away?"

"My fellow employee, Mrs. Hartmann. You remember, I had just visited her when you came to the store the other day."

I nodded. "You said she was suffering from some kind of grippe, but she was improving."

"She was. At least, she seemed to be." Emily's voice cracked. "But she must have had a relapse. Or perhaps she put on a good front for me, because she died the very next day. Such a nice woman too. A widow from Germany. Kind. Highly educated and had worked for Mr. McPherson for years." She lowered her voice and glanced into the back room. "He's very cut up about it. Ned's with him now, helping him get ready."

So Mr. McPherson did have a heart after all.

"I'll leave you then," I said. "My condolences. Should I stop by on Sunday to give you my report, do you think?"

"Yes, yes. By all means," she said, but I could tell she was still distracted. At that moment Mr. McPherson emerged from the back of the shop, with Ned following at a respectful distance.

"Are you ready to shut up shop, Miss Boswell?" Mr. McPherson called. He looked positively hollow-eyed and his face was a mask of distress.

"Very good, sir," Emily said.

"This way, Mr. McPherson, sir," Ned led him forward. "Shall I go and find us a cab?"

I beat a hasty retreat.

EIGHT

Saturday arrived and still no answer. I hoped this Mr. Ketler was still alive and in good health. I hated to be held up like this and paced around the house, wondering what to do next. The words *spring cleaning* did enter my mind, but I realized that I owned no carpet beater, my step was relatively clean, and the most I was prepared to do was take down the curtains and give them a good shaking. I was doing this when Sid and Gus emerged from their house.

"Good heavens, Molly. Such industry," Sid exclaimed.

"I have been shamed into doing my spring cleaning for want of anything better to do," I confessed. "You know me. I simply can't sit around doing nothing."

"Then come with us," Gus said. "We are off to an exhibition of French painters at the Metropolitan Museum."

"Gus is wildly enthusiastic about the

neoimpressionist movement," Sid said with a chuckle. "She has spent the last week trying to paint entirely in little dots like Seurat."

"And all I succeeded in doing was painting a picture that looks as if it has the measles," Gus said.

"Nonsense. I think it's quite good in its own way," Sid said kindly.

"But then you're biased," Gus pointed out. "Anyway, Molly, we're off to get more inspiration. My aim is to paint a masterpiece this year or die in the attempt."

"Don't joke about such things," I said. "Too many people have died this spring. Healthy young people like us. And I was with Emily Boswell yesterday. Her fellow assistant died only this week."

"She's right," Sid said. "Let's have no talk of death. Now, Molly, are you going to put that revolting curtain back where it belongs and come with us?"

"It is rather revolting, isn't it?" I looked at the faded velvet critically in the harsh spring light. "But it came with the house when I bought it. Perhaps my task for this spring should be to make new curtains, although my mother always said my children would go naked if they had to rely on me sewing their clothes." As I said this I took the offending article back inside and climbed on a chair to rehang it. A goodly amount of dust still flew out of it as I threaded the rings onto the rod.

They laughed. "Luckily your brave captain will be able to give you a clothing allowance by the time you have children," Sid said. "Where is he these days? We haven't seen him all week, apart from that brief appearance with lecture on Sunday."

"He's working on an important case that he won't discuss with me," I said. "I've hardly seen him since he was reinstated."

"And how long ago was it that you were complaining that his constant presence was too much of a good thing?" Gus asked sweetly.

"That's right. With me it's either feast or famine."

I took off my apron and went for my coat and hat. Soon we were off on a merry jaunt. We spent a delightful day at the museum. I hoped that Daniel would finally put in an appearance that evening. After all, it was Saturday night. Everybody should have a Saturday night free now and then. But the evening wore on and there was no sign of him. I was feeling thoroughly annoyed until suddenly it hit me: Daniel couldn't actually be enjoying these long hours and no days off. He was only doing what he was required to do, and since he had been in disgrace so recently, he was probably working twice as hard as anyone else. Of course then I felt wretched. Only thinking of myself, as usual. A sudden brilliant idea struck me. I had bought some calves' liver in the hope that Daniel would come to supper one evening. It would go bad if I didn't use it soon. Why shouldn't I go to his place and cook him a nice meal so that he'd find it waiting for him when he returned at whatever ungodly hour.

I put the liver, together with some onions, potatoes, and cabbage, into my basket and traveled northward on the El to Twenty-third Street. Daniel's landlady opened the door cautiously in response to my knock. Chelsea was a fairly safe neighborhood by New York standards, but it was well after dark and she had a family to protect. Her face lit up when she saw me. "Why, it's Miss Murphy. I was asking Captain Sullivan about you only the other day. He said you were doing well and he wished he had time to see you more often."

"I've been feeling the same way, Mrs. O'Shea. Captain Sullivan has been working far too hard, so I thought I'd surprise him with a nice meal."

"Well, I think that's a lovely idea," she said. "Up you go, then. You know the way."

"I don't have a key," I reminded her. "Could you let me in?"

"The spare key's here on the hook, same as always," she said. "Help yourself, my dear. If you ask me, it's time Captain Sullivan had a nice young wife to look after him. Running himself ragged, he is."

"We'll have to see about that." I smiled, then climbed the two flights to Daniel's top-floor apartment. I let myself in and stood in the doorway, savoring the familiar smell of pipe tobacco and polished wood. The living room was meticulously neat, with a dark oak table, a leather armchair by the fire, and shelves of books. Clearly a man's abode. I wondered for a moment whether I had done the right thing and whether Daniel would appreciate my entering his place uninvited and alone. Then I decided that if I was to be his wife someday, he'd have to get used to it.

I took off my coat, unpacked my supplies, and got to work. I put the potatoes and cabbage on to boil and was in the middle of frying the onions when a grotesque shadow loomed over me. I let out a scream at the same time as a voice blurted out, "What the devil?"

I turned to see a bleary-eyed Daniel standing behind me in his nightshirt.

"I came over to make you dinner," I said shakily. My heart was thumping. "I wanted to surprise you."

"You certainly did that," he agreed. "I was up most of last night. I crept into bed in the middle of the afternoon and awoke to the smell of frying onions. I thought I was still dreaming until I heard a noise in my kitchen. You nearly scared the living daylights out of me!"

"That makes two of us." I gave an uneasy laugh. "I'm sorry if I woke you."

"Don't be. Whatever it is smells delicious. I haven't had a proper meal in days."

"It's liver. I thought you needed building up," I said.

"Liver and onions. That's a treat. I'll have to see if I've a bottle of wine that might go with it."

"But Daniel, first you should probably at least put on your dressing gown," I suggested.

He looked down at himself, with his bare legs and feet, and had to laugh. "Lord, I must look a sight."

"Very fetching," I said. "I had no idea you had such nice ankles, Captain Sullivan."

"You know very well what my ankles look

like, so don't play the prim miss with me," he chuckled. "I shall return momentarily."

He disappeared into his bedroom while I finished cooking the meal. The next time he appeared he was in his thick woolen robe and slippers and his hair was wetted and neatly combed. And we women think that we are the vain sex!

I laid the table while Daniel poured red wine into two goblets. "Here's to us," he said, raising his glass in a toast. We clinked glasses. His eyes held mine in a way that was unnerving.

"Don't let my good food get cold," I said. He tucked in as if he had been starving.

"Oh, this is so good," he managed to mumble once. When the plate was clean he put down his knife and fork with a satisfied sigh. "That was so good of you, Molly. I can't tell you how much I appreciated it."

"Your actions spoke pretty well for you." I smiled. "Watching you wolf that down reminded me of my little brothers at home."

Daniel drained his glass. "Drink up," he said and refilled his own. "There's plenty more in the bottle."

"I don't think so, thank you." I was well aware of the effect that wine had on me. "I have to get home. I don't want to be seen staggering up Patchin Place."

I stood up and started to clear away the dishes. Daniel grabbed my arm as I reached for his plate. "Don't go," he said.

"I have to go. It's getting late. Chelsea is fairly safe, but . . ."

"Don't go," he said again. "Stay here with me. I've missed you, Molly. How long has it been since you and I shared more than polite conversation together?"

"Not always so polite," I reminded him. "Last time we met you were yelling at me, I seem to remember."

"Only because I care about you," he said. "You want me to care about you, don't you?"

"Yes, but . . ."

His other hand encircled my waist and he pulled me down to his lap. "I want you, Molly," he whispered. "It's been so long."

God, if the truth were known, I wanted him too. He was nuzzling at my neck in a way that was disconcerting and I felt myself weakening.

"Oh, no," I said, attempting to break free of his grip. "You're not getting me into that bedroom unless and until we're married."

"Then let's get married right away. We'll find a priest in the morning. Any kind of pastor will do."

"And you want me to come and live here?"

"I could move into Patchin Place. There's room enough for two there."

"I haven't agreed to marry you yet, Daniel Sullivan," I said, "and if and when we do marry, I want it done right. My mother settled for less than perfect. She slaved away for four ungrateful males and then she died of exhaustion. What kind of living is that?"

"I'd make everything just right for you," he whispered, gazing into my eyes with that unnerving look. "I promise. Everything's going to be perfect."

"I want it done right, Daniel. A proper proposal, a proper wedding with all the trimmings, and a proper place to live. And we still have some things that need sorting out first."

"We'll sort them out as we go. I need a wife, Molly."

"So that's it, is it?" This time I did break free and stood up. "You want to make sure that someone is around to cook your dinner every evening, and keep your bed warm too."

"I need you," he said simply. "I've been on my own long enough. I've been through the bleakest time of my life. I've been in prison. I've been despised and wrongly accused and I've lost my father, who was my guiding light. Enough bad things have happened to me. I want something to look forward to."

"You've got your job back," I said. "That's a start."

"I want to get married. Start a family. A home of my own."

He must have noticed my sudden reaction. "What is it?" He took my hand. "You don't want these things?"

This would have been the perfect moment to tell him the truth. How hard would it be to say, "Daniel, there's something you should know. When you were in jail, I found I was in the family way." I opened my mouth, but I couldn't make the words come out. The whole horror of that situation came flooding back to me. I had lost the baby when I had to jump off a dock and swim for my life.

"Of course I do," I managed to say. "At the right time. I just don't want to be rushed into anything."

He laughed. "I won't rush you, I promise. I'm going to make it all right for us." He stood up and pulled me to him. Then he took my face in his hands and he was kissing me with unleashed passion. I felt my own passion mounting. I could feel the warmth of his body pressing hard against mine. I wanted him desperately. How easy would it be to stay with him tonight, and if I did find myself in the family way again, then we'd get married in a hurry. God knows plenty of couples had done this before us.

But there was just that germ of hesitation. Daniel's face as he had virtually ordered me to his automobile the other day came into my head and I pushed away from him. "Daniel, I have to get home," I whispered. "What would Mrs. O'Shea think?"

"She's got seven children. She'd have a pretty good idea," he said with a chuckle. "Very well. I suppose you're right. You should go." He slapped my behind. "Go on then, before I weaken and drag you off over my shoulder."

I went for my cape and gathered my belongings.

"Molly, I have day off tomorrow," he said, following me around like a small child. "I thought of going out to see my mother. Would you like to come?"

"I can't," I said. "I've promised to visit a client in the afternoon."

"You blame me for having no time off work, and you're just as bad. Clients on a Sunday?"

"She works all week."

"Your client is a lady? That's interesting."

"Very interesting," I said.

"So what does she want you to do for her?"

I raised an eyebrow. "You should know better than anyone that a professional detective can't discuss her case," I said. "My visit to her shouldn't take too long, as I have little to report so far. So if you'd like to take me out tomorrow evening, when you return from your mother's house?"

"You could cook me dinner again," he said hopefully. "I have eaten on the run for the past three weeks. I long for home-cooked meals. And if you want me to keep saving up to buy you a house . . ."

"All right. I suppose I could cook dinner again," I agreed.

"Wonderful. I'll see you tomorrow night."

"Give my regards to your mother," I remembered to say as I left.

NINE

On Sunday afternoon I made my way to Emily's room on the Upper West Side. It was a delightful spring day and people were out in their Sunday best, strolling in squares amid the bright green of new leaves, or just sitting on stoops, their faces upturned to the warmth of the April sun. I rather wished that I had taken Daniel up on his invitation and gone with him to Westchester to see his mother. It would have been a delightful train ride, and we could have strolled in her large back yard or sat on her lawn drinking lemonade. But I was a professional woman and I'd made an appointment with a client. A man wouldn't have broken it because of the weather, so why should I?

The twin spires of St. Patrick's Cathedral glowed bright in the clear air, and I experienced that twinge of guilt that I had missed mass that morning. Even though I had not been to church in years and felt little love for the Catholic religion, those of us brought up as Catholics have been indoctrinated to believe that you go to hell if you miss mass. I don't suppose I'll ever be able to really shake it off.

Emily lived on the third floor of a rooming house. I suppose if it had been the Ansonia, around the corner, one would have described it as an apartment hotel, but this warranted no more than the rooming house description: tired brown linoleum, creaky stairs, that lingering smell of drains and an old woman's face that peeped out of a door on the second-floor landing. I knocked and the door was opened by a rather flustered-looking Emily, with her hat in one hand and a hat pin in the other.

"Molly!" She sounded surprised.

"Hello. I promised I'd call 'round with news on Sunday afternoon for you."

"Oh mercy me. So you did. I was so upset at the thought of going to Mrs. Hartmann's funeral that I didn't properly take it in. And frankly I never expected you to have anything by this Sunday. You must be a miracle worker. Come on in, do."

She led me into what could only be described as a depressing room. Every attempt had been made to brighten it up. There were net curtains at the window, rugs on the floor, pillows on the daybed, but they couldn't hide the brownish wallpaper, the dark wood trim, and the window that faced the back of another equally dreary building. Emily must have read my thoughts. "Pretty dismal, isn't it?" she said. "But then I'm hardly ever here during the daytime, and it's so convenient and cheap, too. I'm trying to save every penny I can."

"You've made it very nice," I said, trying to sound more enthusiastic than I felt. "Very homey."

"Do take a seat," she said, indicating her one upholstered chair. "Can I make you a cup of tea?"

"No, thank you. I just ate luncheon," I said.

She perched on the daybed, opposite me. "I had been living in a ladies' residential club until recently, but it was expensive, and I tired of all the chatter and gossip and pettiness. You can imagine, can't you, all those unmarried ladies living under one roof? Little notes saying, 'Please make sure you dispose of tea leaves properly. Tea cups belong on the left of the cabinet. Do not hang stockings to dry in the bathroom.' "

"I can imagine," I agreed.

She was looking at me, her face alight with expectancy. "So you've something to tell me already?"

"I don't want to raise your hopes too much," I said. "I've no answers for you yet, but I have located a man who wrote a book on missionaries in China. It seems that they were all massacred during the uprising three years ago."

"Ah yes," she said. "The Boxer Rebellion. We read about it. I paid particular interest because of my parents. When the horrific tales trickled in, I kept thinking that it could have been me."

"The writer lives in Pennsylvania," I said. "I'm not sure if he was a missionary himself, but I have written to him and he will definitely be able to put me in touch with other missionaries. I expect a reply any moment. And I have found where your Aunt Lydia was born."

"Excellent. You have been busy," she said.

Then I became aware of the hat she still held in her hands. "You were on your way out," I said. "I shouldn't keep you."

She blushed. "Yes, as a matter of fact, I was."

"Ned decided to forgo the weekly visit to his mother?"

"Oh no." She smiled. "He'd never do that. He idolizes that woman. She is in poor health, you see, and she relies on him for everything. They are particularly close."

"Did his father die?"

A troubled, almost embarrassed, look crossed her face. "Not as far as I know. He has no father — at least none that we know of. He was an illegitimate child and his mother will never speak of his father. She was cast out, you see, and reared him in terrible poverty. He's done very well to educate himself. He's remarkable, really."

"So you've mentioned before," I teased.

She blushed again. "Actually I'm on my way to take tea with a dear friend," she said. "Fanny Poindexter. She and I were room-mates in our freshman year at Vassar. She was Fanny Bradley then, of course. She married Anson Poindexter the moment we graduated and now she's a respectable and rich married lady." She looked up suddenly as the thought struck her. "Why don't you come along?"

"Oh, I couldn't possibly," I said. "I wouldn't want to intrude in a meeting between old friends, I'd just be in the way."

"No, not at all. Fanny is having an afternoon 'at home' at her place. Other young women will be there. You'd enjoy it, I'm sure. And Fanny would be tickled pink to meet a lady detective."

So I was to be brought along as a novelty!

I was about to refuse, but then I decided that it might indeed be amusing to meet other women with lively minds. "Very well," I said. "I accept your kind invitation."

"Splendid." She jumped up. "Just wait until I can make this wretched hat sit straight on my head. Oh, why wasn't I blessed with good hair?"

"You have striking hair," I said, and indeed she did. It was black and lustrous and today was worn in a thick, smooth roll around her face.

Emily made a face. "But it's so horribly straight and refuses to take a curl. I can have it in curling papers all night and in the morning it drops like a limp rag again."

"I suppose we're never thankful for what we've got," I said. "I just wish my own hair could be tamed and wasn't this awful flaming red."

"Oh, but it's such a magnificent color," Emily said. "Quite startling."

"I'd rather be a little less startling sometimes," I said. "It's hard to blend into a crowd."

Emily stuck a last hat pin into her hair with a fierce jab. "There," she said. "Now we can go."

We set off, arm in arm in the spring sunshine. "You'll adore Fanny," Emily said.

"Everyone does. We had such a good time together at Vassar. I was the shy girl who had been raised by governesses and had no social graces, and she had traveled to Europe and knew how to dance and had the most fashionable wardrobe you could ever imagine. I was in awe of her but she took me under her wing."

"And now she lives close by?"

"She has an apartment in the Dakota, but they are having a house built out on Long Island so they can be among the fashionable set."

"How nice to have money," I said.

"It is she who has the money," Emily confided. "She is a Bradley, of Bradley Freight and Steamship. He has the name. He comes from a distinguished old family, you know. Came over on the *Mayflower,* I believe. But they must be happy about an infusion of Bradley cash. Anson is an ambitious young lawyer, so I expect he will do very well for himself. A good match all around."

We approached the park, which was glowing in leafy splendor. I looked at it longingly, wondering if it would be rude to leave Emily to her friend and go for a walk beside the boating lake. Emily held firmly to my arm as we turned onto Central Park West, and I couldn't think of a polite way to extricate myself. A doorman in impressive livery opened the front door for us. An elevator page took us up to the ninth floor. I tried to remember if I had ever taken an elevator this high before. This was still a new experience for me and I still didn't trust them completely. I'd observed the cable going up and down, and it seemed rather thin to be supporting a large iron cage.

Anyway, such anxieties were put aside as we reached the ninth floor and the operator opened the door for us with a smart salute. We could hear laughter coming from behind the door at the end of the hallway. A maid let us in.

"Madam is in the drawing room," she said, unnecessarily, as a good deal of noise was coming from that direction, and led us in.

"Miss Boswell and Miss Murphy, madam," she said.

We entered a large, light room with windows looking out over the park and beyond. A group of young women was assembled around a brocade chaise on which a gorgeous creature reclined. She looked like a china doll, dressed in delicate baby blue, flaxen curls framing her face. It was almost as if the young women had posed in that grouping for a picture, or rather an advertisement for some kind of cosmetic product in the *Ladies' Home Journal.* They looked up at the maid's announcement, making me instantly aware of the plainness of the outfit I was wearing and the unruly state of my hair.

The gorgeous creature swung herself upright and came toward Emily, arms open wide. "Emily, my dear. You came! I can't tell you how delighted I am. It's been an age."

They embraced. "And how well you look," Fanny went on. "I think that young man must be good for you. You are positively glowing."

"That is from the brisk walk, Fanny," Emily said. "And I've brought a friend along to meet you. Miss Molly Murphy, from Ireland, also a working woman like myself, but with a far more interesting job, as you will hear."

"Miss Murphy?" Fanny stretched out a delicate white hand to me. "I am delighted you could come. Any friend of Emily's has to be a friend of mine. May I call you Molly?"

"Please do," I said as she gave me a most charming smile.

"Do take a seat and let me complete the introductions: Alice, Minnie, Bella, and Dorcas."

A healthy-looking woman with light ginger hair moved over to make room for me on an ottoman, giving me a wary smile. I sat and Fanny continued, pointing at my bench-mate. "Alice is an old school friend, now also married and living in the city, Minnie and I were in Europe together. We attended a dreadful academy in Paris for a summer, didn't we, Minnie, my sweet?"

Minnie was more angular, with a long nose. "We did. There were cockroaches and the Mamselle was a regular tartar."

"But we endured and survived," Fanny said. She put a hand on the shoulder of a worldly looking young woman with red lips and circles of rouge on her cheeks. "Bella is a new friend I have met through Anson's business partners and Dorcas needs no introduction to you, does she, Emily?" Fanny turned to me. "Dorcas shared a suite of rooms with us at Vassar."

"And helped us with our Latin translation," Emily added. "So what are you doing now, Dorcas? Were you at that recent re-union that everybody is raving about?"

"Alas, no." Dorcas looked up with a serene smile. "I couldn't leave my darling

Toodles."

"Toodles?" Emily asked.

"Actually, his official name is Thomas Hochstetter the Third, but Toodles he seems to be at the moment, and he is only two months old."

"You're a mother. How wonderful." Emily beamed at her.

"Yes, it is wonderful, but I suspect my reading will be limited to Peter Rabbit for the next decade or so."

"And to think that we always expected you to wind up as a professor and write brilliant articles," Emily said.

"I've done the next best thing," Dorcas answered serenely. "I've married a professor at NYU. He's a brilliant man."

The maid returned, pushing a trolley that contained a silver tea service, delicate china cups, and a splendid cake stand of various cakes.

"So now we are all happily married," Fanny said. "Except you, Emily. You have to hurry up and join the club. How is this young man of yours progressing?"

"He's doing really well," Emily said. "He's an absolute whiz when it comes to inventing new preparations."

"Preparations?" Alice asked.

"Emily's young man is a druggist," Fanny

explained.

"Just an apprentice at the moment," Emily cut in. "I work for the same apothecary, behind the counter. Mr. McPherson wouldn't let a woman near the actual drugs."

The group chuckled.

"I've popped in there a couple of times and they made me a marvelous mixture for my stomach. Wonderfully calming," Fanny said.

"Do tell where it is," Minnie said. "I am in desperate need of a calming mixture. My nerves are really quite upset since we moved to that big new house. And Frank is so often away that I find it hard to sleep."

"Oh, I'm sure we could make you a great sleeping powder," Emily said. "We're on Columbus, not far from Fanny's."

"Then I must pay you a visit next time I come into the city," Minnie said.

"Oh but girls, I use the absolute best of calming tinctures," Bella said. "My dears, it's almost pure opium. The joy of it! A few drops in water and the world simply melts away."

"I don't think that Anson would approve of that," Fanny said with a frown. "He doesn't like me taking things. He even disapproves of smelling salts. He says it should be mind over matter and that feeling faint is all in my head."

"Of course it's not in your head," I said, and all eyes turned on me. "If you will wear those ridiculously tight corsets, you're going to feel faint any time you're upset, because you start to breathe rapidly and your lungs won't let you take in fresh air. You're actually breathing in your own used breath."

They looked at me as if I was a strange animal. "But everybody wears corsets," Dorcas said. "I'm back in mine already and little Toodles isn't quite two months old."

"I was told one's insides would rattle about if one didn't hold them in place with a corset," Minnie said.

"Well, I've never worn one and never intend to," I said. I could tell they thought I was remarkably odd.

"But don't you want to marry? What man would look twice at a woman with a large waist?" Fanny turned those doll-like blue eyes on me.

"I have a young man and he seems to like me just fine the way I am," I said. I didn't add that he found it hard to keep his hands off me. They might have swooned on the spot.

"So your young man is good at making concoctions, is he, Emily?" Dorcas chose tactfully to change the subject.

"He is. He's been trying his hand at ladies' cosmetics," Emily said. "I think they're marvelous."

"They are," Fanny agreed. "He's absolutely as good as anything that comes from Paris. Emily, don't forget you promised me another jar of that wonderful face cream he makes. I'm almost out of it."

"So I did. I'll remind Ned to make you one."

Dorcas examined Emily's face. "Your complexion is flawless, Emily, and Fanny's is certainly perfection. I'd love to try it too."

"There. You've landed Ned his first order," Fanny said. "And Bella, I wouldn't say no if you brought a little of your magic calming tincture next time we meet. Anson need never know."

"How is Anson?" Emily asked.

"Busy." Fanny frowned. "What with working in the city and then going out to inspect the building of our new house, I hardly see him. If it weren't for you dear friends, and shopping, of course, my life would be one of utter boredom."

"I'm so glad we live in the city," Bella said. "The shopping is wonderful, don't you think?"

"Nothing like Paris," Minnie said. "It's

impossible to buy a decent dress off the peg, and most of the dressmakers are so provincial in their taste. I had to tell mine quite firmly that I had a fine bust and I wanted more of it exposed on my evening dress."

"Minnie!" Alice exclaimed. "And you a married woman, too."

"What's wrong with it?" Minnie said with a self-satisfied smile. "A bigger bust is the one advantage to giving birth to a baby. I had nothing to show off before."

"And what did your dressmaker say?" Fannie asked.

"She turned quite pale and looked at me as if I were a brazen hussy."

We laughed.

"I hope you fired her," Bella said.

"I did, but now I'm lost. What will I wear when the summer season starts out in Newport?"

"You'll be going there for the summer, will you?"

"Oh, definitely. All of Jack's business acquaintances will be there, so there's no point in staying here, and he does enjoy the sailing so."

"I rather wish we were building a house in Newport," Fanny said, "but Anson has insisted on Great Neck or Little Neck or somewhere with an equally silly name. He wants to be close enough to the city to go back and forth with ease. But then we shall move there and I shall know nobody."

"We'll all come and visit you, Fanny dear," Alice said, reaching across to pat her hand. "We'll have such fun garden parties and play croquet."

"And you'll have to come into the city to shop, of course," Bella said firmly. "Speaking of which, did I tell you that I've discovered the most amazing fabric store? It's in the most disreputable part of the city, on Canal Street, but they import silks from China. You have never seen anything like it. My eyes nearly popped out of my head. So I gave them my card and told them to bring me a selection to choose from and next time you see me at a ball, I'll be dazzling in scarlet silk."

"We must all come to your place when the silk merchant is there," Fanny said.

"Oh no. This is my little find," Bella said, laughing. "I have no wish to compete with a bevy of Chinese-clad beauties. You find your own little secret gems."

"And speaking of gems," Alice said, "I must show you Arthur's latest present to me. It's the most divine ruby necklace you have ever seen."

"What was the occasion?" Emily asked.

"No occasion really, although it is close to our second anniversary." Alice blushed. "He just saw it in Mr. Tiffany's window and had to have it for me. Wasn't that divine of him?"

"You'll have to lend it to me for my Chinese silk, Alice," Bella said.

"I'm not lending it to anyone. At that price Arthur probably won't allow me to wear it outside of the house."

I had remained silent since my outburst on the folly of corsets and was following the conversation with interest, mingled with a tinge of alarm. These were presumably all educated women. Two at least had been to Vassar. Yet the conversation had not departed once from shopping and their attire. And their speech had been peppered with such phrases as "Arthur wouldn't allow me to . . ." Fanny's husband was building them a house on Long Island even though Fanny, who supposedly had the money, would have liked Newport. Did all women have to surrender their wits and their power when they married? I tried to picture myself saying, "Daniel would not allow me to . . ."

Fanny must have noticed my preoccupied expression because she said suddenly, "Miss Murphy, please do have a cake or some chocolate, and you never did tell us what manner of work you are involved in."

"You'll never guess," Emily said, with an excited look around the group, "but she's a detective. A lady detective."

"No. Are there such things?" The news caused quite a stir in the little gathering.

"I assure you I'm real," I said, "and yes, I run my own detective agency."

"And are you like Mr. Sherlock Holmes? Do you stalk through New York with your magnifying glass, picking up hairs and cigarette butts and declaring that the murderer was a one-armed Peruvian with a lisp?" Bella giggled as she looked at me.

"I can't claim to have had Sherlock Holmes's success," I said, "but I have concluded some successful cases."

"Not all sordid divorces, I hope?" Alice said primly.

"I rarely touch divorces for that reason," I said. "My cases have ranged from missing persons to proving the innocence of those wrongly accused."

"How terribly exciting," Fanny said. "But isn't this kind of work dangerous?"

"Too dangerous at times," I confessed. "My young man wants me to quit."

"Well, you will as soon as you marry, won't you?" Bella said.

"I don't know."

"She's working for me at this very moment," Emily said. "She's trying to find out the truth about my parents."

"But I thought they were missionaries and they died of cholera," Fanny said.

"So did I. But now I'm wondering if I've been deceived," Emily answered. "Molly is absolutely wonderful. She's already tracked down somebody who wrote a book on missionaries in China and he will put her in touch with everybody who was there at the time."

"Well done, Miss Murphy." Alice patted me on the shoulder.

"Do eat, everybody. Our cook makes the most delicious cakes," Fanny said. The group needed no urging, even though they expressed concern about their figures as the cream cakes disappeared from the plate.

At last we bid our adieus and left.

"So what did you think of Fanny and her friends?" Emily asked as we stepped out of the Dakota. "Isn't she an absolute beauty? And so kind, too."

"She is certainly lovely," I said. "And she does seem kind."

"Of course that kind of life would never be for me," Emily said. "Fanny, Dorcas, and I used to have discussions deep into the night about democracy and the loss of greatness in a democratic society and the justification for colonialism. All kinds of deep topics. We were planning to set the world to rights. I was going to train as a doctor and follow my parents into the mission field. Fanny wanted to be an anthropologist and come with me to Africa to study primitive tribes while I healed their bodies and minds. And Dorcas — she used to read Ovid in Latin for pleasure!"

"And now all they talk about is gowns and cosmetics," I said.

"It is my observation that most husbands do not want brainy wives. They want an adornment, a good mother but not one who will provide any threat to their authority."

"I'm afraid you're right," I said. "I've made my own position quite clear to my young man. I want an equal partnership or nothing at all."

"I expect the same," Emily said. "Ned respects my intelligence too much to think of me as a plaything or a possession."

"Then we will stick up for our rights together," I said. "We will remain the last two intelligent married women in New York City!"

Emily laughed and slipped her arm through mine. We marched, in step, along the side of the park.

Ten

After what I had experienced that afternoon I had second thoughts about cooking dinner for Daniel. Did I want him to become accustomed to seeing me in the role of domestic drudge? After all, I too had been working all week. But then I reasoned that it was up to the woman to do the cooking, however liberated she was. If we waited to marry until Daniel was financially stable again, I should be able to expect at least one servant, presumably one who could cook. So I applied myself to making a good dinner. I had a nice piece of beef that I roasted with potatoes and sprouts. Daniel stood in my hallway, sniffing appreciatively as he took off his hat.

"My, but that smells good," he said.

"Roast beef," I said with a certain amount of satisfaction.

I insisted that he carve. He made rather a hash of it, but I wisely kept silent. Then we sat and ate.

"So how was your client this afternoon?" he asked. "Satisfied with the progress you are making?"

I knew he was curious to find out more about the case, but since he was sharing no details of his own work, I merely gave an enigmatic smile. "Very satisfied, thank you. Recommended me to other women at the gathering in the Dakota."

"The Dakota. So your client moves in high circles."

"She does."

"Fascinating."

I laughed at the expression on his face.

"You're not going to tell me more, are you?" he asked.

"No, I'm not. Not until you tell me about your work."

"Ah, but I'm a police officer. My cases are criminal ones. If I talked about them, I might give a defense attorney grounds for dismissal."

"It's not as if I'll go blabbing to all and sundry," I said. "And a problem shared is a problem halved."

"Nothing you could do, my dear," he said. "Completely outside of your sphere. Gang wars among the Chinese over the opium trade. Bodies in back alleys. Large quantities of opium being brought in under our noses. That's my major concern at the moment, and if that's not enough, I've got cases of apparently random poisonings on my hands."

"What kind of poisonings?"

"Arsenic."

"You're right. Out of my sphere," I said. "And my own case sounds rather boring in comparison. Trying to find out the truth about my clients' parents."

"Interesting," he said, but he didn't sound very interested. "Anyway, enough of work. Tell me something amusing."

So I related my afternoon's experience at the Dakota. "I don't ever want to end up like that," I finished.

Daniel laughed. "No, I can't see you lounging on your chaise, discussing ball gowns. But don't worry, my dear. That will never happen to you."

"Thank you, Daniel." I beamed at him. "I can't tell you how relieved I am to hear you say that."

"Well, it's obvious, really, isn't it," he said. "On a policeman's salary you won't be able to afford ball gowns and jewels. You'll be out hanging the laundry and scrubbing the floors." He ducked as I went to throw a potato at him.

■ ■ ■ ■

The next morning's post brought a reply from Isaac C. Ketler in Pennsylvania.

My dear Miss Murphy:
I am in receipt of your interesting letter of the 12th inst. I personally am not connected with the mission field, although I am personally acquainted with the Simcox family, whose brutal massacre was the impetus for me to write this book. Their parents live close by in Pennsylvania and turned over years of correspondence for my use. I am founder and principal of Grove City College, a small liberal arts institution based on a firm Christian foundation.

I should like to help your friend in her quest for knowledge of her parents and am forwarding to you the names and addresses of each of the missionary organizations active in China. This presupposes that your friend is of American heritage, as there are also missionary societies based in London equally active in Asia.

When you have ascertained with which of the missionary organizations they were affiliated, you may wish to contact some of those names I cite in my book, for more personal details on her parents and their life in China.

If I can be of further service, please do not hesitate to write.

Isaac C. Ketler, Ph.D.

Wonderful. I now had a start. Of course I was a little daunted when I saw the number of missionary societies he had included for me: American Baptists, Bible Society, Board of Commissioners for Foreign Missions, Methodists, Presbyterians, Reformed, Protestant Episcopal, and so on. A whole page of them. I had no idea so many people had a burning desire to convert the heathen Chinese!

Well, I had my work cut out for me. I took out a pad of paper and sat down to write to each of the missionary headquarters. Dr. Ketler mentioned in a postscript the large numbers of Catholic missionaries also operating in China. I saw little point in contacting any Catholics, as they had a surfeit of priests and nuns and wouldn't need the help of lay couples.

As I worked down the list I was pleased to note that some of these societies had their headquarters in New York — two of them

were even on Fifth Avenue, practically around the corner from my own house. Those I could visit in person. It took me most of the morning, including several sheets ruined by inkblots and words that couldn't be repeated in public, before I had my stack of letters to take to the mail.

Now all I had to do was wait. I was itching to do something else, still tempted in fact to visit Emily's disagreeable uncle. I might well have given in to my impulse and done so, but just as I was setting out to visit the two missionary headquarters on Fifth Avenue I received another letter — this one hand-delivered by a messenger.

My dear Miss Murphy:
   It was delightful to make your acquaintance yesterday. I wonder if I could prevail upon you to call on me at your earliest convenience on a matter of great urgency.

Yours sincerely,
Fanny Poindexter
P.S. Please call between the hours of ten and four.

Now this was really intriguing. I had seen Fanny's eyes light up when she heard that I was a detective. The missionary headquar-

ters could wait. I went straight upstairs to put on my most respectable outfit and the one good hat I had rescued from the mud, then I headed uptown to the Dakota.

Fanny was dressed in somber dove-gray this morning, which somehow accentuated the pink of her cheeks and the clear blue of her eyes.

"Miss Murphy!" She sounded breathless. "How good of you to come so quickly. Please take a seat." I noticed I had become Miss Murphy again now that we were discussing business. I followed suit.

"Thank you, Mrs. Poindexter."

I sat. Coffee was served.

I waited. We discussed the weather.

"You have a problem, Mrs. Poindexter?" I said at last. "Something you think I could help you with professionally?"

She was twisting a curl around her finger like a little girl. "I believe that my husband keeps a mistress, Miss Murphy," she blurted out.

"What makes you think this?"

"Silly lies that he has told me. Once he claimed that he was dining with Bella's husband on a business matter, and later I found out from Bella that she and her husband had been out of town that night. And all those trips to oversee the building

of our new home . . . surely no building needs to be overseen that frequently. And the crowning piece of damning evidence. I saw a piece of jewelry in Cartier's and asked about it and found that such a piece was already purchased by my husband. But I never received it, Miss Murphy."

"Maybe he is saving it for a special occasion and plans to surprise you with it?"

She shook her head. "No, I'm ashamed to say that I searched the places he'd be likely to hide it and it wasn't there."

"At the bank, maybe?"

She shook her head again, violently this time. "No, I'm sure, absolutely sure it wasn't meant for me. Anson isn't the sort of person who would buy a piece of jewelry to surprise me with later. He buys me presents for my birthday but apart from that he has never surprised me with flowers even. He does his duty but no more."

"How does he treat you? Is he not affectionate?"

"At the beginning of our marriage he was — well, to put it bluntly, rather keen in bedroom matters. But I believe that had more to do with wanting an heir than with me. And now over two years have gone by and I have failed to produce that heir, and I noticed his interest waning. Recently he scarcely notices my presence and only comes to my bedroom when he is drunk."

"Dear me," I said. "Have you confronted him with any of this?"

"Oh no," she said. "I don't want him to have any inkling that I suspect him. I want you to provide the evidence, and if it's true, I plan to divorce him."

"Divorce him? Give up all this?"

"Miss Murphy, the money is from my family. Without me Anson would be living in a dreary side street with no hope of a home on Long Island." She leaned closer to me. "To be honest with you, this match was arranged by our families when we were still children. Anson is — well, a very attractive man. What sixteen-year-old would not be excited at the thought of marrying someone as dashing as he? I agreed to the match before I knew anything about life."

"And he has not proved to be dashing and exciting?"

"He sees me as a useful adornment, Miss Murphy. Someone to dress up and show off at his business functions. And someone to buy him the house of his dreams. But I do not believe he cares for me one iota. I am a prisoner in a beautiful cage."

"Do you mean that, Mrs. Poindexter? You have your own life and friends, surely?"

"Anson is a very forceful man," she said. "He expects to control every aspect of my life — what I wear, whom I meet for luncheon. He wants to know where I am going and with whom. He has to approve of my friends before they come to the apartment. My sister wanted me to accompany her to Paris, but I am not to travel without him. He likes to keep me under his thumb. I am one of his possessions now, Miss Murphy. No more, no less."

I looked at her with compassion. "Do you have any idea who this woman might be?"

"No, I have no idea. It may even be one of our set. Will you take my case, Miss Murphy? Will you find out the truth for me?" She reached out that delicate white hand, adorned with a perfect, square-cut emerald. I took it and she gripped mine tightly.

"I'll do my best, Mrs. Poindexter," I said.

"Please, make sure he doesn't see you." Fanny grabbed my sleeve with sudden vehemence. "He must not know about this."

"I am a professional and skilled in such matters, Mrs. Poindexter," I said.

"Because if he found out I had hired a detective and was planning to divorce him — I don't know what would happen," she said in a small voice.

"You can rely on me," I said.

ELEVEN

I left the Dakota armed with the details of Mr. Anson Poindexter's life — his place of business, his club, the names and addresses of his business partners and friends. I had been shown several likenesses of him and Fanny gave me a small photograph to carry in my purse. Now I had to do some of that old-fashioned surveillance work that is the backbone of any detective agency.

So I found myself with two cases to juggle again. I was clearly a glutton for punishment. But on this occasion I didn't think they would overlap very much. Anson Poindexter would be working as an attorney during the daytime hours. It was after work that he would need to be observed and followed. So that gave me the rest of the day to do the more mundane task of visiting missionary societies. I smiled at the incongruity of this — the mistress and the missionaries. What interesting bedfellows!

Before I went home, I decided to check out for myself where Anson Poindexter worked during daylight hours. His chambers were in a solid brownstone on Pearl Street, just around the corner from Wall Street and the stock exchange. I wondered if he had his own carriage or would take a cab or even walk to the nearest form of public transportation, which would probably be the South Ferry station of the Ninth Avenue and Third Avenue trains. I rather thought the cab and looked for cabs waiting nearby. Questioning the drivers proved of no value. None of them knew Mr. Anson Poindexter by name.

"I don't ask questions. I just drives them where they wants to go," one of the drivers snapped. "If they pays their money then they could be one of P. T. Barnum's freaks for all I'd care."

So much for that line of inquiry. I had been hoping to find a friendly cabby — one who would, for a small fee, let me know where he had taken Mr. Poindexter recently. But so far I couldn't see this working out. All in all they were a surly bunch. Maybe sitting up on a cab in all weather, exposed to the elements, would make the best of men surly. And maybe after a few days of visiting this location, I could soften them up a little. I resolved to go home and bake cookies, knowing that the way to a man's heart is through his stomach.

That much accomplished, I decided I still had time to visit the two missionary head-quarters before they shut up shop that evening. I arrived at lower Fifth Avenue and paid a call on the Methodist Missionary Society, at number 150.

I was greeted politely and told my tale. The bewhiskered gentleman listened attentively. "Boswell?" he said. "The name doesn't immediately ring a bell. Are you sure of the denomination?"

"Not sure at all," I said. "All we know is that they were missionaries in China and died in a cholera epidemic about twenty-five years ago."

"Let me check for you." He got up and went to a shelf full of ledgers. After searching for a while he shook his head. "No, they do not appear to be connected with our church. I'm sorry I can't help you further. I wish you good luck."

One down, about twenty to go. I came out and walked a few paces up the street to the Presbyterian Board of Foreign Missions, at 156 Fifth Avenue. It was next to a fine Presbyterian church. Those Protestants certainly knew how to build some grand edifices. This time there were two gentlemen in earnest conversation when I entered. One was similarly elderly and distinguished-looking, the other a more robust-looking fellow with a fine set of muttonchop whiskers, in a black frock coat. I was offered a chair and they listened attentively while I told my story.

"Boswell?" the older man said. "I don't recall the name as one of ours, do you, Mr. Hatcher?"

"I can't say that I do," the man with the muttonchop whiskers replied, "but I haven't been in the service as long as you, Dr. Brown."

The older man nodded. "I have certainly been part of this missionary effort for more than twenty years. But let me go and check the ledgers for you, my dear young lady. Please take a seat and I'm sure our Mr. Hatcher will keep you entertained." He disappeared into a back room while the other man leaned over to me. "So you're doing all this for a friend, are you? That's what I call real Christian friendship. Is the poor dear lady suffering from an infirmity?"

"An infirmity? No, she's in good health. Why do you ask?"

"I just wondered, because from what you said it sounded as if she was not able to make the inquiries herself, so I thought that perhaps she was of frail constitution."

"No, not at all," I said, smiling, although there was something about the man's overly friendly manner and the fact that he had moved his chair closer to mine that was beginning to annoy me. "The answer to that is simple. She is a working woman, supporting herself with no family behind her. She has neither time nor leisure for this sort of undertaking."

"Oh, I see. Then you must be a lady of leisure yourself."

I was tempted to tell him it was none of his business, but I controlled the urge and reasoned he was only trying to make polite conversation while we were waiting for the search through the ledgers. Perhaps he wasn't used to dealing with young white women any longer, and his gushingly friendly manner went down well among the heathen.

"I happen to have enough time to help out a dear friend," I said. "Isn't that what the Bible tells us to do?"

"Absolutely. Oh, indeed, yes, it is. You sound like you'd be an ideal candidate for the missions yourself, Miss — ?"

"Murphy," I said. "And I think I'd be the last person to want to serve as a missionary.

First, I happen to be a Catholic, although not the most devoted to my religion, and, second, I have no wish to live in a mud hut and be massacred by savages or die of cholera or typhoid."

"I assure you it is not as bad as you make it sound," the gentleman said. "I myself have been harvesting souls for the Lord for quite a while and have come through unscathed, as you can see. Although I was lucky to have been home on leave during the terrible massacre three years ago. You must have read about it. I lost a lot of good friends."

"It must have been awful," I said. "I have just read Dr. Ketler's account of it. Your fellow Presbyterians Mr. and Mrs. Simcox and all their little children."

"Yes, indeed. But they are now reaping their reward at the feet of their maker, aren't they?" He took out his handkerchief and blew his nose noisily. "So tell me, are you still unattached yourself then, Miss Murphy?"

Really, was he interested in me or just plain nosy? "I expect to be married in the near future," I said.

"And your young man, is he in some kind of philanthropic field? Does he have good Christian leanings like yourself?"

I chuckled. "Some might find his profession a philanthropic one. He is a policeman, sir."

"A policeman? Fancy that. One hears some terrible stories about corruption among the police. Let us hope that a young Christian girl like yourself can keep him on the straight and narrow."

"I assure you he is of an honest and upright nature, Mr. Hatcher," I said.

"That is reassuring to hear, my dear. I am glad to know that there are honest policemen in New York City and that we citizens can sleep sound in our beds. So tell me . . ."

At that moment mercifully the older man returned. "Ah, I see you two have had a nice chat. You've had a chance to talk with our Mr. Hatcher, then, Miss Murphy. One of our most devoted missionaries. He works in the city of Shanghai, among the most depraved of souls in that port city. I can't tell you the number of souls he has saved for Jesus."

I decided that I might have been uncharitable. Obviously the man's approach was more successful among the Chinese. The thought crossed my mind that he might have been looking for a wife to take back to China and might have seen me as a likely candidate. The idea made me grin.

"Oh come now, Dr. Brown," Mr. Hatcher

said, twiddling his mustache in embarrassment. "It is Jesus who saves the souls. I am merely an earthly vessel."

Dr. Brown sat down at his desk again. "Well, I regret to tell you, Miss Murphy, that we have no record of a couple called Boswell ever having been part of our mission to China."

I got to my feet. "I see. Thank you for your time, Dr. Brown. And it was pleasant chatting with you, Mr. Hatcher."

"You've asked Hatcher about the Boswells, then, have you? The man knows China like the back of his hand."

I looked up at Mr. Hatcher as he gave a regretful shrug. "I can't say I ever ran into a couple called Boswell. Of course, you said you were speaking of twenty-five years ago, and I have only been working in the Orient for the past eighteen years."

"But perhaps you might have heard tales of a missionary couple who died in the cholera epidemic and a baby who survived."

"Which year would that be?" Hatcher asked.

"Eighteen seventy-seven or -eight."

Hatcher frowned. "There was no cholera epidemic that I know of that year. I remember when I arrived in the mid-eighteen-eighties a sister of the Catholic mission said how fortunate they had been to have been cholera-free for the past ten years. But of course the disease is never completely eradicated and China is a huge country. If your couple had been working far from civilization then they would have been exposed to all manner of foul diseases."

"I'm sorry we couldn't be of more help, Miss Murphy." Dr. Brown shook my hand.

"Maybe the young lady should leave you her card," Mr. Hatcher suggested. "Then we could contact her if we happened to hear anything that might be of use to her."

"You're most kind," I said. "And maybe if you could possibly put me in touch with any missionaries who were working up-country at that time?"

"I could probably do that," Dr. Brown said. "Leave your card with me and I'll go through my records to see which of our missionaries might now be retired and easily available. I'm afraid most of them are so devoted to the cause that they die out in China. So many poor heathen souls waiting to know the Lord, and the workers are so few, you know."

I fished in my purse and offered him my card. I noticed Mr. Hatcher leaning forward in his seat to get a look at it. Really, it was amazing that the man's nosiness had not gotten him into trouble in a place like China!

Having completed my missionary inquiries, I went home, grabbed a bite to eat, and hastily changed into a more fashionable outfit. It was a little cold for the shantung two-piece costume I had acquired from famous actress Oona Sheehan while working on an assignment for her, but I was prepared to shiver a little to make sure I looked right. I caught the El down to South Ferry and lurked out of sight until I saw Anson Poindexter emerge from his office building. I noticed which cab he hailed, but couldn't hear the directions he gave the cabby. As soon as the cab pulled away, I went into the building and up the stairs to Farnsworth and Poindexter, Attorneys at Law. As I had hoped, a young male clerk was still hard at work. He looked up in surprise as I entered.

"I'm sorry, ma'am. We're actually closed for the day. I'm just doing some filing."

"Oh, dear me, how vexing. So Mr. Poindexter has gone then, has he?" I tried to play the spoiled upper-class miss.

"Yes, ma'am. Left just a few minutes ago."

"Oh, what a pity. I took tea with his wife this afternoon and I promised her I'd pass him a message, as I was going to be visiting my accountant in this area. And now I'm too late and I've let Fanny down. You don't happen to know where Mr. Poindexter went, do you?"

"I believe he said he was going straight home, ma'am." The clerk was looking at me strangely.

"Really? Because Mrs. Poindexter was under the impression he was going to the theater."

Did I notice the hint of a reaction to this last word?

"No, I'm pretty sure he said something to Mr. Farnsworth about 'heading home.' "

"In that case my services weren't needed and I can go about my business with a clear conscience, can't I?" I gave him my most charming smile.

I suspected that Anson Poindexter would have said he was heading home even if his intentions were quite different. I had no choice but to go home myself. Not for the first time, I lamented the fact that I was a woman. A male detective could follow a man to his club, could chat with a cabby more easily and blend among men without arousing suspicion. I had taken this assignment blithely confident that I could carry it out. Now I started to wonder exactly how I

was going to keep tabs on the wandering
Mr. Poindexter.

Twelve

The next day I decided I would have to resort to subterfuge. My former employer, Paddy Riley, had been a master of disguise. It was something I seldom used but this might be a good moment. Accordingly, I found my oldest clothes and topped them with a truly awful hat from the used clothing store on Greenwich Avenue. Then I made sure my face was good and dirty with the help of some earth from my back yard. I stopped in at the Jefferson Street market and bought enough flowers to fill a basket, then made my way back to Pearl Street, this time as a flower seller.

I had actually made four sales — three buttonholes and a posy — by the time Mr. Poindexter emerged. I studied him as he came toward me. A dashing fellow indeed — the classic tall, dark, and handsome, with a strong jaw unadorned by side-whiskers. He carried himself with an air of authority, almost a swagger. I could well see how sixteen-year-old Fanny had fallen for him. He hailed a cab and was about to climb in when I approached him.

"Buy some flowers for the special lady in your life, sir?" I pleaded with the right amount of humility and desperation in my voice.

He glanced at my hand, which now held out a posy of primroses and jonquils. His face broke into a charming smile.

"Good idea. Why not?" he said, fished in his pocket, and dropped a silver dollar into my hand. Then he leaped into the cab.

Unfortunately, at the very moment he was giving his instructions to the cabby, a large dray passed with a loud rumble and the clatter of horses' hooves. I thought I heard the word Broadway, but I might have been mistaken. I hesitated a second, then decided to act. I rushed to the nearest cab waiting in the rank opposite. "Follow that cab," I said.

The cabby gave me a queer look. "Here, what's your game, girlie?"

"I'll make it worth your while not to lose him," I said, in the process of hauling myself and the flowers on board.

"You better have the money to pay for this," he said.

"Do you want the job or not?" I demanded, angry now as Poindexter's cab was fast disappearing up Pearl Street. "Should I take another cab?"

"Okay, I guess. Climb in," he said.

I did and we set off. I have to confess it was rather exciting. The horse even broke into a canter at times and we rocked around a bit. But as we headed uptown and reached Broadway the traffic increased. Several times I thought we'd lost him. The ride took forever and I began to wonder whether Mr. Poindexter was extravagant enough to hire a cab to take him all the way home. This was fast turning into a very expensive cab ride, and I realized that I had yet again failed to establish my fee before I agreed to take the assignment. Still, Fanny Poindexter had claimed she was rich in her own right. She ought to have enough money to pay me.

At last the cab turned into Forty-fourth Street and stopped outside an imposing building.

"Stop here," I called to the cabby. Luckily, there was a line of cabs pulling up and disgorging passengers ahead of us, so I could descend without Mr. Poindexter noticing me. I paid the rather exorbitant amount the cabby demanded. I saw his eyes open wider when he glimpsed my purse, and then an idea struck me.

"Your normal place is down on Pearl Street, is that right?"

"That's right, miss." He was more friendly now that he had been paid. "What's this all about then, keeping an eye on your wayward husband, are you? You're no more a flower seller than I'm the president of the United States."

"You're right," I agreed, because it was easier than telling the truth. "Get a good look at him as he goes into that building, because there's a dollar in it for you if you can report to me any address to which he takes a cab."

"A dollar?" he sounded disgusted.

I bit the bullet. "Five dollars then. How about that? I'll give you five dollars if you can come up with valuable information for me. Is that a deal?"

He looked at me long and hard. "I don't know what your game is, lady, but I reckon it's none of my business." He reached down his hand. "You got yourself a deal."

I left him and approached the building into which Poindexter had disappeared. It turned out to be the New York Yacht Club. Personally, I thought it was a strange site for a yacht club, with no water within sight

149

in any direction, but I knew from what Fanny had told me that he was a member here, as well as at the Columbia Club and the New York Athletic Club. I wondered if he had just popped in for a quick drink and how long I should keep watch. The problem was that this wasn't the sort of street where a flower seller could remain inconspicuous. There were no crowds, for one thing, and the passersby were well dressed. I discarded the basket of flowers and the hat, and cleaned my face with my handkerchief. But I still attracted the attention of a passing constable. He eyed me from the other side of the street, and when he came around again, he crossed over to me. "Waiting for somebody, miss?" he asked. I was clearly not dressed well enough to be a street-walker.

I tried to come up with a good answer to this question. "I'm a writer," I said. "I'm thinking of setting a scene of my next novel on this very street and I'm soaking up the atmosphere." All right, it wasn't good, but it was the best I could do on short notice. The constable seemed to buy it, anyway. He smiled and shook his head and went away muttering something about women writers.

It became quite dark and cold. I hopped around a bit until finally Poindexter emerged from the club. He didn't look pleased with himself this time but annoyed. He hailed a cab and swung himself up. "The Dakota," he snapped.

After all that, he was simply going home. I was about to do the same, as I was cold and hungry and my feet were hurting me, but I had a flash of inspiration. We were very close to Delmonico's, a well-known haunt for late-night suppers in very private rooms. It was just possible that Mr. Poindexter had entertained his lady friend there. It wasn't until I entered the front door and saw the look of horror on the face of the maître d' that I remembered how I was dressed. I don't know if he thought I was begging, seeking customers, or simply wanting to make a nuisance of myself, but he marched over with that jaunty, bouncy step that only Italians can master and muttered that I should probably leave. He made sure of this by signaling one of the waiters, who escorted me out the front door.

I waited until we were outside and then took my chance. "Listen," I said in a low voice. "I'm trying to trace somebody. If I show you a man's picture, could you tell me whether he's been seen in the restaurant recently with a woman?"

The waiter looked horrified. He was one

of those sad-looking men with longish black hair, parted down the middle, and a droopy black mustache. "I'm sorry, miss, but it is more than my job's worth to give out any information on our clientele. We pride ourselves on our discretion. So run along, please."

I could sense the maître d' watching me, but just then a couple of bona fide diners entered and I took my chance again, whipping out the photograph. "This man," I whispered. "Has he been to the restaurant lately?"

"I told you, miss. I couldn't divulge anything like that."

I moved the photograph just enough for him to see that the dollar bill lay beneath it. "More than my job's worth," he said again.

But I had seen from a momentary change in his expression that he had recognized Anson Poindexter.

"So you couldn't describe the woman who was with him?" I asked.

"With whom?" He stared at me blankly. The dollar bill still rested in the palm of my hand.

"The man you've never seen," I went on. "I just wondered what sort of woman might have been with a man like that, had he decided to come here without your seeing him."

The ghost of a smile twitched on his lips. "Exotic-looking," he said. "Not the type you'd bring home to Mother."

I reached out my hand to shake his. "You've been most helpful," I said and felt him slip the bill into his own palm. "She wouldn't have a name, this exotic woman?"

"They never have names, only kitten, sugar, or honeybun," he said, really smiling now.

I came away feeling more optimistic. Exotic-looking. The type you don't bring home to Mother. That definitely implied the theater to me. It so happened that I knew a bit about the theater life. While I had been working undercover in a theater, I had seen the stage-door Johnnies in operation — those rich young men who hung around theaters, plying leading ladies and chorus girls alike with champagne and flowers. Maybe Mr. Poindexter had met his lady-love this way. Tomorrow I'd start to make the rounds of the theaters and see what turned up.

Now that I had a plan I felt more satisfied as I made my way home. I let myself into my house with a sigh of relief and turned on the gas in the hall. As I was about to go upstairs to get out of this most unattractive of outfits, I glanced into my sitting room and froze. There were some sheets of paper on my floor. I confess to not being the most tidy of individuals, but I would never go out leaving papers on the floor. I went in cautiously and lit the gas bracket. I picked up the papers and examined them. They had been on the stack on my table — of no significance in themselves except that I hadn't seen them for a couple of weeks. And the papers that had been on top of the stack were there no longer. I could come to only one conclusion — somebody had been in my house.

Of course the moment I came to this realization, the next step was to wonder whether the intruder was still here. I checked the windows but found them shut as before. There was no sign of a forced entry. I hesitated to go upstairs, but when I finally got up the courage, I found the windows up there were likewise shut. Daniel had a key, so that was the most obvious of explanations. Maybe he had found himself near Greenwich Village and had stopped by for a few minutes' rest. But why would he have gone through my papers? To see if he could find out the truth about my client?

No. I shook my head. I could not think that of him.

So who could have gained access to the place, and for what purpose? I crossed the street and knocked on Sid and Gus's door.

"Molly, how nice," Sid said. "We were about to eat. Why don't you join us."

I felt embarrassed then, as if she might have thought that I only showed up for food. "I don't want to trouble you," I said, "but I wondered whether you happened to notice anybody outside my house at any time today."

"I'm afraid we'd be of no use at all," Sid said. "I have been fully occupied writing letters. I'll have you know that I have been in correspondence with none other than the great Susan B. Anthony."

I wasn't quite sure who this person was but I nodded as if impressed. Sid went on, "And Gus is painting up a storm. Now she's inspired to do a mural. She wants to portray oppressed people, starting with the children of Israel in Egypt and ending with the women of America seeking the vote."

I tried not to smile. "And where would she do this mural?"

"That's the problem. We need a large white wall and ours are all papered and full of knickknacks. So now we have to find a

155

friendly white wall somewhere in New York."

"I have one in my bedroom," I said, "but I don't think I'd like to wake up to the struggles of oppressed people."

She laughed merrily. "Molly, you are so amusing. Come and have some dinner, do."

I was tempted. My stomach reminded me that I hadn't eaten for quite a while. "But this is serious, Sid. I think someone has entered my house while I was away."

"Broke in, you mean?"

"There is no sign of a break-in, but my papers have been moved."

Sid smiled. "I'm sure you're imagining things, my sweet. It is easy to move a few papers while our thoughts are on something else."

I shook my head. "But the papers I had just been dealing with were no longer on top of the pile."

"Was anything taken?" She looked concerned now.

"Not that I could see."

"So someone entered your house without breaking any locks, disturbed your papers, and then vanished again?"

"It does sound improbable. Maybe it was only Daniel, who had a few minutes to kill and . . ." I broke off, not wanting to say this out loud.

"Amused himself by rifling through your desk? Surely not."

"I sincerely hope not," I said. Then I remembered Fanny telling me that she had searched through her husband's drawers looking for the necklace he had bought. Did husbands and wives do this regularly?

Sid took my sleeve and pulled me into the house. "We can ask Gus if she spotted anybody from her studio window, but I'm sure she was too absorbed in her painting to notice a thunderbolt descending on New York. Now, for heaven's sake, come and eat."

This time I allowed myself to be led into the kitchen.

THIRTEEN

When I got home I conducted a thorough inspection of the house and found nothing missing or in any way disturbed. I now concluded that it was just possible I had sent papers flying in my hurry to leave and that my overactive imagination had done the rest. But just to make sure I penned Daniel a note, asking if he had visited my house while I was out that evening.

The next morning's mail delivery brought the first replies from various missionary headquarters. Not one had ever employed a couple called Boswell. I decided it was time for a little more subterfuge. I put on my business two-piece, twisted my hair into a severe bun, placed a pair of spectacles on my nose to complete the bluestocking effect, and set off for the mansion of Mr. Horace Lynch, a notebook clutched in one hand. I was told by the butler that Mr. Lynch was in his study, and after a brief consultation he returned to say that he would see me.

I was taken down a hallway decorated with Greek and Roman statues and shown into an impressive wood-paneled study. Mr. Horace Lynch was sitting at a splendid mahogany desk. He was older than I had expected. I had known that he was older than Emily's Aunt Lydia, but this man must have been well into his sixties. He was almost bald, with unattractive strands of hair combed across his pate. A gold watch-chain was stretched across an impressive paunch, and he had a face like a British bulldog, with large, sagging jowls. He did not rise as I was shown into the room.

"Well, what's this about?" he demanded. "I'm a busy man. And if you're angling for a subscription to some charitable organization you're wasting your time. I never give to charities."

"Nothing of the kind, sir. I will not waste your valuable time. I am just seeking some information for a book I'm writing." I tried to eliminate my Irish accent and speak in a most refined manner.

"Information, huh? Of what nature?"

"I am writing a book on the history of the Christian missions in China. I am especially focusing on those missionaries who made the supreme sacrifice of giving their lives for the faith over there." I detected an instant change in his demeanor. His gaze was suddenly sharp, almost wary. I continued with my rehearsed piece. "One of my classmates at Vassar was your niece, Emily, and I recall she told me that her parents had died in a cholera epidemic while serving as missionaries in that country."

"That is correct," he said.

"How very tragic for your family. I wondered if you could give me details of their lives in China, or if you have any photographs I could include in my book."

He rose to his feet now, his paunch extending over the desktop. "I'd like to help you, Miss Murphy, but I'm afraid this couple were only distant relatives of my wife. I never even met them, or had any kind of contact with them."

"Oh, I see," I said. "Maybe you could let me know where I might locate relatives of your wife who could supply me with more information."

"I'd like to help you, but my wife's parents died when she was a child. She was raised by a great-aunt who has since died and I understood that she has no other living relatives — which was why we had to take in the child, of course. My wife was of a very tender nature and wouldn't hear of it going to an orphanage." A spasm of pain crossed his face as he said this.

"It was very noble of you," I said.

"It was indeed," he said. "Now if you will excuse me, Miss Murphy. I am due to meet a man at my club within the hour. My butler will show you out."

"If you could just supply me with the basic facts about them, then I could pursue my inquiries through the appropriate missionary society," I went on, maybe unwisely. "Their full names, where they came from. You must know that much from Emily's birth certificate, surely?"

His face was now decidedly red. "She had no birth certificate, damn it. The child was the only survivor of a cholera epidemic, so we understood. Whisked to safety by a devoted Chinese servant. I'm sorry, but I can be of no further use to you. I suggest you focus your story on other missionaries who will prove easier to trace. Good day to you. Jenkins!" He bellowed this last word. "This young woman is leaving."

I had no choice but to be escorted out. So I was none the wiser, or was I? One thing I was now sure of was that Mr. Horace Lynch did know more about Emily's parents. He just wasn't willing to share that information with me. So far my investigation into Emily's past was getting me nowhere. I hoped for more rapid success in my assignment for Fanny Poindexter, or I wouldn't be making enough money to pay the rent.

As far as Emily's family history was concerned, I wasn't sure where to go from here. Wait until I got a reply from all the missionary societies, of course. But then? I knew where her Aunt Lydia had been born. I would have to find the time to pay a visit to Massachusetts, but I couldn't do that until I had fulfilled my obligation to Fanny. I made my way back to Pearl Street and located my cabby. He had nothing to report. Mr. Poindexter had not left his office all day, as far as he could tell. It seemed that he had roped in some of his fellow cab drivers to keep watch when he had a fare, so I felt confident that the building was being well covered. I suggested he pay particular attention to listening for the name of a particular theater.

I was on my way to do the rounds of the theaters when it suddenly struck me that I had sources within the theater who might be able to supply me with information. The first of these was Oona Sheehan, who had rooms in the Hoffman House, a swank hotel on Broadway and Twenty-fourth. Miss

Sheehan's maid informed me that her mistress was resting prior to the evening performance and was not to be disturbed. I decided that Miss Sheehan owed me a favor or two after what she had put me through on the way to Dublin, and sent the maid to tell her that Molly Murphy needed to see her.

This produced results. I was shown into Miss Sheehan's boudoir and found her draped in a delightful green silk robe, trimmed with feathers.

"Molly, my dear —" She held out a languid hand to me. I wondered if she was playing Camille. She patted the bed beside her. I sat and explained briefly what I wanted. She frowned prettily. "Poindexter? The name does ring a bell. I believe he sent me flowers, years ago. A good-looking boy, I seem to remember."

I produced the photograph. She nodded. "Yes, I do remember him."

"I don't suppose you've heard any rumor about who might be the current object of his affection?"

"My dear child, I haven't the least interest in who is bedding whom if it doesn't concern me."

"She was described as exotic looking," I prompted.

She gave that delightful, tinkling laugh. "Aren't we all, darling? Aren't we all?"

None the wiser, I went to my second source in the theater, the irrepressible playwright Ryan O'Hare. I found him in his rooms at the Hotel Lafayette, just off Washington Square.

"Molly, my darling. Aren't you a sight for sore eyes," he said, rising from his desk to embrace me. He was dressed in a white peasant shirt with ruffles at the cuffs and the front open to reveal his chest. His black hair was unkempt and he looked delightfully Byronesque. "Where have you been these past weeks? Devoting all your time to that brute of a policeman, I expect."

"Not at all. I've been working."

"Working. Exactly what I've been doing myself. Working feverishly on a new play. Best thing I've ever done, Molly. The theater world will be stunned. Amazed. Agog."

"I'm glad for you. When is it to open?"

"Ah, now there's the rub. I'm still without a backer. I had a certain man-about-town in my pocket, my dear. Ready to shell out millions for me and then — disaster."

"He died?"

"Worse. He went back to his wife."

I had to laugh. Ryan joined me.

"At least life is never dull with you, Ryan,"

164

I said, and told him of my current mission. He looked at me, then burst out laughing. "Now, Molly, my sweet. Why on earth would I show any interest at all in young men who hang around stage doors to pick up women?"

There was nothing for it but to visit every theater, one by one. I headed for Broadway and began to show Mr. Poindexter's photograph at the various stage doors. Luckily stage doors are guarded by wise and fierce old men who usually keep a fatherly eye on the welfare of the female members of the cast. This includes keeping away unwanted admirers and taking up gifts from those in favor. I showed Poindexter's likeness at one theater after another, with no luck. One or two of the stage-door keepers thought they might have seen him, but they had to confess that handsome young men in top hat and tails tend to look alike.

After several hours of walking the streets around Broadway, I was feeling tired and dispirited. I hadn't begun to visit every theater, not to mention the vaudeville houses and nightclubs. This could take me days, if not weeks. What I needed now was a piece of luck.

On Thursday my generous tip to the cabby paid off. The day before, Mr. Poindexter had left the office in the middle of the afternoon and had been gone for just over an hour. My cabby himself had driven him to an address on East Twenty-first Street. I took a less expensive means of transportation to that street myself, walked up to the front door, and rang the bell. A French maid opened it.

"Hello," I said in friendly fashion. "Would this be the house of Mrs. James Delaney?"

"No," she said in distinctly foreign tones. "Zis is zee residence of Mademoiselle Fifi Hetreau."

The name rang a vague bell. Something I had seen on a billboard, maybe? I took a stab at it. "Fifi Hetreau? Isn't she a dancer?" I asked.

"Mais oui," she said. "You have heard of her? You like to attend the theater?"

"It's my brother who's rather keen on the theater," I said confidentially. "And he is a great admirer of Mademoiselle Fifi, I gather. Do you think she'd give me her autograph for him?"

"She is not at 'ome, miss," the maid said. "I'm sorry."

"No matter. Do you think she'd give him the time of day if he came to visit in person?"

"I am sure she would give him an autograph, miss, but zat is all. She has a beau who would be very jealous," She wagged her finger in a very French manner and laughed.

I departed then and headed straight for the Dakota. At last I had something to report. I had no proof as yet, but I would certainly be able to produce the necessary snapshot in due time.

I was just approaching Fanny's front door when it opened and Dorcas, one of the young women from last Sunday's little gathering, came out. She looked startled when she saw me. "Oh, Molly, isn't it?"

"That's right," I said. "Is Mrs. Poindexter at home?"

"She is, but I'm afraid she's not well."

"Oh dear, what's wrong?"

"They think it's the influenza that's been going around. The doctor was just here."

"I see. Would I be permitted to see her, do you think?"

She glanced warily into the hall. "I was only with her for a couple of minutes before her mother arrived and shushed me out, so I suspect the answer to that is probably no."

"Oh dear," I said. "I had some news I wanted to share with her, but it will have to wait for another time."

"You could leave her a note," Dorcas suggested. "Ask the maid to bring you a pen and some writing paper."

"That's a good idea," I said. "I'm sure she'll make a swift recovery with all that attention."

"I'm sure she will. Fanny always liked to give the impression of being delicate, but she's really the toughest of any of us." Dorcas smiled. "I'd better be going. I want to see little Toodles before Nanny puts him to bed."

I was in the process of asking for writing paper when a matronly woman came out of a door and looked at me in surprise. "I came to see Fanny," I said. "You must be her mother. I am Molly Murphy, one of her friends, but I gather she's not well enough for visitors at the moment."

"I'm afraid she's not," the older woman said in that sort of imperious voice that upper-class matrons develop. I could see her checking out my clothing and clearly making the decision that I was not of her daughter's class. "In fact I've asked the doctor to hire a nurse for her. I have a social engagement this evening and I do not think she should be left alone. And that husband of hers is out again. Not that men are any good around a sickbed, are they?"

We exchanged a smile. "I thought I might

write Fanny a note. I had a message for her I'd like her to have."

"I would be happy to deliver a message, if you so desire," Fanny's mother suggested.

"I think I'll write it, if you don't mind," I said. I had no idea whether she had shared any of her suspicions about her husband with her family, and certainly didn't want to stir up trouble.

"Very well. Come into the drawing room and I'll have the maid bring you a pen and writing paper." She ushered me through, seated me at a little table, and hovered over me while I wrote. I thought carefully before I wrote,

Fanny, you were right about our little discussion. My best wishes for a speedy recovery. I will come to visit in a few days, and hope to have more information for you then.

Since I had claimed to be a friend I signed it, "Yours sincerely, Molly."

Then I had nothing else to do but to go home.

FOURTEEN

I had no trouble locating the theater at which Mademoiselle Fifi was performing. The show was a revue called Fun-Time Follies, at the Miner's Bowery Theater. From what I could see it wasn't as respectable as the theaters that were springing up around Broadway. Mr. Poindexter was clearly not the most upright of young men.

After that it was merely a question of waiting for the right moment. I took my camera — a nifty little Brownie I had inherited with the business from Paddy Riley — and lurked near Mademoiselle Fifi's house on East Twenty-first. Fortunately it was not too far from Sixth Avenue, with its department stores: Simpson, Crawford & Simpson was on one corner and Hugh O'Neill on the other, so there was a constant stream of pedestrian traffic, which made me less conspicuous. I walked up and down with my shopping bag, pretending to be interested in shop windows, occasionally going into a baker to buy myself a bun. But Mr. Poindexter did not appear at all that day, nor did he visit the theater that evening. Since my camera did not operate in the dark and I had no kind of flash equipment, it made little sense to watch and wait outside Mademoiselle Fifi's that night. Besides, I'd had enough for one day.

I came home exhausted at eleven and fell asleep with no supper. The next day it was raining and I worried about there being enough light for my snapshot. It was also Saturday, and I wondered whether Mr. Poindexter would be working at his office or maybe taking a trip out to Long Island to oversee the building of his new home. I took an umbrella and lingered within view of Mademoiselle Fifi's house for most of the day, feeling thoroughly cold, damp, and uncomfortable.

At last I decided that I was wasting my time and that I would go home for a hot cup of tea. I had just reached the corner of the block when a cab turned into the street, moving at a lively clip. Before I could do anything sensible, Mr. Poindexter himself jumped down from the cab and ran to Mademoiselle Fifi's front door. I moved back quickly and took up position outside the house. After a few minutes he came out again, slammed the front door behind him, and ran down the steps to the cab, which was still waiting. It was all over so fast that I didn't have a chance to snap more than one picture — probably so blurred that it would be hard to prove who it was and which street it was on.

I wondered whether I should go and see if Fanny had recovered enough to receive visitors. At least now I had seen her husband at Fifi's house for myself, although his stay was certainly not long enough for a lover's tryst. Maybe he was there for the purpose of arranging such a tryst, although from what I saw during my brief glimpse of him, he had not looked happy or excited. In fact, *grim* would have been the word to describe his face.

As I left Twenty-first Street to go home, I glanced back once more and saw Mademoiselle Fifi's maid emerge from the house and come running toward me. It was still raining and she was in her maid's uniform, with no hat or coat. I lowered my umbrella to conceal my face and she ran past. On the corner she hailed a cab and rode in it back to the house. A few minutes later I was treated to the sight of Mademoiselle Fifi herself, emerging, draped in a glorious sable coat. I snapped a picture of her, though I'm not sure exactly why. I tried to move close enough to hear the directions she gave the cabby as he assisted her into the cab, but the street noise was considerable and I heard nothing. I watched them drive away, wondering if I should try to find a cab of my own to follow them, or whether she was going on some simple errand, or even to a matinee at her theater. In any case, by the time I had reached the end of the street and spotted an empty cab, they were gone.

I went home, feeling somewhat satisfied. I had seen Poindexter for myself at Mademoiselle Fifi's house. That would be enough for Fanny to have ammunition to confront her husband. Of course, I had no way of knowing whether the news would be welcome or not. Did she want to get out of a confining marriage in which she saw herself as a prisoner, or did she want her husband to start paying her more attention? One never knew with women. We don't always fall in love with the right men. I can attest to that. Either way, I decided I should probably wait until Monday to visit Fanny, as her husband would most likely be spending his Sunday at home.

I spent a quiet evening alone. No sign of

Daniel, and Sid and Gus were off to the theater. On Sunday morning I slept in late and was just fixing myself a leisurely breakfast of scrambled eggs and toast when there came a thunderous knocking at my front door. I was still in my robe, so I paused to make myself respectable before opening it. Emily Boswell stood there, a look of absolute distress on her face.

"Emily, my dear. What is it?" I asked.

She staggered into the hallway. "She's dead. Fanny is dead," she said, gasping.

"Fanny's dead?"

She nodded, then drew out a handkerchief and pressed it to her mouth.

I put a tentative arm around her shoulder and steered her into my kitchen. "My dear Emily, I am so sorry," I said. "I knew she was sick, but this is such a shock. When did it happen?"

"During the night," she said. "I went to visit her yesterday, as I knew she had been sick. Her servant came to our shop earlier in the week and asked for some of our stomach mixture that she liked. I gathered that she was suffering from influenza, so I took the medicine over myself, as well as some aspirin, as it is so effective at bringing down fever." She looked up at me for confirmation. I nodded and eased her onto

174

one of my kitchen chairs.

"And how did she seem then?"

"She was looking flushed and seemed weak but only what was to be expected with the flu. I tried to cheer her up and mixed some of the aspirin for her. She made a fuss about taking it and we laughed at what a baby she was about medicines and sickness.

"I had no time to visit her until yesterday. I went to visit her after I finished work and was told she was sleeping, and this morning I got a message that she had died during the night."

"How very sad," I said. Although I was no longer the best Catholic in the world, I had an overwhelming urge to cross myself. "This influenza seems to be particularly virulent, doesn't it?"

She looked down at her hands for a long moment before she said, "I can't get this awful thought out of my head, Molly. I can't stop thinking that he killed her."

"Who? Who killed her?"

She looked up now. "Her husband, Anson."

"Anson? Surely not." I gave an uneasy laugh. "She had the flu, Emily. You know yourself that healthy people have been succumbing to complications of the flu. Even the woman who worked with you at the drugstore, remember?"

She frowned.

"I know it sounds awful to say this, but he never really loved her, Molly. I've always known that. I've always been convinced that he married her for her money."

"But if he killed her, surely that would be a good way of cutting off the supply of money from her family?"

She shook her head. "Her father settled a large sum on her at her marriage. Anson will be a wealthy man whatever happens now."

I was in a quandary. Should I tell her what I knew? Did she know that Fanny was planning to divorce him? I decided that Fanny was my client, even if she was now dead. I decided to tread cautiously. "Emily, are you sure the marriage was unhappy? Weren't they looking forward to moving to their new house on Long Island together?"

She shook her head violently. "On the surface she acted as if all was well with their marriage, but beneath she was deeply unhappy. She didn't talk about it much, but I could tell. He was a bully and a domineering tyrant."

"Emily, however black his character was, he could hardly have given her influenza, could he?"

"I don't doubt the influenza," she said, "but when I saw her earlier in the week, she wasn't that ill. As I said, she was always a baby about sickness. Even the smallest cold or splinter in her finger was cause for great drama. I think he took advantage of her weakened state to finish her off. Stomach complaints aren't a usual part of influenza, are they? And yet she requested our stomach mixture. I'm wondering if he wasn't feeding her something like arsenic."

"That's a serious charge," I said, "and I don't know how you'd prove it." As I spoke, an awful thought crept into my mind. I had left her a note. I had tried to make it as general as possible, but perhaps a clever man could have put two and two together.

"That's why I came to you," she said. "I'm only a friend, and Anson never liked me. I was too clever and too independent for him, you see. I tried to persuade Fanny not to marry him when we were roommates at Vassar. But you are a detective. You know how to set about these things. Will you not try to find out the truth? I won't rest until I know for sure."

"Emily, this would be a criminal case. A matter for the police. I shouldn't be meddling in it."

"But you know what the police would say,

don't you? Female hysteria." She sounded almost hysterical herself now. "They'd say it was influenza and I was imagining things."

I thought this was all too probable.

"Listen," I said. "My young man is a senior police detective. I'll mention the matter to him and he'll know what to do."

"Thank you, that would be helpful," she said, "but I'm wondering — if there was any kind of foul play, shouldn't we take a look for ourselves before he has a chance to get rid of the evidence?"

I thought privately that any clever murderer would probably have destroyed the evidence instantly, but Emily went on. "I want to go over there right now to pay my last respects. Won't you come with me? You'd know what to look for."

"Emily, I should warn you that I know nothing about arsenic or any other kind of poisoning, but I'll be happy to come with you. I'd like to pay my last respects too."

I poured her a cup of tea while I went upstairs to find my one black dress.

The maid who opened the door to us at the Poindexter home looked as if she had been crying.

"Oh, miss. Oh, miss," was all she could manage.

"We came to offer our condolences," Emily said, "and to say a last farewell to dear Fanny."

She nodded and let us into the hall. We waited while we heard voices in the drawing room and presently Anson Poindexter himself came out. He looked haggard and disheveled, as if he hadn't slept all night, and was still wearing a maroon silk robe.

"Ah, Miss Boswell," he said, extending his hand to her. "How good of you to come. You must excuse my appearance. I'm finding it hard to function."

"This is Miss Murphy, another of Fanny's friends," Emily said.

I saw a flicker of interest or suspicion cross his face. "Miss Murphy? I don't believe I've had the pleasure of making your acquaintance before." He held out his hand to me in civil enough fashion. "Are you another of the fearsome Vassar ladies?"

"No, sir. My acquaintance with your wife is fairly recent."

"I brought her to one of Fanny's at homes," Emily said. "They hit it off really well."

"I'm so glad," he said. "She had some wonderful, true friends. She was well loved, wouldn't you say?"

"Very well loved," Emily said.

"Her parents are here." Anson Poindexter looked back at the drawing room door. "They are absolutely devastated, as you can imagine. Fanny was the light of their lives. Their adored only child." He paused and cleared his throat. "As she was the light of my life, of course."

"We were with her only last Sunday," I said. "And she seemed so bright and healthy then. The disease took its toll so quickly."

He nodded. "The doctor said he'd seen so many cases this year in which a simple influenza turned to pneumonia overnight."

"That's what she died of then, was it?" Emily asked. "Pneumonia?"

"That's what's on the death certificate," he said. "It was her lungs, in any case."

"Not her stomach?" Emily asked.

"Her stomach?" He looked surprised.

"She sent a note to my pharmacy requesting her favorite stomach mixture on Tuesday."

"Did she? Well, I suppose there was some vomiting, but I put that down to the high fever. No, I'm sure it was pneumonia."

"Was the progression very rapid?" I asked, trying not to sound overly interested.

"It must have been rapid," he said. "You see, I was away from home on Friday night. I had to visit a client out of town. When I

180

left on Friday morning Fanny was weak and feverish but seemed cheerful enough. I didn't get back to the city until late last night. I arrived home to find the doctor here and Fanny's mother in a terrible state. Fanny was close to death, her breath coming in rasping gasps. She only lasted an hour or two after that. It was horrible." He paused and coughed again. "Now, if you'll excuse me, I find this too painful a subject to discuss at this moment."

Emily stepped forward. "Might we just see her, to say good-bye?" she asked. "She was my dearest friend, you know."

"Of course." He nodded solemnly and walked toward the bedroom door. "You'll forgive me if I don't come into the room with you. I simply can't —" He left the rest of the sentence hanging.

We stepped into the darkened room. The heavy velvet drapes had been drawn, making it hard to see anything. I could dimly make out the white figure in a vast carved mahogany sleigh bed.

"I hope they won't mind if I open the drapes for a minute," Emily said. She went across to the window and pulled them back. Bright spring light flooded in. Pigeons rose, flapping in alarm from the balustrade of the balcony outside the window where they had been sunning themselves. The light fell directly on the figure who lay on the bed. She looked absolutely lovely, like a marble sculpture in an old church or medieval painting of the Virgin, her face serene and her glorious golden hair spread out across the pillow.

Emily gave a stifled sob and went over to her. "Fanny," she whispered. "Oh, Fanny."

I felt similarly upset but I reminded myself that I was here for a reason. I started to look around the room, seeing if there was any sort of unwashed coffee cup or medicine glass that I could spirit away for testing. There wasn't. An impressive row of perfumes and jars of cream sat on her dressing table, along with a silver-backed brush set. I moved quickly to check the door at the far end of the room. It led to a dressing room with wardrobes around the walls, and that room in turn led to a bathroom. There was a glass on the marble table but it looked to be clean and unused. The bottle of mixture, labeled with the directions "One teaspoonful as needed to calm the stomach," sat on a glass shelf. Apart from that there were few medical preparations: smelling salts, headache powders, liver pills. Mrs. Poindexter clearly had not been one to worry about her health. I was sorely tempted to take them with me but I couldn't justify doing so. Besides, I didn't want to make her husband in any way suspicious and spoil an official inquiry later.

I came back out again to a most touching scene. Emily sat on the bed with Fanny's head cradled in her arms. "I can't believe I'm saying good-bye to you," she whispered. "We had such good times together, didn't we? The happiest days of my life."

Then she saw me standing there and lowered Fanny again to the pillow, before rising guiltily to her feet. "We should go, I suppose," she said. "And I should close these drapes again."

As she walked over to the window I noticed her jacket. "You should brush your jacket," I said. "You have Fanny's hairs all over you."

"So I do," she said. "I wonder if hair falls out after death?"

Instead of brushing the hairs to the floor, she picked them off, one by one. "I'm going to keep these, as a token to remind me of her," she said. "Maybe I have enough here to weave into a ring or a brooch."

I nodded. Darkness fell over the room again and we closed the door quietly behind us.

FIFTEEN

We took the elevator down to the ground floor.

"Well, what did you think?" Emily asked. "Did you find anything at all to arouse your suspicions?"

"Not in the way of used coffee cups or glasses," I said. "There was the stomach mixture that came from Mr. McPherson, her smelling salts, and some liver pills. They should all be tested, I suppose."

"The thing I found suspicious was that Anson was conveniently out of town until the moments before her death," Emily said.

"Yes, I have to agree that was suspicious," I said, still debating whether to tell her what I knew.

"So where do we go from here?" Emily asked.

"I think I should present the facts to Captain Sullivan and let him proceed. We should not interfere in case we spoil an official criminal investigation."

"When can you see him?"

"Good question," I said. "He is working on a couple of big cases — one of them involving arsenic, by the way — and I've scarcely seen him in weeks. But I'll leave a note for him at his apartment on my way home."

"Thank you." She reached out and took my hand. "I am so glad you're going to take this on for me, Molly. If you have to put my own investigation on hold, I quite understand. Justice for poor Fanny is more important to me right now."

I left her making her solitary way home and I took the El to Twenty-third Street and went straight to Daniel's residence. When Mrs. O'Shea opened the door she looked more flustered than usual.

"Oh, Miss Murphy. The captain's not at home again."

"That's all right, Mrs. O'Shea," I said. "I just want to leave a message for him."

"Do you mind if I don't accompany you upstairs," she said. "I've got sick children and frankly I'm run off my feet."

"I'm sorry to hear that. Is there anything I can do for you?"

"You're most kind, my dear, but I don't want you catching anything. Go on up then,

185

will you?"

I nodded and made my way up the stairs. At Daniel's desk I found writing paper and asked him to call at Patchin Place at the earliest possible moment, as I had a matter of great urgency in which I needed his help. As I was writing I couldn't help thinking of the last time I left a note for somebody, and couldn't fight back the feelings of guilt that swept over me. If Anson Poindexter somehow got wind of the fact that Fanny had hired a detective to keep tabs on him, and that she was planning to divorce him, might I not have forced his hand? I remembered when I had seen him on Saturday afternoon — his grim face as he ran up to Fifi's door and then left again. And then Fifi had left soon after him. Had he warned her to get out of town?

I felt quite sick as I went down the stairs again and made my way home. I was tempted to go to police headquarters and see if I could seek out Daniel there, but I decided against it. I didn't want to be known as the annoying woman in Daniel's life who wouldn't leave him alone at work. So I waited patiently — or rather not too patiently — until that evening. When I had just decided to fix myself some supper, he showed up on my doorstep.

"Molly, are you all right?" he asked, bursting into my house with a look of concern on his face.

"I'm just fine, thank you," I said.

"But your note. I got the feeling that something was horribly wrong."

"Not to me," I said, "but I have a case that I think might be a matter for the police."

"Really?" He came into my kitchen. "My, but that smells good."

"It's only some neck of beef I'm making into a stew. There will be plenty, if you like to stay."

"I'd like to but I should really get down to headquarters," he said. He pulled out a kitchen chair and sat down with a sigh of relief.

"Have they made you work all of Sunday again?"

"Actually, not today," he said. "I went out to Westchester to see my mother."

I told myself that I was a petty sort of person to feel jealous that he had wanted to spend his one day off with his mother again, rather than with me.

"That was nice of you," I managed to say. "So how was she?"

"Not doing too well, as a matter of fact. Still grieving terribly for my father," he said.

"Those two were married for forty years, you know. It's not going to be easy to adjust to life without him."

"Forty years, fancy that." I tried to picture myself and Daniel after forty years together. Did one not grow tired of the other person after all that time?

"Can you picture us after forty years together?" Daniel asked, echoing my sentiments. "We'll probably have killed one another by then!"

"So about this case," I said, hastily changing the subject. "It's a suspicious death, possible poisoning."

"Poisoning? How on earth did you get yourself involved with something like that?"

I told him the basic details of my dealings with Emily and Fanny Poindexter.

"And what grounds does your friend have for thinking this Mrs. Poindexter was poisoned by her husband?" Daniel asked.

"Intuition, mainly."

"Intuition?" He uttered a disparaging *humpf*. "I'd need more than that to call a death suspicious. And you tell me she came down with influenza and died of breathing complications?" He shook his head. "What has that to do with poisoning? Didn't I tell you about the number of cases I've seen of healthy people dying from this flu?"

"You did," I agreed, "but apparently she was having stomach troubles as well and Emily thought that Fanny's husband might have taken the opportunity of her weakened condition to get rid of her."

"And why would he want to do that?" Daniel asked.

"To get his hands on her fortune and to be free of her." I glanced up at him. "This is strictly between the two of us, but Fanny Poindexter hired me last Monday because she suspected that her husband was keeping a mistress. If that did prove to be true, then she planned to divorce him, and her money would go with her."

"I see," he said. "A strong motive then. And does he have a mistress?"

"He does. A dancer called Mademoiselle Fifi. I saw him going into her house and she was described to me by one of the waiters at Delmonico's."

"You're getting quite good at this detective business, aren't you?" he said with a smile.

"I don't know about that, Daniel," I said. "I left a note for Fanny the other day because she was sick and they wouldn't let me see her. I was careful not to say anything specific in it but I'm now worrying that her husband deduced something from the note that made him realize she was on to him. I'm really concerned that I precipitated her death."

"Presumably a doctor signed a death certificate?" he asked.

"He did, I'm sure. But he wouldn't have thought to check for arsenic or any other kind of poison, would he?"

Daniel sighed. "Molly, I'm snowed under with work. I've got Chinese tongs trying to kill each other to gain control of the opium trade, I've got opium smuggling that we can't stop and I've got random arsenic poisonings all over lower Manhattan."

"So what would the symptoms of arsenic poisoning be?" I asked.

"Severe gastric distress. You had it yourself, remember?"

"I remember very well," I said, my thoughts going back to that mansion on the Hudson and the vomiting that had brought me close to death, "but would there be any hints left on the body?"

"An autopsy would reveal traces of arsenic in the system," he said. "The stomach would appear inflamed. And if the victim had been fed small doses so that death didn't occur immediately, then it would affect the liver and the victim would appear jaundiced."

"Meaning that her skin would look yellow?"

"And her eyes. Bloodshot and yellow probably. It can also produce a blotchy rash."

I shook my head. "She looked perfect. Like a white marble statue."

"I really don't think you have enough to go on to warrant investigating further here, Molly," he said. "It all boils down to one woman's intuition and I have to tell you that female intuition is not as reliable as word would have it." He smiled and patted my hand in a rather annoying way.

"So you're not going to do anything?" I asked.

He sighed. "I could go and see her doctor if it would make you happy. I expect I can find the time to do that for you. If he shows any concerns at all about the cause of her death, then I'll move to the next step."

"Which would be?"

"Ordering a test for poisons. But from the way you described the body, I think we can rule out the other common poisons — strychnine, cyanide, as they usually leave signs of extreme distress on the face. And the skin could looked flushed as well or the lips have turned blue."

"She looked serene," I said.

"As I said, I suspect this is all the result of an overactive imagination on the part of your friend." He got up again. "I really should be going. Give me the name and address of the deceased woman and I'll do what I can."

"Thank you." I went across the kitchen and lifted the lid from the pot on the stove. "This is just about ready," I said. "Can you not stay long enough to have a bite to eat?"

"I suppose I could do that," he said. He glanced back longingly at the stove, then sat down again. "By the way. What was that strange note I received from you asking if I had been inside your house while you were out?"

"I came home to find the pile of papers on my table had been disturbed," I said. "Some of them were on the floor."

"And you thought that I might have sneaked into your house and gone through your papers?" His voice rose angrily. "To what purpose? To spy on you?"

"Keep your hair on, Daniel," I said. "Of course I didn't mean it like that. It's just that I know you have a key and I couldn't otherwise explain the papers on the floor."

"I can think of several reasonable explanations myself," he said. "Your skirt brushed them as you passed. A wind came from the front door as you opened it? The pile was too high and collapsed."

"I know," I said. "I suppose you're right and I got upset over nothing. I just had this horrible feeling that someone had been in my house."

"And why would they be doing that?"

"I don't know," I said.

He gave me a long, hard look. "Molly, is there something you've not been telling me? You're not working on any dangerous cases at the moment, are you?"

"Not at all," I said. "Finding out about some missionaries is hardly dangerous."

"And were there any signs of breaking and entering?"

"Not at all."

"Then I'd say it was another case of overactive imagination," he said with a relieved smile. "No, don't throw that spoon at me!"

"The police have ways of collecting finger-prints, don't they?" I insisted. "We could check my door and windowsills and my desk to see if someone had been here."

"And what good would that do, my sweet?" he asked. "Unless we have a crimi-nal's fingerprint on file to compare the prints, we'd be no nearer to telling you who had been here. And frankly I suspect that we'd find a good many fingerprints on your window ledges and doors — don't look at me like that. I know you dust as well as anyone else, but it's true. The mailman and the milkman and the window cleaners would all have put their hands on your door at some time. And your friends and neighbors and acquaintances." He smiled. "To be frank, fingerprinting is not all it's cracked up to be. It's never been allowed as evidence in court, either. I can see that one day it will be a marvelous tool, but until we've built up files in the way we have with Bertillon measurements, we can take prints but we can't easily compare them."

"I see," I said. "I suppose that means no."

"If your door had been bashed down, your window broken, and your belongings scattered in disarray, I'd be happy to take fingerprints for you. But in this case I have to say that you'd be wasting police time and resources."

"Hmmm," was all I could think of saying.

SIXTEEN

I suppose I should have been content to leave everything to Daniel after that. But never having been of a patient disposition, I was itching to do something myself. I wouldn't have been as willing to agree with Emily's suspicion had not Mr. Poindexter claimed to have been out of town from Friday morning until Saturday evening, when I knew very well he was in the city on Saturday afternoon. It seemed that he had gone out of his way to establish this alibi for himself — although of course he might have spent Friday night with Fifi and not have wished to disclose that fact.

I paced around my house, trying to think through how a real detective would approach this matter. Obviously test for the poison, which I couldn't do. Interview the attending physician, which Daniel was now doing. But if Anson Poindexter was away, then he would have relied on someone else to deliver the fatal dose. I could probably find out more by speaking to the Poindexters' maid. Unfortunately, I didn't think it would be as easy to get the servants alone in a large apartment building as it would have been in a private house, where I could simply slip around to the servants' entrance. I'd just have to play it by ear and take my chances. I put on my black dress again, arranged a black lace shawl over my shoulders, and went uptown to the Dakota.

On the way there I decided that I should go first to Emily's and let her know about my meeting with Daniel the night before. She might also want to come with me to Fanny's place during her lunch hour, and two of us might be a distinct advantage. I glanced into the shop window, with its intriguing glass globes that glowed in the morning sunlight and its displays of various preparations. I wondered if one day I'd have money to spend on my appearance and if I'd ever be as concerned about my appearance as Fanny and her friends seemed to be. Maybe there was something to an existence of hardship like mine. At least I was seldom bored!

The bell jangled as I opened the door. I was surprised to see Ned at the counter.

"Miss Murphy, wasn't it?" he said, giving

me a friendly smile.

"Oh, hello, Ned," I said. "I just stopped by to give Emily a message. Is she out making deliveries again?"

"No, ma'am. She's off sick today. That's why I'm finding myself manning the counter."

"Off sick? What's wrong with her?" My face must have registered alarm.

"I don't know," he said. "She just sent a message with a neighbor's son to say that she wasn't well and she wasn't coming in. Mr. McPherson wasn't pleased, I can tell you." He glanced into the back room, where his employer could be seen with his back to us, opening one of those tiny drawers.

"Oh dear," I said. "I better go and check on her, I think."

"You've gone quite pale, Miss Murphy," he said. "Can I get you a glass of water?"

"No, thank you. It's just that one of her friends has just died and . . ."

"And you suspected that what she had might be catching?"

"Well, yes," I said, not wanting to hint at the real reason for my concern. "She died of complications of influenza, so we were told. Very sad. A young woman who had everything. Life isn't fair, is it?"

"No, it isn't," he said with such vehemence

197

that I looked up. "Take Emily," he went on rapidly. "She is turned out into the world through no fault of her own while her friends live in palaces. And she is such an angel that she never complains about the unfairness of it all."

"We all have our crosses to bear," I said. "I've been struggling on my own, as I know you have, and yet we're coming through quite well."

"So — who was this friend who died?" he asked. "Someone who lived close by?"

"Her name was Fanny Poindexter. I believe you've heard Emily talk about her."

"Indeed I have," he said. "Formerly Fanny Bradley. She was Emily's roommate at Vassar, wasn't she? Married well and lived not far from here."

"That's right."

He made a face. "Poor Emily, that will be a cruel blow to her. Fanny was like a sister to her. A cruel blow to Fanny's family too, I shouldn't wonder."

I nodded. "I gather she was an only child. Her parents are taking it very hard."

"Yes, I expect they would." He glanced back nervously at the inner sanctum again, to see if Mr. McPherson was about to reprimand him for gossiping. "So it was the influenza she died of?"

"So it appears."

He nodded. "I knew she wasn't well because Mr. McPherson had me make her up some of the stomach mixture she liked last week, but there was no hint that it was so serious. Dear me, that is a shock, isn't it?"

"Of course we don't know yet whether it was influenza or something more serious," I went on.

"What do you mean? A doctor was called, wasn't he?"

"Oh yes, and he signed a death certificate, but no autopsy has been —"

"Autopsy? Why should there be an autopsy?"

I realized I had let my mouth run away with me again. "No reason at all," I said quickly. "It's just that you don't expect healthy young people to die of influenza, do you?"

"This year they are seeming to," he said. "If I had more resources, I'd like to be working on a cure, instead of wasting time here making up stomach mixtures and tonics for ladies who don't need them."

"Do you think someone will discover a cure for diseases like influenza one day?"

He nodded. "One day they're bound to. Now that we're in the scientific age."

A cough from the back room made Ned jerk to attention. "I'd better get back to work," he muttered. "Let's hope Emily hasn't come down with the same influenza. Tell her I'll try and visit her tonight after work, will you?"

"I will indeed. Thank you, Ned."

"My pleasure, miss."

As I left the shop a thought crossed my mind. I wondered if Ned might have the knowledge and equipment to test substances for traces of arsenic or other poisons.

I knocked on Emily's door and waited what seemed like an eternity. My heart started to beat faster. Had our visit yesterday made Anson Poindexter suspicious? Was there any chance that Mademoiselle Fifi and her maid had seen me and described me? A redheaded Irish woman does rather stand out in a crowd.

"Emily?" I called through the keyhole at last. "It's me. Molly. Are you all right?"

At last I heard slow footsteps and the bolt slid back from the door. Emily stood there, blinking in the light, a blanket around her shoulders. She looked terrible.

"Emily, what is it?" I asked nervously. "Are you very ill?"

She frowned and put a hand up to rub her forehead. "Just one of my sick head-

200

aches, I'm afraid. I've always been prone to them when I'm badly upset, and seeing Fanny yesterday was just too hard to bear."

"Is there anything I can do for you?" I asked. "Can I bring you something from your chemist's shop?"

She shook her head with a tired smile. "There's nothing that works for it apart from resting in a darkened room until it passes, I'm afraid."

"I went to McPherson's to see you and I can't tell you how worried I was when I heard that you were ill. Ned's worried about you too. He sends his best and says he'll try to visit you this evening after work."

"He's such a sweet boy." She managed a smile. "What did you want to see me about?"

"Nothing too important. Just to tell you that Daniel has agreed to speak with the doctor."

"That's good."

"And I am going to see if I can talk to Fanny's maid. I came to see whether you wanted to come with me, but obviously not today. Should I postpone it until you're well, do you think?"

"No, please go, by all means," Emily said. "I wouldn't know what to do there anyway and I really don't think I could handle seeing Fanny again."

"I understand," I said. "Should I make you a cup of tea or coffee before I go?"

She shook her head. "Nothing, thank you. I can't keep anything down at this stage, so it's a waste. Sleep is the only thing."

"Then I'll leave you to sleep," I said. "I'm sorry to have disturbed you."

"Not at all. Thank you for coming." She made her way back to bed while I went to the Dakota.

Fanny's maid looked surprised to see me.

"I'm so sorry to disturb you," I said, "but I rather fear I dropped my glove while I was here with Miss Boswell yesterday, paying our last respects to your mistress. Have you found a glove, by any chance?" I held up the black leather glove I had brought with me for the purpose.

"Oh no, miss." She let me in and closed the door behind me. "But I don't think anybody's been in to the mistress's room since you were here."

"Are you home alone?" I asked hopefully.

"No, miss. The master is off making funeral arrangements with Mr. Bradley, but Mrs. Bradley is still here."

"No need to disturb her," I said. "If you could just come into Mrs. Poindexter's room with me and help me look for my glove."

"Go into the mistress's room?" She looked quite alarmed.

"Is her body still here?"

"Yes, miss. The gentlemen should be coming back with the undertaker any moment to have her removed."

"I can see that it must be very distressing for you. I can do it alone. No matter," I said. "What is your name?"

"Martha, miss, and yes, I'm finding it awful hard to realize that she's gone."

"Well, Martha, I'm sure it's a consolation to you that you did everything you could to ease her suffering."

"I did, miss. I really did. I'd have sat with her night and day but her mother wanted to be with her toward the end."

"Martha, I wondered," I began. "Maybe you could tell me, did she eat anything during the last day or so that might have made her sicker?"

She frowned at this. "I don't think so."

"Did you bring her her food?"

"Not for the last few days, miss. Like I said, her mother took over everything toward the end — fed her like a baby, she did. Not that she was eating much. She couldn't keep anything down, you see. But her mother had cook make her a good ox-tail broth, and some barley water and calves' foot jelly, and she fed her a little of those. Not that they did any good —" she pressed her hand to her mouth. "She just slipped away from us, miss. No matter what we did, she just got worse and worse and slipped away."

"And no medications helped at all?"

She shook her head. "The doctor said it was no good prescribing anything while she couldn't keep it down. Just sponge baths for the fever and liquids. That's what he said."

"I'm so sorry," I said. "I didn't know her that well, but she was a sweet and lovely woman."

"That she was, miss."

"So Mr. Poindexter was away when she died, then?"

"No, miss. He came back just before the end. Awful cut up about it, he was. 'Why didn't somebody tell me how bad she was? Why didn't you send someone to find me?' he shouted. 'I'd never have taken that stupid trip if I'd known.' "

I moved toward the bedroom door. "In here, wasn't it?"

She nodded.

"I'll only be a moment," I said. "I must have dropped my glove when I went to open the drapes to take a last look at her."

Martha opened the door and we stepped into the gloom. The odor of death was now more pronounced. I couldn't exactly describe it, but once you've smelled it, you recognize it forever more. The sweet, sickly scent of decay, to put it bluntly, I suppose. I saw Martha visibly recoil.

"It's all right. You really don't have to be here with me," I said. "If you could just show me where to turn on the electric light."

She did, and harsh yellow light flooded the room.

"I'll only be a minute," I said. "I'll turn the light off again when I'm done."

I moved quickly, pretending to search around the floor, not sure whether she was watching me or not. When I couldn't see her I darted into the dressing room and quickly dipped a piece of cotton wool I had brought with me into the stomach mixture. I was just about to drop it into the greaseproof pouch I had made for it when a booming voice demanded:

"What is going on in here?" Mrs. Bradley appeared in the doorway.

"Miss Murphy?" she demanded, her eyebrows raised.

"I'm sorry, Mrs. Bradley. I came back because I thought I had dropped my glove when we came to pay our last respects to Fanny yesterday." I spoke slowly, trying desperately to come up with a good reason for being in her dressing room. "And Emily felt faint yesterday so I went into the bathroom to wet my handkerchief for her."

"She doesn't carry smelling salts like any normal woman?" Mrs. Bradley still didn't look entirely convinced.

"I don't know. I just acted on the spur of the moment. I always find that cold water works wonderfully well for me." I closed my purse and moved quickly toward the door. "I'm so sorry to have troubled you. I must have dropped my glove somewhere else. On the train, perhaps. I'm always losing gloves."

I came out into the hall. Mrs. Bradley stood with arms folded across an impressive bosom, watching me.

"Martha was telling me that poor Fanny just couldn't keep any food down toward the end and that you fed her yourself from a spoon."

She nodded curtly. "I did everything I could to keep her alive. It wasn't enough."

"I'm so very sorry," I muttered again, feeling like an awful fraud and completely out of place in this house of sorrow. "Please excuse me. And if you could please let me know when the funeral will be held, I should certainly like to attend."

"Of course." She nodded again.

Then I made a hasty retreat.

SEVENTEEN

On Tuesday morning I received a message notifying me that the funeral was set for Thursday at the Trinity Church Cemetery on Riverside Drive. I was still waiting for news from Daniel. If the doctor was absolutely sure that Fanny died of complications of influenza and that there was no chance of foul play being involved, then I could get on with my life and take the next step in Emily's case — which would be to go to Massachusetts and the area where her Aunt Lydia was born. She might not have any surviving family members, but surely someone there would have known the family well enough to have heard of cousins who went out to China — or not, as the case may be.

At noon Sid came to my door and literally dragged me across to their house. "Gus insisted. You have to come and see our latest achievements," she said. I allowed myself to be dragged, then followed her up two flights of stairs to Gus's studio on the top floor.

"There, what do you think?" Sid demanded with obvious pride in her voice. "Isn't it a masterpiece?"

As with all of Gus's paintings I didn't quite share her enthusiasm.

"It's interesting," I said, not wanting to ask what it was depicting. "Very powerful." It was indeed powerful, with great splashes of red and purple and what looked like a smashed boiled egg in the middle with ants crawling out of it.

"It is womankind, shaking off the shackles of oppression and domination to assume our rightful place in society," she said. "And has Sid told you about her latest triumph?"

"No."

Sid shrugged modestly.

"She has been asked by none other than Susan B. Anthony to write for *The Revolution*."

"Excellent," I said, not having a clear idea of either of these. "I congratulate you both."

"Anything to make society in general more aware of our cause," Sid said.

I then allowed myself to be persuaded to stay for what they called a "peasant lunch" of crusty bread, smelly cheeses, olives, and onions, washed down with a glass of Chianti, and came home again feeling rather mellow.

A note was waiting for me in my mailbox. Miss Molly Murphy. By Hand.

Inside was Daniel's bold black scrawl.

Molly. I'm sending this with a constable. Saw Dr. Larson today. He says he's sure cause of death was pneumonia. Vomiting caused by high fever. Absolutely no cause for autopsy. He was furious at the suggestion and told me he'd been the family physician for thirty years. He went on to say that Mrs. Poindexter had been ministered to most diligently by her mother who had overseen every aspect of her care. I hope this allays your suspicions. Daniel.

So that was that. I didn't know whether to be relieved or annoyed. Maybe Emily did suffer from an overactive imagination. She was obviously extremely fond of Fanny, and devastated by her death. She also suffered from the kind of constitution that laid her low with sick headaches when she got upset. All in all it seemed she was an emotional young woman who could well be prone to hysteria. I decided to see if she had returned to work and, if she had, to risk the wrath of

Mr. McPherson by delivering Daniel's message to her at the shop later that afternoon. There was no answer at her apartment, so I proceeded around the corner to the shop. Emily was behind the counter, busy serving an elderly man. She looked pale but seemed in good spirits as she chatted with him. "These are to be taken twice a day with water," I heard her say as I opened the door. "And no more port until the gout subsides."

The old man chuckled and said something that made her smile. Then he raised his hat to me as he passed me.

"Molly." She glanced around warily.

"Sorry to disturb you at work, but I thought you'd want to know."

"You have news?" she whispered. "From your policeman friend?"

I nodded.

"And?"

"The doctor is sure the cause of death was pneumonia."

"But what about the gastric problems?"

"Brought on by extremely high fever."

"So they're not going to do any testing?"

"No."

Emily chewed at her lip. "She's going to be buried on Thursday, and then it will be too late."

"I went to Fanny's place yesterday," I said.

"And I did manage to take a sample of the stomach mixture."

"Stomach mixture?" She looked aghast. "You don't suspect us, do you?"

"Of course not. But someone could have added a poison to it. It was the only thing in her bathroom that could easily have been tampered with."

"Oh, I see."

"So we can have that tested. And you know what?" Another brilliant idea hit me. "You have some of her hair. I'm sure doctors can test hair for traces of arsenic."

"What's this?" Ned appeared at Emily's side. "Who wants something tested for arsenic?"

"We do," Emily said. "We have hair that we'd like tested for arsenic. Is that something you could do, Ned?"

Ned frowned. "You suspect someone of arsenic poisoning?"

"Probably not, but we'd just like to make sure. Is that the kind of test that you could conduct for us?"

"I think so," Ned said. "It's a simple enough test, I gather. Not that I've ever been called upon to run it, but I have to warn you that traces of arsenic often show up in a person for the most innocent of reasons. For example, wallpaper often contains arsenic, especially the new green floral papers that are so popular."

"But you mean someone would have to soak wallpapers and make a person drink the liquid?" I asked.

Ned shook his head. "No, they give off fumes."

"Mercy me," Emily said, looking quite alarmed. "So you're saying that most people will show some trace of arsenic in their systems?"

"Probably," Ned said. "And don't forget that many tonics and medications contain a small amount. It's used to treat plenty of diseases, too — including syphilis."

Emily blushed. "Oh, I don't think there's any question of . . ."

"Of course not." Ned grinned. "But all I was suggesting was that a trace of arsenic in hair would not necessarily mean a person was being poisoned."

"I see," I said. "But more than a trace?"

He grinned. "Ah, then that's a different matter altogether. So bring me the hair, Emily, and I'll see what I can do, all right?"

"Thank you, Ned," she said, gazing at him adoringly.

I left them and went home, content that I had done everything I could. If arsenic showed up in the hair sample, then we'd have to test the stomach mixture. Again, all we had to do was wait. By now I had received replies in the negative from all of the missionary societies, although the Baptists had shown a couple called Bosman on their books some thirty years ago. Was it possible that Emily's kin had somehow got the name wrong? It seemed unlikely. One thing I was sure of was that Horace Lynch had known more than he was willing to tell me. There was something about Emily's background that needed to be kept from her. And then, of course, I couldn't help thinking about her complete collapse with a sick headache yesterday. Was there some kind of mental instability in the family — a parent in a mental institution, perhaps? I was keen to take that journey to Aunt Lydia's hometown to find out the truth for myself, but I realized that it wasn't a trip I could make there and back in one day. And attending the funeral was important. Perhaps I would learn something from the demeanor of those who came to it.

So I spent my free day finding out how to get to Williamstown, Massachusetts. I was surprised to find that it was not at all in the direction I had expected it to be. I had thought of Massachusetts in terms of Boston and a train ride up the coast, but it seemed that Williamstown was in the far northwest of the state and would be reached by traveling due north from New York — nowhere near Boston. It seemed as if it would be a long journey, with a change of trains in Springfield, and then I would have to find a cheap place to stay. I reminded myself that Emily was not able to pay me much — unless I could prove that she was the rightful heiress to a fortune, in which case I'd ask for more. I also reminded myself that my last client had just died without paying me a cent.

The funeral morning dawned bright and breezy — that typical April weather with white puffy clouds racing across the sky that makes one want to be outdoors. I found that the Ninth Avenue El went all the way to the northern tip of the island and spent a pleasant half hour looking down on city life as we progressed northward. The Trinity Church cemetery was one of the only cemeteries still operating within the city itself. Only those with powerful connections could be buried there, and it seemed that Poindexters owned an impressive family mausoleum. Aside from the tragic circumstance that brought us there, the cemetery was a delightful spot to be. Tree-lined

215

walkways and marble statues made it a pleasant oasis and escape from the hubbub of the city. On one side, vistas of the Hudson River opened up, with great strings of barges and jaunty river steamers sailing past. And on the far Jersey shore the Palisades rose, sheer and forbidding from the river's edge.

I was glad that my one black hat was an old-fashioned bonnet with a bow that tied under my chin, as the wind whipped fiercely and several hats were sent flying. A large crowd had gathered at the gravesite, all dressed in the height of fashion. Fanny's mother and other female members of the family were hidden under heavy veils, and I wouldn't have been able to recognize her had she not been approached and addressed by name. So much for watching expressions.

At least the men's faces were clearly visible beneath their top hats. Anson Poindexter stood between two men who must have been his father and Mr. Bradley. Both of them fine figures still — carrying themselves with the grace and control expected of people of their station. I noticed Mr. Bradley intercepting well-wishers so that he could spare his wife as much of the ordeal as possible. His face was grave but pleasant as he shook hands just as he would at any party or in any reception line, and one would never have known from his face that this was his daughter's funeral. He was a handsome man, as dark as his daughter was fair — his black hair and sideburns now tinged with gray.

My attention turned to Anson Poindexter. In contrast to his father and father-in-law, he was clearly ill at ease, and glanced around with jerky head movements. He was clearly distracted as well, having to be nudged by his father when well-wishers tried to speak to him. Did this indicate a guilty conscience, I wondered, or simply that he found the situation so uncomfortable he was looking for a way to escape? He had, after all, found every excuse to escape from his sick wife's bedside.

Emily arrived and came to stand beside me. "Old McPherson wasn't going to let me off," she said, panting as if she had had to run to get here on time, "but Ned talked him into it. Oh, and Ned has run the test on Fanny's hair. He says there was no trace of arsenic at all. I suppose that's good news, isn't it."

"Yes, it is," I said. "It would be awful to watch her being buried and always wondering if someone had gotten away with murder."

She looked around. "A good crowd, wouldn't you say? I don't see any of Fanny's other friends — oh, yes I do. There's Alice, and that must be Minnie with her under that veil. Come on, let's join them."

She made her way through the crowd to where the two women were standing.

"Emily!" Alice held out her hands. "I'm so glad you could come. What a terribly sad day, isn't it?"

Emily nodded.

"I still can't believe it," Minnie said, nodding politely to Emily and me. "Was it only less than two weeks ago that we were all together in Fanny's living room, talking about ball gowns and complexions?"

Emily was still looking around. "I don't see Bella or Dorcas," she said.

"Bella was with us a moment ago." Alice's eyes scanned the gathering crowd. "But Dorcas won't be coming. Haven't you heard? She's quite ill. They're worried about her."

Emily and I exchanged a glance.

"What's wrong with her?" Emily asked.

"That's just it. The doctors don't know. Worrying, isn't it?"

"Is she up to receiving visitors, do you think?" Emily asked.

"I really couldn't say," Alice answered.

"And of course now they are worried that her baby will catch whatever she has."

"Poor Dorcas," Emily said.

"You know what I'm wondering." Minnie leaned closer to us. "I'm wondering if Fanny wasn't coming down with something when we were there and Dorcas caught it from her."

"Fanny's doctor says she died of complications of influenza," I said, joining in this conversation for the first time, "and this strain of flu is supposed to be horribly virulent."

"Then let's hope the rest of us don't follow suit," Minnie said.

"I'm all right," I said. "I went through it a month ago and I don't think you can get it twice."

As soon as she could, Emily dragged me aside. "We must visit Dorcas," she whispered. "We must find out if Anson Poindexter came to see her."

I frowned as I realized what was going through her head. "But even if it's remotely possible that Anson killed his wife, what motive could he have for wanting to kill Dorcas?"

"Maybe she found out. I know she went to visit Fanny last week. What if she discovered something and came to Anson to share her suspicions?"

"I really think you're going a little far," I said. "We've heard from Ned that there was no trace of arsenic in Fanny's hair. The doctor says he is convinced that he correctly diagnosed her illness and we know that her mother and only her mother ministered to her during her last days. What more do you want?"

Emily sighed. "I really don't know. I guess you're right and I'm just being silly."

"Not silly," I said with more enthusiasm than I felt. "But maybe overly concerned."

I turned to look as the minister arrived and the mourners began to gather around the gravesite. I picked out Anson Poindexter, then I froze. Bella was standing beside him, her hand on his arm. As she looked up at him a momentary glance passed between them. I had seen that look before. It was a look exchanged by lovers.

EIGHTEEN

Now I was really confused. Could I have made a mistake about Anson and Mademoiselle Fifi? Had his real mistress been right here, under my nose all the time? They moved apart instantly but I had seen enough to be sure. And Bella had been to visit her poor sick friend during the week. Perhaps she had brought something with her — some calves' foot jelly, a special tonic? And taken the vessel back with her afterward? But then I shook my head. That was ridiculous. Why would Bella want Fanny dead? She wasn't free to marry Anson.

The ceremony continued. I watched Fanny's family — her mother hidden beneath her veil and yet her carriage proud and erect, her father staring out toward the Hudson, his face stoic. I felt for them — their beloved only child, with a life so full of promise ahead of her, taken from them. And all the money in the world couldn't save her.

The final blessing was concluded, the coffin was carried into the vault, and the mourners drifted away.

Emily was already tugging at my arm. "Can you come with me to see Dorcas now?" she whispered. "Mr. McPherson won't know how long this ceremony has taken, so I can probably be away for another half an hour. And Dorcas's house is on the way."

I no longer knew what to think. I still didn't have Emily's overwhelming conviction that her friend had been murdered or that Dorcas was now in grave danger. As I tried to look at it logically I could see that Anson Poindexter did have a strong motive for wanting Fanny dead. If she had divorced him, he would have lost her money and his current, very pleasant, lifestyle. But I couldn't see why he would want to kill Dorcas, unless she had discovered something at Fanny's house that made her suspect him. In any case, it was better to know the truth and to ease Emily's fears. And it was a lovely bright morning and I had nothing better to do.

"All right," I said. "I'll come with you — or would you rather that I went alone?"

"What do you mean?" she asked.

"Didn't it occur to you that both Fanny and Dorcas really might have caught this horrible influenza and you might not want to expose yourself to it again? I, on the other hand, have had it."

Emily smiled. "My dear Molly. I work in a drugstore. Every day I serve people who are coughing and sputtering all over me. If I haven't caught anything yet, I'm not going to. Besides, Dorcas is a friend from college. I have to do everything I can to save a Vassar sister."

So we left the cemetery together and soon found ourselves on the east side of the park.

"I see that Dorcas married well too," I said, as we passed one impressive mansion after another, some with carriages waiting outside and liveried footmen standing beside them. Crisply starched nannies pushed baby buggies and led well-scrubbed toddlers by the hand. I wondered if one of the passing buggies contained little Toodles, Dorcas's baby son. "But I thought she married a professor."

"She did," Emily agreed, "but a professor from an old New York family. So she has the best of both worlds — an intelligent husband and the money to enjoy life." She smiled, then went on, "Now that I recall, hers was a real love match. He was a student at Columbia, and they met at a dance. And they don't own one of these mansions — they live with her in-laws."

As we walked I noticed Emily suddenly quicken her pace, striding out and staring straight ahead. It took me a moment to register that we were passing her old home. Maybe soon I'd be able to settle her mind with the truth about her parents. We went up the front steps of a square, gray stone house and were admitted by a butler.

"Please wait here and I shall inquire if Mrs. Hochstetter Junior is feeling well enough to receive visitors," he said.

We waited in an impressive entrance hall decorated with shields, swords, and various strange weapons brought back from foreign parts. It seemed that the Hochstetters were a much-traveled family. At last the butler reappeared. "She would be delighted to see you. Please follow me."

He led us up a broad central staircase and ushered us into a grand but old-fashioned bedroom, liberally decorated with knick-knacks. In the midst of china statues, brass vases, artificial flowers, and a cage containing a stuffed bird, Dorcas lay, propped up on several pillows. Her eyes were sunken and she looked flushed but she held out her hand to us.

"Emily, Molly. How very kind of you to come to see me."

"We were at Fanny's funeral when we heard that you had also been taken ill, so we felt we had to come immediately," Emily said.

"Poor Fanny. I wanted so badly to attend, but of course I'm too weak to go anywhere. How was it?"

"Very moving," Emily said.

"And a beautiful setting. The trees were all in blossom."

"I know. It's a delightful place, isn't it? Our family also has a plot there."

She gave a gentle sigh.

Emily perched on the bed beside her. "So how are you? I was so worried . . ."

"Feeling a little better, thank you," Dorcas said. "I've had a horrible high fever and some nasty vomiting but today I've actually kept some barley water down, so one can hope that I'm on the mend."

"That is good news," Emily said. "Is there anything you'd like? Anything we can bring you?"

"No, thank you." She lay back and sighed. "My mother-in-law looks after me so well. I have everything I need and my friends have been most kind. Bella brought me those lovely grapes and Honoria was here and gave me those daffodils you see blooming on my windowsill. So cheering, don't you think?"

"Honoria? Fancy that. I haven't seen her in ages. Not since she became famous, anyway. How is she?"

"Flourishing," Dorcas said. "When I'm well again we must go and see her perform."

"Have you had any other visitors?" Emily asked, trying to sound casual.

Dorcas frowned. "Thomas's aunt and cousins a few days ago. That's about it. My mother-in-law has been trying to keep visitors away so that I have peace and quiet to recuperate. She's out at the moment or she wouldn't have allowed you two in to my room. She can be quite a tartar when she wants to."

"Anson Poindexter didn't come to see you, did he?" Emily asked.

Dorcas looked up in surprise. "Anson? Why would he come to see me? I hardly know him. I've met him at a couple of dinner parties with Fanny, that's all."

"Did Bella bring you anything else beside the grapes?" I asked, quickly changing the subject.

Dorcas looked surprised again. "Bella? No, she wasn't actually allowed up to see me but the maid brought up the grapes from her."

I couldn't see any way to tamper with grapes but I had to make sure. "They look absolutely delicious," I said. "And what a luxury at this time of year."

"Please help yourself," she said, as I had hoped she would. I picked off a couple and managed to put them into my pocket, while pretending to eat with expressions of delight.

"Presumably the doctor has been to see you," Emily said, with a glance in my direction.

"Of course. Every day. He's been giving me the most horrible medicine that he says is effective against influenza, but it tastes ghastly, and frankly I don't think it's been helping at all. Finally I told him I couldn't keep it down and I wasn't going to take it anymore."

"So he definitely thinks this is influenza, does he?" I asked.

"Well, yes."

"Even though stomach distress is not normally part of the flu?" I asked.

She paused, considering this. "I think he was slightly puzzled, but when he heard I visited Fanny last week he said it was obvious I had picked up the same microbe that caused her illness."

"I see," I said. "I just wondered if you could have eaten something that disagreed with you, in addition to the flu, I mean."

"Oh no," she said. "I've hardly eaten a thing since I came down with this. I haven't felt like food. I haven't even touched those grapes yet. Literally barley water and a little chicken broth. That's about it for days now. The only thing that has disagreed with me has been that disgusting influenza medicine." She made a face. "I told him it tasted like arsenic and said was he trying to poison me." She laughed. "He said it tasted like arsenic because it had arsenic in it and no, he wasn't trying to poison me but to cure me."

"I wonder if it was the same mixture we've been selling at the store," Emily said.

"I wouldn't know. I had my maid take it away," Dorcas said.

"I'm afraid I have to get back to work," Emily said. "My boss will make a frightful stink if I take too long. I had to really plead with him to go to the funeral in the first place."

"It must be so hard for you to work for such a man," Dorcas said. "I advise getting married as soon as possible and letting your husband face the outside world. I can truthfully say that with Thomas and little Toodles I am quite content."

As we went to make our good-byes, Dorcas moved restlessly. "I seem to be slipping down again," she said. "If you could just plump up my pillows for me again."

Emily eased her into a sitting position while I plumped the pillows. As I replaced the top pillow I noticed something — it was liberally strewn with long, dark hairs.

"She doesn't seem to be too bad, does she?" There was relief in Emily's voice as we left the Hochstetter mansion. "I was so worried that we'd find her dying or dead like Fanny."

"Yes, I know you were." I put my hand on her shoulder. "So now perhaps we can put Dorcas's illness down to coincidence and Fanny's death down to pneumonia following the flu, and I can get on with solving your own little mystery."

She smiled prettily. "Why, of course. What do you plan to do next?"

"Go to Massachusetts to the place where your Aunt Lydia was born," I said. "If the family comes from around there, then someone will know something — a childhood playmate or an old servant. Someone always remembers."

"I hope so," Emily said. "I can't tell you

229

how painful it was to walk past my old home just then, even though it holds no particularly happy memories for me. But it did remind me that I now have no place to call my own, and it's a distressing feeling."

"I feel rather the same," I said. "I had to flee from Ireland and can no longer go back there, so I, too, have no home."

"But a family — you still have a family, don't you?"

"I lost my father and my oldest brother. I still have two brothers alive. One is in exile with the Republican Brotherhood in France and the other has been taken in by a kind family. So I don't know if or when I'll ever see them again."

"Oh Molly, I'm so sorry. You must miss them terribly."

"Actually I found them annoying and ungrateful when I had to look after them, but it seems to be true about absence making the heart grow fonder."

I looked at Emily and we shared a smile.

"I am concerned about my youngest brother, Malachy," I said. "I don't like the thought of his being raised by strangers, but I don't quite know what to do about it. When I'm settled I would like to see if I can bring him to America, but I don't know if he'd even want to come."

Emily took my hand. "So we are both alone in the world. Then let us be sisters, linked with a common bond. I recognized you as a kindred spirit the moment I saw you in that parade."

We parted company as she went across the park to the Upper West Side and I took the Third Avenue El to Grand Central Terminal to inquire about trains to Williamstown. I booked a ticket for early the next morning and started home to prepare for the journey. I was just crossing Greenwich Avenue toward Patchin Place when I heard the thunder of approaching horses' hooves. A woman's voice screamed, "Lookout!" I turned to see a carriage bearing down on me at great speed.

"Holy mother of —" I exclaimed. The vehicle showed no sign of slowing. I flung myself aside, tripped at the gutter, and would have gone sprawling had not passersby grabbed me and hauled me onto the sidewalk as the carriage passed, mud flying up from the hooves and wheels. I got an impression of a black, enclosed carriage of the type often seen around town, owned by the smarter families. From what I saw the driver was all in black, wearing no particular livery by which I could later identify him. But in truth the whole thing was a blur and my heart was beating so fast that it was all I could do to stand there, gasping for breath.

"Are you all right, miss?" a woman asked.

"Should be locked up," a man beside me muttered, and waved his cane at the rapidly disappearing carriage.

"I'm fine. No harm done, thanks to you." I looked at their concerned faces. "If you hadn't grabbed me, I'd have been under those hooves."

"It's happening more and more these days," another woman said. "Reckless drivers all over the place, electric trolley cars, and now these new automobiles. A person isn't safe crossing the street any longer."

The crowd began to melt away, the hope of a spectacle now over. I also went on my way and turned into Patchin Place. I found my hand was shaking as I put my key in the lock. As I put on the kettle for a cup of tea, that scene insisted on playing itself over and over in my mind. And as I replayed it an alarming thought surfaced. That carriage had headed straight for me — accelerating, not slowing. I was the target, not a random victim.

Which made me wonder who could possibly want me out of the way badly enough to risk running me down in broad daylight on a busy street. I found myself wondering if Anson Poindexter was still at the funeral banquet. Maybe I couldn't put Fanny Poindexter's death behind me just yet.

When I went to bed that night I tried to reason with myself that recklessly driven carriages cause accidents every day in the city. It must just have appeared that the carriage was headed for me. It had been unlucky timing, nothing more. But I couldn't shake off the nagging doubt and was rather glad that I would be out of town for the next couple of days.

NINETEEN

I set off for Williamstown on a blustery morning with clouds that promised the chance of rain. We passed green fields and apple trees in blossom. We stopped in Hartford and then I had to change trains in Springfield. From now on the terrain became hilly and I found my enjoyment in being in the leafy green of the countryside turning to nostalgia. These sweeping green hills and racing brooks reminded me of home. When an April shower peppered the train window the picture was complete. Then I told myself that I really didn't want to go home again, even if I could. My life was here and there was nothing much wrong with it.

I alighted in Williamstown and stood on the platform taking in the crisp air. I was so used to the sooty, city air of New York that it was delightful just to breathe here. The town was surrounded by green hills. During my hours in the train I had tried to formulate a plan. I hadn't expected the town to be quite so large. I had rather pictured it like Westport at home in Ireland — a little country town set amid green fields. This looked to be quite a large, bustling metropolis, and, as I soon discovered, it was a college town to boot. Students walked past me, deep in earnest discussion. Others rode past on bicycles. I had decided to start at the church with the baptismal records. Surely a woman who married such an important man as Horace Lynch would have been from a prominent family in the area. But then I saw the mill, with the tall chimneys rising against the hills. And then of course I remembered Emily saying that her Uncle Horace owned mills in Massachusetts. Was it possible that he owned this very mill? I made my way there through back streets and went in the front entrance to a central courtyard. Around me was the clank and groan of heavy machinery. Mill girls hurried past, chattering away, their shawls around their shoulders against the chill wind as they crossed the courtyard and disappeared into a building at the rear. I found an office and asked my question. No, I was told. This mill belonged to a Mr. Greeley, but the mill in North Adams was owned by Mr. Lynch.

This was an annoying discovery as I had just come through North Adams on the train. It had been the stop before Williamstown, some six miles away. So it was back to the station and another train ride. I'm sure those who do not make their living as detectives have no appreciation for the amount of time we take coming and going. The job turns out to be hours of travel, hours of nothing happening, coupled with the odd minute of excitement every now and then.

North Adams was less prosperous-looking, and terraces rose up the slopes of an impressive mountain. The mill itself dominated the town, a square red brick building, with white-framed windows and tall chimneys. I made for it and was shown into the office of the mill manager.

He was a large, florid man with a perpetually worried expression but he greeted me cordially enough.

"Now, what can I do for you, miss?" he asked.

I told him I was sorry to trouble him but I'd been asked to track down any surviving relatives of Lydia Lynch, née Johnson. I understood that Mr. Lynch owned the mill.

"He does," the man said, "but he doesn't come near the place often these days. Leaves

236

all the running of the business to me."

"So have you been here long enough to remember Mrs. Lynch?" I asked.

"Aye, I've been here twenty-two years, man and boy," he said, staring out past me with a wistful look. "I started here as an apprentice and I've worked my way up. Haven't done at all badly for myself, have I?"

"I'd say you've done very well." I gave him an encouraging smile. "So what can you tell me about Mrs. Lynch? Did the family come from around here?"

He nodded. "From Williamstown," he said. I tried not to let my annoyance show. As usual my impetuous nature had driven me to leave that town before I'd asked the right questions. I probably could have saved myself a journey.

"Williamstown. I see. I don't suppose any Johnson relatives are still living in these parts?"

"No relatives that I know of," he said. "There was only her parents, and I believe they'd come over from Scotland when her father was a young man. He made quite a fortune for himself with this mill —"

"Wait a minute," I interrupted. "He owned this mill?"

"He did. He and his missus were killed in

237

a buggy wreck when Miss Lydia was a young woman. She married Horace Lynch soon after. He took over the mill and they moved into the old Johnson mansion."

"And when did they move away from this area?"

"Ah, well." He sucked through his teeth. "That would have been more than twenty years ago. They hadn't been married long. Mr. Lynch had done very well for himself. He'd got other business interests down south and he wanted to be closer to them. At least, that's what I heard. So they upped and moved to a swank part of New York City. I expect it was Mrs. Lynch's doing — she always was one for parties and dances and smart society. There wasn't much for her in Williamstown or North Adams, that's for sure."

"They must have moved away when they took on the baby," I said.

"Baby? I never heard of no baby," he said. "That was one of Mr. Lynch's disappointments, that he had no heir."

"Not hers," I said. "A cousin's orphan. She took over the rearing of a cousin's baby. Its parents were missionaries in China, so I've been given to understand. They died in a cholera epidemic and Mrs. Lynch took on the baby."

He frowned. "Maybe I did hear something about that, but Mr. Lynch isn't one for conversation when he comes here. And since she died, he never mentions her. He's not one to show his feelings, you know. All business and then he's off again. And he's not the easiest man in the world to work for, but by and large he's fair. He pays a decent wage."

I couldn't think of anything else to ask. I stood up. "Thank you for your time," I said, and we shook hands.

So it was back to Williamstown and the old Johnson mansion. By now it was obvious that I'd need to stay the night somewhere in the area, so I booked myself at an inn on Main Street near the college. The landlady looked at me suspiciously to begin with as she showed me up to a clean but spartan room.

"Are you visiting a sweetheart at the college?" she asked.

"No, I'm a businesswoman from New York City," I said. "I'm here checking for relatives of the Johnson family."

"Johnsons? You mean the old Johnson mansion?"

I nodded.

"There's nobody here now," she said.

"The old couple died, of course. Tragic accident."

"What happened?" I asked.

She sucked in air through her teeth. "Their buggy went off the road in a storm. They were both swept into the creek and drowned. And then their daughter married and moved away."

"What about the house? Who owns it now?"

She shrugged. "As far as I know Miss Lydia's husband still owns it. I never heard of its being sold and it just sits there, going to ruin. I can't see why. He'd have got a tidy sum for that when it was in good condition, years ago."

This didn't tally with the picture of Horace Lynch that I'd been given — a man who was keen on money would surely have sold a vacant property, wouldn't he?

"So where is this house?" I asked. "Is it in town?"

"On the edge of town on the Petersburg Road. You just follow Main Street and you'll get there. About a mile's walk, I'd say."

"So I'd have time to go there today?"

"If you're not afraid of a good walk."

I smiled. "I'm from Ireland and we thought nothing of walking five miles into the nearest town."

240

"Ah well, then. Off you go, but you'll find nothing there but weeds and a ruin. Supper's at six o'clock sharp."

I set off, quite enjoying the pace of a small town, the passing buggies, the men chewing the fat outside the barber's shop, a group of Williams College young men in earnest discussion as they crossed the road. I thought they might be debating Plato or Shakespeare until I heard one of them say, "Of course the beer isn't better there, but the barmaids do make up for it, don't they?"

I smiled to myself as I walked on. At first there were college buildings on either side of me, then shops and businesses until Main Street became Petersburg Road and meandered out of town. At last I came to a high brick wall. I continued along it until it was broken by a wrought-iron gate. Ivy grew up the wall and spilled over the top of the gate. I pushed the rusty latch and the gate swung open with much creaking and groaning. Cautiously I stepped inside. A gravel driveway led to a tall mansion in the neo-Gothic style. Tall Scotch pine trees surrounded it and creepers covered much of the walls. It looked like the house from one of those dreadful Gothic novels and I half expected to see the heroine, clad only in her nightgown, run screaming from the front door, pursued by a man with an axe. I could see why Lydia Lynch had been keen to leave Williamstown for the elegance and bright lights of New York City.

I tiptoed up to the house itself and peered in the windows. The rooms were almost empty, apart from an occasional piece of furniture, hidden under a dust sheet.

As I walked around I was overtaken by the stillness and the melancholy. Sounds from the lively world outside did not penetrate this forgotten estate. I could tell that there had been lovely gardens here once, but the flower beds were an overgrown tangle of brambles, the lawns were full of weeds, and shrubs had grown rampant to form an impenetrable barrier across the back part of the yard. Why had Mr. Lynch let the place go to rack and ruin, I wondered. If he no longer wanted it, then why not sell it? And surely he must come here occasionally to check on his mill, so why not keep a suite of rooms open in readiness? I knew he had a reputation for being a skinflint, so perhaps he would regard the latter as an extravagance, but letting a valuable asset go to waste did not ring true to his character as described to me.

As I peeped through an arbor that was now a tangle of wild roses, I glimpsed a pretty little lawn area beyond, with a swing hanging from the branch of an old oak tree. And I imagined young Lydia Johnson sitting on that swing, dreaming about the world that she longed to see.

I let myself out of the gate and closed it behind me again with a final sort of clang. The melancholy of the place was overpowering and I walked quickly to get away. Was it the tragedy of Lydia's parents' untimely death that still lingered here? I crossed the street to distance myself from it and came upon an old man, digging in his yard. On impulse I went up to him.

"That house over there," I said. "I take it that nobody lives there anymore."

He looked up, squinted at me, then grunted. "That's right. Don't take a genius to see that."

"But it used to be owned by the Johnson family? Have you lived here long enough to remember them?"

"I was born in this very house, miss," he said. "And I remember that house when it was newly built. William and Mary Johnson — foreigners they were, from Scotland. He spoke with such a thick accent you could hardly understand him. But it seemed he'd made a killing in timber up in Vermont and he bought the mill over in North Adams,

243

and had himself this fine house built."

"And they had a daughter?"

His grim face softened. "Pretty little thing, and the sweetest, gentlest nature you could imagine. I did some gardening and heavy work for them over there and she used to come out and talk to me. She'd swing on her swing and chatter away." A smile crossed his face. "I don't suppose there was much lively conversation with those parents. Dour, that's what would describe them. They belonged to one of these religions that thought that dancing, singing, merry-making were a sin. I don't believe they even celebrated birthdays. And Miss Lydia — well, she was a friendly little soul. She just loved to dance and sing. I don't understand why she married that Lynch fella. He was a good deal older than her and about as unpleasant and dour as her father was. Well, maybe I do understand it — her pa had just died and she was looking for another father figure, I suppose. There's no accounting for taste, is there?" He chuckled.

"So you were closely connected with the place," I said. "Did you happen to meet any of the Johnsons' relatives ever? I'm trying to trace a couple called Boswell, who were mis-sionaries in China. I'm just wondering if they ever came to visit or you heard anyone speak of them."

"I don't recall any relatives coming to stay," he said. "Those Johnsons pretty much kept themselves to themselves. But I can well believe they had relatives who were missionaries. Very much into their religion, they were. They used to make a terrible stink if anyone hereabouts made music or had a party on the Sabbath."

"Lydia and Horace took over the rearing of these relatives' baby when they died in China," I said. "So they weren't living here when that happened?"

He shook his head. "I never saw a baby at that house. They must have already upped and gone to New York."

"So they moved to New York, did they?"

He grunted again. "I'm not sure if that was her doing or his. Some said he'd acquired a whole lot of other business enterprises and wanted to be in the thick of things. Others said that she'd bullied him into going because she wanted to be closer to society and the bright lights. I think it was probably a bit of both. You'd have thought it would have suited them both but I heard that she took sick soon afterward and died. Great pity, that. As I said, she was a lovely little thing. She deserved a better life."

"And when they went, they just left this place untouched, did they?"

"That's right. They'd kept a pack of servants and gardeners and whatnot. They just fired them all. Didn't take a single one to New York with them. I suppose none of us was grand enough for their new life. Always did have airs and graces, that Horace Lynch."

"So you lost your job with them?"

"I was never a regular employee with them. I worked at Paine's Lumber Mill for forty years. I only helped out at the Johnsons' and then the Lynchs' on the side. So it didn't affect me much, but I can tell you that a lot of noses around here were put out of joint. Servants that had been with the family for twenty years or more, kicked out without so much as a thank-you. Still, that was Horace Lynch for you. Good riddance, I say."

I thanked him and left him, my mind fully occupied with what he had told me. If the Johnsons came from Scotland then I'd probably been searching for my missionaries in the wrong places. Now I'd have to start from the beginning again and contact all the missionary societies in England and Scotland. I sighed. Perhaps I could save time by contacting some of the names I had been supplied of missionaries who had worked in China. Surely the British missionaries and their American counterparts must have worked in cooperation with each other. I thought of the men I had spoken with the other day at the Presbyterian missions headquarters, but I couldn't remember their names. I'd have to go back there and ask them.

Then my thoughts turned to the Johnsons and their daughter, who liked to sing and dance and have fun, and the unpleasant Horace Lynch. It didn't seem like a love match and I wondered if Horace had been more interested in acquiring her mill, her mansion, and her money. Either way, I felt sorry for Emily and her miserable upbringing.

TWENTY

Supper was a good hearty pot roast with plenty of root vegetables, followed by an apple betty and fresh cream. I ate enthusiastically.

"So did you find the old Johnson place?" the landlady asked as she brought in a pot of coffee.

"I did. It seems such a shame that it's being left to fall down."

"A waste, that's what I'd call it," she said. "Sarah here recalls what it was like in its heyday, don't you, Sarah?" She addressed this remark to the large, red-faced woman who was clearing the dishes from the table.

"I do," Sarah confessed.

"Sarah was a maid there, you know."

"Really?"

She smiled. "That's right. I went to work for the Johnsons when I was fourteen and I stayed with them until they left. I helped look after Miss Lydia when she was a girl.

Sweet little thing she was. Sweet and gentle and eager to please."

"I heard she didn't take any of her servants when they moved to New York. She didn't ask you to go with her?"

"No, miss. Didn't take a single one of us, not even Cook, who had been with the family all those years. But then it wasn't Miss Lydia's decision, I'm sure of that. He ruled the roost from the moment he showed up, didn't he?"

My landlady nodded. "Pity that the Johnsons had to go and die."

"It was. It was a grand place to work at one time," Sarah said wistfully. "The house always just so and the gardens were really lovely. Old Mr. Johnson loved his garden, didn't he. Employed a pack of gardeners — mostly foreigners . . ."

' "I remember you were sweet on that one Italian gardener," my landlady said, giving Sarah a nudge in her amply cushioned side. "What was his name? Antonio?"

Sarah snorted, then chuckled. "Go on with you. That was just girlish fantasies. He never looked at me twice, even though I have to say I was a good deal slimmer and better-looking in those days. If you ask me, it was Miss Lydia he was sweet on. Not that anything could have come of it, given the

249

difference between their stations. But I remember how he used to push her on the swing and she'd look up at him, just so. . . . My, but he was handsome, wasn't he?"

"What happened to him?" the landlady asked. "Did he go back to Italy?"

Sarah's face clouded. "No, don't you remember? He was killed. They reckon he drank too much at the saloon and fell off the bridge on his way home. His body was found floating in the river. Poor man. So young, too."

She picked up the tray of dishes. "I dare say I'm better off with my Sam. Even if he's not a barrel of laughs." She chuckled again as she carried out the tray.

The landlady and I exchanged a glance.

"So would you know of any families around here who were friendly with Miss Lydia and the Johnsons?" I asked. "Someone must have stayed in touch with her when she moved."

She stood, the coffee pot poised in one hand, and a cup in the other, thinking. "I never had dealings with the family personally, you understand, but Miss Lydia and I were around the same age, so I did hear of her from time to time. Those Johnsons kept a close rein on her, I can tell you. She wasn't allowed to parties and dances like the other girls. And any young man who showed up on the doorstep was deemed unsuitable. Old Pa Johnson thought the world of her. No man was going to be good enough for her."

"But she chose Horace Lynch," I said, thinking of the unpleasant, bald-headed face and the sagging jowls.

"After her father died," my landlady said. "I think she needed someone to boss her around the way her father used to. It's funny how we women make the same mistakes over and over, isn't it."

"But as to friends around here?"

"The Johnsons were not what you'd call social people," she said. "He was caught up in his work and she was a shy thing. I suppose they must have given dinner parties and ladies' teas like anyone else but I can't tell you who they invited to them. I wasn't of that class. And as to the daughter — well, she went to the ladies' seminary with the other girls of good families. Miss Addison's, it's called."

"It's still in operation?"

"Oh yes. Miss Addison — she's an institution around here. On Buckley Street. That's to the right off Main. I'm sure she's kept a list of past pupils and will be able to help you."

I drank my coffee, nodded to fellow guests, and went up to my room. That night a fierce storm blew through, rattling the window frames and howling down the chimneys. I lay awake in the unfamiliar bed, trying to think things through. What was I doing here? What did I hope to discover? I had heard the basic facts — Lydia's parents died. Any remaining family was in Scotland. She had married Horace Lynch and moved to New York to be near the bright lights and high society. End of story as far as Williamstown was concerned. My thoughts turned to Fanny Poindexter, and her friend Dorcas. If Fanny's husband had killed her, we'd have no way of proving it. I was glad Dorcas looked as if she was on the road to recovery, or my life would become impossibly complicated.

By morning the wind and rain had abated and a lovely spring day awaited me as I came out of the inn, my stomach full of hotcakes, sausage, and maple syrup. The hotcakes and maple syrup were a new experience for me, one that I looked forward to repeating. I soon realized that it was Saturday. The college was not bustling with students as it had been the day before. No doubt they were enjoying sleeping in after a hard week of study, or a harder night at the taverns!

I turned off Main Street as directed and found myself on Buckley. Miss Addison's was announced on a painted sign swinging outside a dignified old white clapboard house. I went up the path and knocked on the front door. A maid opened it and immediately I heard the sound of girlish laughter coming from a back room. I explained my mission and was admitted to a parlor, where I was soon joined by Miss Addison herself — a venerable old woman with upright carriage, steel-gray hair, and steely eyes. I explained my visit.

"You remember Lydia Johnson?" I asked.

Her face softened. "Indeed I do. A bright girl. Very bright indeed. Loved to read. Absolutely devoured books. And not just light, fluffy novels that most girls of her age love. She'd wade through the biographies and the histories, finish them in no time, and beg for more. She wanted very much to go to college but her father wouldn't hear of her going away. We tried to persuade him that a ladies' institution like Vassar or Smith would be suitable and safe, but he wouldn't bend. It's always a shame when a good brain goes to waste, I think."

"I agree," I said. "So would you happen

to know of any women who were Lydia's friends while she was here, with whom she might have kept in contact after she moved away?"

"I couldn't tell you with whom she corresponded," Miss Addison said, "but I could take a look at her class records. Let me see. She would have been the class of seventy-seven, wouldn't she? Please take a seat."

She went and I amused myself by looking at graduation pictures of past years — all similar young girls in white, holding sprays of flowers like brides, their faces alive and hopeful, also like brides. How many of them went on to use their minds and pursue their dreams, I wondered. There was a squeal outside the door and a girl rushed in, her red-blond curls tied back in a big bow, a gingham pinafore over her dress. She saw me, started with a look of alarm, and turned bright red.

"I'm sorry," she said. "I didn't realize anybody was here. We were just —"

"I'm going to get you, Mary Ann," another girl's voice shouted outside. "You just wait and —" It fell silent.

"Letitia. Young ladies never raise their voices. How many times do I have to tell you?" came the headmistress's deep voice.

"Sorry, Miss Addison," came the muttered

response.

Mary Ann slunk out of the room as Miss Addison reentered. "I apologize for that little outburst," she said with just the hint of a smile. "It is Saturday and the girls do need to let off steam occasionally." She came to sit beside me on the sofa. "Now, where were we? Ah, yes. Here we are. Lydia Johnson. Now let me see. Rose Brinkley — she's still in town. Married a professor at Williams. What was his name? Sutton. That's it. And Jennie Clark. She married locally. Herman Waggoner. He's a doctor. Went into partnership with his father here in town. And Hannah Pike. I seem to remember that she and Lydia were good friends. She hasn't married but she became a professor at Mount Holyoke ladies' college. A proud moment for me, as you can imagine."

I was rather afraid she'd go down the whole list, giving me the history of each graduate, so I interrupted. "So were any of these girls Lydia's particular friends, do you recall? How about Rose Sutton, née Brinkley?"

"Yes, I think she and Lydia were tight. And Lydia and Hannah Pike, of course."

"Would you know how I could locate Rose Brinkley?"

"He's a professor of history here at the college, so the history department should be able to give you that information. And Doctor Waggoner has his practice on South Street, if you wish to speak to Jennie, his wife."

"Thank you for your time." I stood up and shook hands. "This should give me something to go on. If I learn nothing from the women here in Williamstown, then maybe I can write to the professor at Mount Holyoke."

We shook hands and she looked at me with that piercing gaze. "A woman in business for herself. I like that. Maybe I can persuade you to come and address our students one day. They tend to accept the role of wife and mother all too compliantly."

"I will certainly come if I am able," I said and walked out, tickled pink at the thought of myself as a role model for young ladies at a seminary.

I went to the history department at the college first and came away with Professor Sutton's address. As I opened the gate to their front yard the door opened and a woman of about the right age came out, followed by several boys ranging in age from teens to six or seven.

"Come along, Wilfred. Don't dawdle," the

woman looked back and called.

I introduced myself and stated my purpose.

"I'm afraid I haven't the time to talk at the moment, as you can see," she said, separating two boys who had started to scuffle. "We're off to buy new boots for the boys. They get through them in no time at all. But you can walk with us, if you've a mind to."

We started down the street, the boys running ahead, kicking rocks and generally behaving like boys anywhere.

She turned to me with a tired smile. "I never thought I'd be the mother of seven sons. Not a daughter in sight. And they eat us out of house and home."

I turned the conversation back to Lydia.

"Yes, I remember her well," she said. "We were good friends in school. Everyone was friends with Lydia. She was just that sort of person. She loved to laugh and dance and have fun. Of course her parents forbade that sort of thing so we'd have to sneak her to our parties under false pretenses." Her face became quite young again and she giggled.

"Miss Addison says she was a good student, too."

"Very bright. She and I talked about going to Vassar — we thought that would be so glamorous to be near New York and on the Hudson — but her father said no and mine couldn't afford it. I did the next best thing and married a professor. I thought we'd have long, intellectual discussions, but most of our time seems to be spent separating fighting boys. William, Henry, stop that at once," she yelled.

"When she moved away, did you keep in touch with her?"

"I didn't, and I've since regretted it," she said. "Of course it was all done rather suddenly. One minute they were here, the next packed up and gone."

"Any idea why that was?"

"I heard a rumor that she became sick. From what I gathered she developed consumption and her husband was sending her out west to a hot, dry climate to try to cure her," she said. "But then later I heard that she had died anyway, poor thing."

"Consumption? Do you know where he sent her?"

"They usually send them to Pasadena, don't they? Or to the Arizona desert. But, no, I was busy with a baby at the time and you know how it is — you intend to stay in touch but you don't."

So that was why Lydia had turned from a fun-loving, vibrant young person into the invalid that Emily remembered. She had never fully recovered from her illness.

I left Mrs. Sutton shepherding her brood down the street. I wondered if I should also contact the doctor's wife to see what she had heard about Lydia's disappearance. It was easy enough to locate the offices of Drs. Waggoner and Waggoner, in a solid square brick house, just off Main Street. There I learned that Mrs. Waggoner was not home but that the doctor could maybe see me between patients. I was shown in. Dr. Waggoner was a tall, rangy man with a shock of graying hair. We shook hands and I explained my mission. He nodded seriously.

"Yes, I remember Lydia Johnson well. An attractive young person. My father used to be physician to her family. I was surprised when she married that Lynch fellow, and even more surprised when I heard that she'd been sent out west, apparently diagnosed with consumption."

"So your father wasn't the one who made the diagnosis?"

"No. I'm trying to remember if Lynch used the services of another doctor in town. I don't believe we ever treated him, or her after her marriage. But maybe they were never sick until that moment. She certainly always seemed full of life when I saw her.

And I understand that the stay out west didn't cure her, either."

I shook my head. "She died a few years later."

"Such a terrible wasting disease," he said. "As a physician one feels so powerless. Essentially we can only let it take its course." He looked up as his nurse indicated the next patient was waiting. I got to my feet and shook his hand again.

"I'll let my wife know that you stopped by to visit."

I wasn't sure what to do next. It all seemed rather cut-and-dried here. Lydia had married Horace, contracted consumption, and moved away. But the thought did cross my mind that it was rather a risky undertaking to bring a baby into a home with consumption, because she obviously hadn't been cured by her stay out west.

I debated as I walked down the street and decided that the next thing to do would be to visit the county seat and see if any Boswells might have lived in the area within living memory. If Lydia had never been to Scotland, she was hardly likely to take on the child of relatives she had never met.

I was on my way to the courthouse, thinking gloomily that Boswell was a common enough name, as was Johnson, when it suddenly hit me. I stood stock-still on the sidewalk, oblivious to the pedestrians who had to walk around me. How could I have been so completely blind? When I started to put together the facts, suddenly they all added up. Lydia Lynch, née Johnson — the fun-loving girl who loved to dance and go to parties but was overprotected by her strict parents. The girl who was described by her school principal as a gifted student, always with a book in her hands. And the handsome Italian gardener who had pushed her on a swing and then had so conveniently fallen off a bridge and died. And she had been sent out west in a hurry. And I knew that I probably wouldn't find any Boswells at the courthouse. As I had suspected all along, the only person who could clear up this matter for me would be Horace Lynch. I didn't look forward to facing him again, but I had to try out my hunch on him.

I marched straight back to the station and caught the next train home, having bought a copy of the *New York Herald* to keep me occupied during the long journey. I sat impatiently as the train steamed southward and tried to read. Then suddenly I saw an article that caught my eye:

YOUNG OPERA STAR'S TRAGIC DEATH.

THE NEW YORK MUSIC WORLD IS MOURNING THE LOSS OF ONE OF ITS BRIGHTEST YOUNG HOPES, THE SOPRANO HONORIA MASTERS. MISS MASTERS, SCION OF A SOCIETY FAMILY WHO LEFT THE GLITTERING LIFE OF THE FOUR HUNDRED TO PURSUE AN EXACTING CAREER ON THE OPERA STAGE, DIED YESTERDAY OF A BRIEF, UNEXPLAINED ILLNESS. THE TWENTY-FIVE-YEAR-OLD MISS MASTERS MADE HER DEBUT AT THE METROPOLITAN OPERA A YEAR AGO AND WAS SCHEDULED TO SING WITH THE GREAT ITALIAN TENOR ENRICO CARUSO WHEN HE COMES TO AMERICA LATER THIS YEAR.

There was something about the article that bothered me and at first I couldn't think what it was. Then I realized it was the name Honoria. Not the most common of names, and it had come up in conversation recently. Of course. Dorcas had said that Honoria had been to visit her and Emily had said that she hadn't been in touch with Honoria since she became famous. It had to be the same person. And she had visited Dorcas and she had died.

TWENTY-ONE

When I got home the first thing I found was a note in my mail slot. It was from Emily.

> I must see you at once. Dorcas died suddenly today.

I paused only to wash the grime of the trip from my face, then I went out again, straight to Emily's drugstore. It was by now half past five. I didn't know how late she had to work on Saturdays, but most stores had closed by this time. McPherson's hadn't. I glanced at the globes in the window and then went inside. Emily was at the counter, her face looking pale and strained.

"Oh, Molly, you came. Thank heavens." She came around the counter to greet me and grabbed both my hands. "I went to see you yesterday evening but you weren't home."

"No, I was up in Massachusetts, working

on your family background."

"And did you find —" She looked up expectantly then shook her head. "No matter about that now. It's not important. Not when my friends are dying. First Fanny and now Dorcas. There has to be something to it, Molly."

"Unless it's a very powerful disease."

"But Dorcas was getting better. You saw for yourself. She didn't seem to be at death's door."

"No," I agreed, "she seemed like anyone else with influenza — under the weather, but not dying. But I don't see why Anson Poindexter or anyone else would want to kill her."

"She went to see Fanny the week before, that's why." Emily had been keeping her voice down. Now she raised it without thinking, looked around at the men still occupied in the back room, and lowered it again. "Fanny may have been suspicious. She may have told Dorcas something damning."

"Well, even if she had, that wouldn't explain Honoria, would it?"

"Honoria? What has she to do with this?"

"Honoria Masters — is that the woman you were speaking about the other day?

Comes from a good family and now sings opera?"

"Yes, that's her." Emily smiled. "She was one of our Vassar classmates, you know. She had a lovely voice, even in those days. Then she went to study in Italy and the rest, as they say, is history."

"She's dead. I read it in the paper today. 'Brief, unexplained illness,' it said."

Emily put her hand to her throat as she gasped. "And she went to visit Dorcas last week. I suppose she could have caught whatever microbe it was that killed Fanny and Dorcas, but . . ."

"She had no connection to Fanny Poindexter, did she?"

She shook her head at this, puzzled. "Only that we used to be students together. I don't think she was part of Fanny's current circle. They are mostly young married women like Fanny herself. Honoria was too busy with her career."

"Well, then. We have to put the deaths down to a nasty sickness and nothing more."

She nodded. "I suppose so. But I can't rest until I'm absolutely sure. Maybe I'm being an hysterical female. Maybe I cared about Fanny too much, but . . ." She paused and looked at me strangely. She had obviously read from my face what I was thinking.

Because I had just remembered something I had not taken into account until now. Somebody had deliberately tried to run me down the other day — somebody in a big black carriage. There could be no other explanation for this except that someone didn't wish me to arrive at the truth.

"I don't think you are the hysterical type, Emily," I said. "What time do you get off work? Maybe we could visit Dorcas's family to offer our condolences this evening."

At this she blushed bright red. "I'm afraid. You see, Ned and I — well, he asked me to go with him to a show and . . ."

I smiled. "Of course you must go on your outing with your young man. We can visit Dorcas's family in the morning. It would probably be more seemly, in any case."

We arranged to meet in the morning. I took the El train home and was just walking up Patchin Place when I heard my name called and turned to see Daniel behind me. "Ah, there you are," he said, quickening his pace to catch up with me. "I was just coming to call on you. I'm glad to find you home for once. I had a free evening yesterday and I came over, all prepared to take

266

you out for the evening, and you weren't there."

"No," I said. "I was in Massachusetts."

"Massachusetts? My, you do get around these days. Quite the globe-trotter." He sounded a trifle annoyed.

"Just checking some details for a case I'm working on."

I opened the front door and he followed me inside. The setting sun was shining in through the front windows, giving the whole place a pleasant rosy glow.

"And how is this case progressing?" he asked.

"Well, thank you. I think I've pretty much got it solved."

"Good for you. You're turning into quite the detective, aren't you?"

I looked up at him to see if he was being sarcastic. He read my look and laughed. "No, I mean it. You'll be an asset to me in my profession, I can see that."

"Not if you won't share your cases with me."

"Ah, well, when we're married it will be different." He came over to me and slipped his arms around my waist, drawing me close to him. "In many ways," he added. "I can't wait until we can be together, Molly."

"You haven't asked me yet," I said. "I may

be so successful that I'll turn you down."

"Don't tease me like that," he murmured, his lips nuzzling into my hair. "You know I'm waiting until I can do it properly."

I pushed him away. "Then we should wait until you can do it properly," I said, giving him a meaningful glance.

He laughed at my double meaning. I put my hand up to his cheek. Why did his closeness still have this effect on me? I could feel the roughness of his skin and the warmth of his breath on my face and hand.

"So what brings you here?" I asked, attempting lightness as I moved away and sat at the kitchen table. "Don't tell me you've two free evenings in a row?"

"As a matter of fact, I have," he said. He pulled out a chair and sat opposite me.

"You've solved all of those complicated cases?"

"Not solved. Put new men on them. We weren't getting anywhere. And with the Chinese tong murders I suspect we'll never get anywhere. They'll not betray their own. Frankly I don't really care if they go around killing each other, but I'd surely like to know who is their opium kingpin. Someone's bringing it into the country in large quantities and not for medicinal purposes but to keep the opium parlors supplied."

"Speaking of opium," I said. "You remember the suspicious death I spoke to you about?"

"Which didn't turn out to be suspicious at all," he said. "I interviewed her doctor, remember?"

"Yes, I know. But something strange has happened. Two of her friends, both society ladies, have died under similar strange circumstances."

"I told you, this flu has been a killer, Molly. That's why I was so worried when you insisted on running around just when you were recovering."

"But there's a chance it wasn't influenza, Daniel. The symptoms weren't typical. I went to visit the second woman and she was suffering from considerable gastric distress as well as a high fever."

"So what are you saying — that they were poisoned somehow?"

"It is a possibility."

"For what reason?"

"I told you the first woman was planning to divorce her husband because he had a mistress. That was a good enough motive. If they divorced, he'd lose her fortune."

"And the second and third women? Were they also planning to divorce their husbands?"

"You're not taking me seriously, Daniel," I said angrily.

He patted my hand, which I found annoying. "I'm thinking that maybe you're letting your success as a detective go to your head and seeing crimes where there are none. The thing to ask yourself in any murder case, Molly, is 'who benefits?' "

"In the case of the first victim, obviously the husband, in many ways. He keeps her fortune and is free to marry his mistress if he wants to." As I said this I found my thoughts wandering to that graveyard scene. Would Anson Poindexter really want to marry Mademoiselle Fifi? Hardly likely given their difference in class, and given that look I had seen pass between him and Bella.

"But the other two?" Daniel insisted.

"It's possible that the first woman told her friends what she planned to do, or that she suspected her husband was trying to kill her."

He shook his head. "Not a strong enough motive. First, how would he know what she'd told her friends?"

"He overheard her?"

"Unlikely that she would have revealed such a suspicion with him in the house. And second, why would he need to kill them? The first death was so well carried out that the doctor was convinced she died from natural causes."

I sighed. "You're right, of course. We managed to obtain some of her hair and there was no trace of arsenic in it, so that rules out the most obvious poison."

He looked at me, surprised. "You obtained her hair? How did you do that? Yank it out of her head when she was dead? Or did you ask her for it when she was still alive?"

"We didn't have to do either. Her hair came out with the high fever. It was all over the pillow."

"Interesting," he said. "And who tested this hair?"

"My friend Emily's young man. He's an apprentice to a druggist."

"An apprentice druggist? I wonder if he has the facility and knowledge to run a test like that."

"He's very smart," I said.

"Yes, but . . ."

"If you're volunteering to retest it for me, I'm sure I can get more hair from Emily. She was planning to weave it into a mourning ring. And there's something else you could do," I added as I remembered. "It just happens that I have a sample of a preparation that was never tested," I said. "It was a bottle of stomach mixture. I poured some onto a ball of cotton wool."

"Quite the daring opportunist, aren't you," Daniel said. "But I wasn't actually volunteering to do either. Until you can come up with a good motive for someone needing all three women out of the way, then I'll have to believe that they died of natural causes."

"You'll not even volunteer to test a strand of hair for me then?"

He stood up again and came around the table to me, putting both hands on my shoulders. "Molly, why don't you give up on this? You are grasping at straws, or rather you're being influenced by someone else's vivid imagination. Is she paying you to look into this? If not, then you're wasting valuable time and can achieve nothing by it. In my job we find it hard enough to prove a case of poisoning unless it was so obvious that the victim was practically frothing at the mouth. I'm sure skilled poisoners get away with murder every day in New York City. We may be dealing with one ourselves, because we still haven't found any link between quite a few deaths from arsenic poisoning."

"You've tested everything they ate or drank?"

"Of course. And looked into any motive

the family members might have had for wanting to get rid of them. But nothing. In most cases the victims were poor and had nothing to leave."

I looked up at him suddenly. "What color was their wallpaper?"

He laughed. "Their wallpaper?"

"That's right. This young druggist was saying that some wallpaper contains arsenic, especially the green one with roses that is so popular."

Daniel was still smiling. "Yes, but even if it contained arsenic, it wouldn't be enough to kill somebody unless they actually licked it. And if it gave off fumes, it would have made the rest of the family sick."

"Just a thought," I said. "I know nothing about it personally."

"Which is why you should stop sticking your nose into this business of the three women. If there were a real poisoner, then your bumbling attempts would warn him to be on his guard. It might even drive him to kill again. So be careful. You've had enough narrow scrapes — including almost stepping under the wheels of my automobile."

"That's it!" I shouted, making him jump. "That's what I wanted to tell you. That's the reason I'm inclined to believe Emily."

"What is?"

"Someone tried to run me down the other day. A big black carriage came right at me as I was crossing the street."

"I'd put that down to a bad driver," Daniel said, "and to your not looking where you were walking."

"No, it was deliberate, I'm sure. He came right at me and didn't attempt to slow or swerve."

"So you think someone, in a city as big as New York, was waiting and lurking on a street, just on the off chance you'd pass by and he could run you down?"

"It wasn't just anywhere in New York City," I said. "It was around the corner from Patchin Place, just by the Jefferson Market building."

"All the same," he said, "I'm still inclined to believe that some coachman was not looking where he was going, or had been told to hurry by his master and was driving rather too fast."

"But he came right at me, Daniel. He didn't attempt to rein in the horses or to swerve away. In fact I think he almost steered toward me."

He was looking at me with a look I couldn't quite fathom — was it humor or concern, or maybe a bit of both?

"You don't believe me, but it's true," I said.

He sighed. "If it's true, all the more reason to back down, Molly. If you really think that someone would be desperate enough to try to kill you in this way, then that person must suspect that you are coming too close to the truth. As I've said before, criminal cases should be left to the police."

"Aren't you the police?" I demanded. "But I've presented you with the facts and you're doing nothing." I shook his hands from my shoulders and spun around to face him. "You could at least volunteer to test that hair for me."

He sighed. "I suppose I could have that done, if it would finally satisfy you."

"Thank you." I gave him a peck on the cheek. "I'll ask Emily when I see her tomorrow and I'll try to get a strand or two from the second dead woman."

He shook his head, smiling. "Molly, you're like a terrier. You hang on and shake and won't let go."

"Not until I've reached the truth." I stood up to face him. "So where are you going to take me this evening?"

"I thought the theater," he said.

"Any particular one?"

"What would you like to see?"

"I'd rather like to see the revue starring Mademoiselle Fifi," I said.

He raised an eyebrow. "Rather risqué for a respectable young woman, don't you think?"

"But I hear she is a wonderful dancer," I said, eyeing him steadily.

He came over to me and put his hands on my shoulders again. "Molly, you are up to something. You have an ulterior motive for going to this show."

"Really? Don't be silly. And don't tell me you'd not enjoy watching the dancing of Mademoiselle Fifi."

"Of course I wouldn't mind watching her," he said, looking decidedly uncomfortable, "but . . ."

"Well then, what are we waiting for?"

TWENTY-TWO

Mademoiselle Fifi's revue was indeed quite entertaining, and quite risqué. I felt decidedly uncomfortable sitting beside Daniel as she danced wearing not much more than a corset and black suspenders. Daniel was also embarrassed about having me beside him, I could tell — although I'm sure he wouldn't have complained had he been there alone.

As it was, his eyes were riveted to the stage, which gave me the chance to look around the audience and see if Anson Poindexter was there. He wasn't, of course. It would have been unthinkable for a newly bereaved husband to go to the theater. In fact I had no idea really why I had insisted on going to this theater. Just wanting to see Fifi in the flesh, I suppose. And I certainly saw large quantities of that. But I saw nothing else that aroused any suspicions and I wasn't sure what to do next, if Emily and I were going to pursue the matter. Visit Dorcas's home, of course, and find out who had been to see her or sent her gifts of food in her last days. Also try to visit Honoria Masters's home and see if there was anything that linked the three women in any way.

Now that I had time to consider, it did seem a little improbable that a respectable man like Anson Poindexter would go around killing women willy-nilly, just on the off chance that his dead wife had told them something suspicious. After all, the doctor had signed a death certificate with no qualms. Fanny was buried in the family tomb. He had essentially gotten away with murder, if that was what it was. So why risk two further attempts?

I made up my mind that I would go with Emily to Dorcas's and then I would close my files on the case. After all, I wasn't being paid, and I had another case on my hands that I had almost concluded. All that was needed now was a visit to Horace Lynch, and I planned to fit that in tomorrow afternoon. Then I would be able to tell Emily the truth about her parents.

On Sunday morning I met Emily as arranged and we walked together to Dorcas's house. To tell the truth, I felt most uneasy about intruding in this way on a family I hardly knew. The Hochstetter mansion was clearly in a state of mourning. Black drapes swathed the windows. We stood in a darkened front hall and after a while Mrs. Hochstetter Senior came down the stairs to us. She was dressed all in black.

"Miss Boswell?" She held out a hand. "I believe we have met before. You were our daughter-in-law's friend from Vassar, is that not correct?"

"I was indeed," Emily said. "And this is my dear friend Miss Murphy, who also knew Dorcas. We came as soon as we heard the terrible news, to offer our condolences."

"You are most kind." She put a black lace handkerchief up to her lips. "She was a lovely young woman and we are desolate to have lost her. My son is beside himself with grief and of course young Thomas will now be without a doting mama."

"What exactly did she die of?" I asked. "When we came to visit her last week, we heard that she had influenza. She seemed sick and weak but she told us she was on the road to recovery."

"Influenza, that's what the doctor said it was." Mrs. Hochstetter fought to retain her composure. "Simple, stupid influenza. We did everything. The doctor was here, I nursed her myself, and she just slipped away from us."

"So tragic," I muttered, feeling like a hypocrite. "I wondered whether anything she had eaten might have made her condition worse."

"Eaten?" she demanded sharply. "The poor woman couldn't keep any food down. She took nothing except for barley water and a few sips of broth."

I couldn't think of a way to ask if the servants were trustworthy and the cook had prepared these items herself. "I expect her friends came to visit as we did and brought her all kinds of lovely foods she couldn't eat," I said. Even as I said it I had to agree that it sounded strange.

"I gave strict orders that she was to be allowed no visitors as soon as I saw how weak she had become," she said firmly.

"Of course." I nodded.

"Mrs. Hochstetter, might it be possible to say our final farewell to Dorcas?" I asked. "Her body has not been taken away yet, has it?"

"She still lies in her marriage bed," Mrs. Hochstettter said. "I have not allowed anybody in there, on account of the virulence of the sickness. Anything that can kill a healthy woman in a few days should be given a wide berth and certainly not allowed to spread."

"Of course not," I said. "But as it happens I have recently recovered from the same influenza and I understand that one cannot catch it twice. And Emily works in a drugstore and deals with sick people every day."

Mrs. Hochstetter was still regarding us with a quizzical stare. "If you insist, then I suppose you know what you are doing."

"She was my Vassar sister," Emily said.

"Very well." Mrs. Hochstetter smoothed down her black skirt before ringing a little bell on the side table. "Soames. These young women wish to say their farewells to Mrs. Hochstetter Junior," she said. "Please escort them to her room."

"Very well, madam." The butler indicated we should follow him. Up the stairs we went, along a hallway that was bathed in gloom and made the statues in niches look like disembodied heads glaring down at us. He opened the door to Dorcas's bedroom with obvious reluctance.

"Mrs. Hochstetter Junior is at repose in here."

We stepped into a room that was as dark as the hallway had been. The odor of death came to greet us and we both recoiled a little, Emily giving me an alarmed glance.

"Are you young ladies sure you wish to go inside?" he asked.

"Vassar would expect it of me," Emily said. "May we turn on an electric light?"

"Certainly not. This house is in mourning," Soames said.

"I really would like to take one last look at my friend," Emily said. I was impressed she could be so persistent. Soames was quite an intimidating figure. "May I then open the drapes just a little?"

I thought he was going to say no to that too, but he sighed. "I will open them a crack for you, if you really insist, but it is highly improper."

He held open the curtains just an inch or two, sending a thin stripe of bright sunlight across the darkness.

"Thank you." Emily went to stand by Dorcas's bed. The body was covered in a white sheet. Emily pulled back the sheets and let out an audible gasp. "Poor Dorcas," she whispered. "Poor, dear Dorcas. She was the brightest of us all."

She bent down and kissed the dead cheek before pulling up the sheet again.

While she had been occupied at the bed, I had tried to observe everything in the room. Given the almost complete darkness and the clutter of stuffed birds, artificial flowers, and every other kind of knickknack, it was hard to see anything. I didn't know what I should be looking for anyway. There was hardly likely to be a bottle of poison sitting on the bedside table. But as my eye moved over Dorcas's dressing table I felt I was looking at something I had seen somewhere else before. I looked again and couldn't for the life of me decide what that was.

"I think you should depart now," Soames said, letting the drapes fall into place again and plunging us into complete darkness.

We did as he requested and walked in silence down the stairs. We encountered nobody in the front hall and stood blinking in the blinding light of the street.

"Well?" Emily said. "What do you think?"

"I don't see how she could have been poisoned," I said. "Her mother-in-law guarded her fiercely. You heard her yourself. She was allowed no visitors during the last days and she took no food apart from barley water and broth."

"Well, I have some strands of her hair, just in case," Emily said.

"Emily!"

"It was easy enough. It came out in my hand. I didn't even have to yank it hard."

"We'll see if Ned turns up anything."

"Emily, what is he likely to turn up?" I

found myself getting a trifle annoyed. "It was quite obvious that Anson Poindexter had not been near the place. Bella came and brought grapes but they were not touched."

"Bella? What has she to do with it?" Emily asked sharply.

I realized that I had not told her what I had observed at the funeral — that intimate look that had passed between Bella and Anson when they thought that no one was looking. I decided to stay mum.

"Nothing at all," I said. No good could come of yet another complication, but I resolved to pay Bella a visit, just in case. If she had wanted to assist Anson in getting rid of a rich wife he didn't love, as well as a friend who had been told too much, then it would have been easy enough to tamper with something in the room — the glass of barley water, for example.

"I tell you what, if you'd like to give me that hair sample, my friend Captain Sullivan can have it tested in the real police laboratory — just to make sure."

"Oh, but Ned can test it for us," she said. "He's able to do this kind of thing, in fact he loves a challenge like this. He told me so."

"Then how about we divide the sample," I said. "You give half to Ned and I'll give half to Captain Sullivan and we'll compare results. That is what any good scientists would do and I'm sure Ned would not object."

"Of course not," she said. "I'll tell him about it today."

"I thought he went to visit his mother on Sundays."

"He does." She blushed bright red. "But today he wants to take me with him. Isn't that wonderful? I'm now the girl that a young man brings home to meet his mother."

"That is wonderful," I said. "I'm happy for you."

"So am I," she said. "Things finally seem to be going right for me. And now I remember that you were going to tell me what you discovered in Massachusetts." She slipped her arm through mine. "I am all agog. You really found out the truth? Were they really missionaries? Am I really an heiress?"

"I can't tell you anything until I have made one more visit," I said. "I have to verify the facts first. But with any luck you should know the truth this week. Of course, I might be barking up the wrong tree, but I don't think so."

Her face was alight with hope and I felt guilty. If my news were true, then I'd hardly be making her happy, would I? Still, it's always better to know the truth. I've found out that much in life.

TWENTY-THREE

After Emily and I parted, I walked up and down the quiet, elegant street several times before I finally plucked up the courage to knock on the door of Mr. Horace Lynch. His butler reported that Mr. Lynch was indeed at home but was due to leave for a luncheon engagement in a few minutes.

"This will not take long," I said. "It is a matter of great importance."

I was shown into a morning room, where Mr. Lynch was just pouring himself a glass of whiskey from a decanter. He scowled as if trying to place me.

"Yes, what is it? Asking for a donation for the poor and destitute, are you? Then you go right back and tell them to get a job and earn an honest living for themselves, you hear me."

I realized then that I was dressed all in black and that my hair was hidden under my black hat with its half veil. He hadn't recognized or remembered me.

"Mr. Lynch. You may not remember me but I visited you a week ago, asking for details of your ward Emily's parents."

His scowl deepened as he recognized me. "You again? I thought I made it quite clear to you that I could be of no use to you at all regarding those missionaries."

"Ah, but I'm sure you can be of use to me, Mr. Lynch," I said. "May I take a seat? I won't keep you long."

I perched on the nearest chair without being asked. I saw his face flushing an angry red. "Are you dim-witted or something? I told you quite clearly that I had no knowledge of these people. They belonged to my wife's family, not mine."

"I think you do have knowledge, Mr. Lynch. You're just not willing to share it. I went up to Williamstown, you see."

The color now drained from his face. "What exactly is it that you want?" he demanded. "Blackmail? Is that it? Because if so you're going to be sorry you came here."

"Blackmail? Good heavens, no. I just want the truth, Mr. Lynch, and I want to hear it from your lips."

"I've told you the truth — as much of it as I know."

"I don't think so," I said. "I spoke with various people in Williamstown and I think I've discovered the truth. Shall I share my thoughts with you and you can correct me if I'm wrong?"

He was still scowling horribly. His face now looked even more like that of a bulldog. "Go on, damn you."

"Such language, Mr. Lynch," I said. "Very well. When I was in Williamstown I learned of a lovely, vivacious young girl called Lydia Johnson. I learned that she loved to dance and have fun but she was raised by strict Scottish Calvinists who did not allow her normal girlish pleasures. I learned that she was a very bright girl who loved to read and wanted to go to college — Vassar, to be exact. Are you with me so far?"

"Go on," he growled.

"Her parents might have agreed to a college education but then a terrible tragedy struck. Her parents were both killed when their buggy went off the road. She was left with no one in the world, her only relatives being back in Scotland." I glanced up at him again. He was sitting as still as a statue, his whiskey glass in one hand.

"That was when you came on the scene, wasn't it, Mr. Lynch? You were an ambitious man and you summed up the situation correctly and seized the moment. You sensed that she needed to replace that domineering father figure, and you grabbed your chance to get your hands on her fortune and the mill. So you courted her and she agreed to marry you while she was still vulnerable and grieving for her parents. She didn't love you but she needed someone to take care of her. Am I correct so far?"

"Get on with it," he snapped.

"But Lydia was a romantic. She longed for balls and parties and you were as strict as her father had been. You had her money but you were a bit of a skinflint, weren't you? And you were not the romantic husband she had dreamed of. She was ripe to fall in love when you hired a handsome Italian gardener — Antonio, was that his name? She fell madly in love with him. They had a passionate affair and she found herself in a difficult and embarrassing position. She was going to have a child. Am I right in my hunch so far, Mr. Lynch?"

I waited for him to react to this but he sat there as if carved from stone.

"Now, I don't know if she was just honest by nature or she knew that the darker-skinned baby would never pass as yours or" — I looked at his face and made a stab at the truth — "that you couldn't father a child

290

of your own?"

He flushed beet-red again.

"Anyway, she told you the truth. You were enraged, but you couldn't throw her out and risk the scandal, or risk losing her money. She might have run off with Antonio but he died tragically and fortuitously by falling off a bridge. So now she was at your mercy, wasn't she? You acted the forgiving and magnanimous husband. You would keep her, but you weren't going to keep the child. She pleaded and at last you cooked up a scheme. You sent her away to the West Coast and when she returned she brought the child of relatives who had conveniently died in China. Is this how it went so far, Mr. Lynch?"

Again he sat staring past me.

"But you never forgave her, did you? You made it clear that you'd hold it over her for the rest of her days and make her life a misery. The birth, plus her grief over the loss of her love, had weakened her. She never regained her strength and she died of a broken heart. And you never forgave Emily either just for being born. You showed her not one ounce of love or affection and turned her out at the first possible moment."

"And how did you come up with this

preposterous idea?" he sputtered.

"I suppose the germ of the idea was planted when I heard about Lydia's character — so bright and fun-loving but married to you, described as a dour old skinflint by one person I spoke to. And the mention of the handsome Italian gardener who was sweet on her, and his convenient death, and the rumor that she had been sent out west because she had contracted consumption. A healthy, vibrant young lady, living in comparative isolation — how would she have contracted this foul disease? But what gave it away was the name she chose. Boswell. Her name was Johnson, you see."

"And?"

"Boswell's *Life of Johnson* is a very famous book. She was quite a scholar, according to her old headmistress."

There was a long pause, during which I was conscious of the slow tock-tock of the grandfather clock in the corner.

"May I ask your purpose in this?" he said at last. "It goes rather beyond writing a book on Chinese missionaries, I take it?"

"It does indeed. I did this on behalf of my friend Emily. I am a detective, Mr. Lynch. I felt she deserved to know the truth. She also deserves some of her mother's money, and yours, as a child born in wedlock, to a married woman."

He looked at me and smirked. "You'd never be able to prove any of this rubbish."

"But I think I would, Mr. Lynch. I believe I could easily produce the doctor in Williamstown who confirmed her pregnancy, or the friend to whom she confided the truth. No woman keeps her pregnancy completely secret, you know. And if necessary I could retrace her steps out west and find the place where she gave birth to the child and where, presumably, a birth certificate has been filed. I might also find a witness who saw you follow Antonio home from the bar that night and push him off the bridge."

I looked up and our eyes met. "And the buggy," I went on as this thought crystallized in my head. "You might also have tampered with the buggy that killed her parents . . ."

He rose to his feet then and came toward me. He was a big man, powerful for all his flabbiness. "In which case you are a very foolish young woman to come here and find yourself alone with a murderer, aren't you?"

Of course, I hadn't considered this. I had been saying these things as they popped into my head — putting together the pieces of the jigsaw puzzle as I spoke. One of my major failings. "Not at all," I said, in what I hoped was a jaunty manner. "I have just now left Emily Boswell, or should one say Emily Lynch, with instructions to call for me in half an hour. If I fail to appear, she will most certainly go for the police."

I waited to see if he would call my bluff. He turned and walked over to the window, pulling back the drape and staring out. I wondered if he was checking to see if Emily was standing there, but after a long silence he said, "I am no murderer, Miss Murphy. I was raised on the Bible and I am a God-fearing man. I have never, to my knowledge, broken any of the commandments. Those two accidents were accidents and nothing more. Fortuitous for me, I have to admit. Oh, and I did jump in and take my chances with Lydia, but not entirely for the reason you stated. I loved her, Miss Murphy. She was the most beautiful creature I had ever seen. When she agreed to marry me, it was the happiest day of my life. But I soon discovered that I couldn't — uh — satisfy her, that she didn't love me. And then the nightmare with the child. Everyone would have looked at it and known it wasn't mine. Hate and despair consumed me, Miss Murphy — have consumed me for years."

"But you have your salvation waiting for

you, salvation you have refused so far."

"What are you talking about now?"

"Emily, Mr. Lynch. The daughter you refused to acknowledge."

"She is not my daughter." He spat out the words.

"You say you loved Lydia. You could still see part of Lydia alive and flourishing in Emily. Wouldn't that be better than nothing?"

He was silent.

"You hated Emily for something that wasn't her fault. Is that what a good Christian does?"

He turned away again. "If you think I'm welcoming her with open arms and handing over my money to her, you are mistaken."

"I'm not saying you should do either, Mr. Lynch, although I think we could make a good case in court for a share of Lydia's money. But Emily has suffered from loneliness all her life and so have you. I thought maybe you might find that you could be solace for each other. You could at least give it a try."

He crossed the room and stared at himself in the mirror above the fireplace. "I'm an old man, Miss Murphy. Set in my ways. What you're asking goes too much against the grain."

"Then at least start by making her a small allowance so that she doesn't have to live in one room in a seedy boarding house."

"Is that what she does?"

"She has a job but the pay isn't wonderful and it's hard for a woman alone to find somewhere respectable and safe to live."

"And a young man?" he asked. "Does she have a young man?"

"She does, but he is also struggling to make his way in the world. He is apprenticed to a druggist and learning that profession. I understand he's very smart and ambitious. Rather like yourself at the same age, I suspect."

"I see," he said. "You'll now tell her everything you told me, I suppose?"

"Unless you'd like to tell her yourself."

"I don't think I could bring myself to do that."

"Then I'll tell her."

"She'll hate me, won't she?"

"I don't think she's brimming over with love for you at the moment," I said, and he laughed.

"You're a rum one, Miss Murphy. And you've got guts, I'll say that for you."

"So may I tell her to call on you if she wants to?"

"I suppose so," he said at length.

Twenty-Four

One case closed most satisfactorily, I said to myself as I left Horace Lynch. I like it when the threads all tie up neatly. And if all went well, Emily and Horace might find some companionship. I wanted to go straight to Emily and tell her the truth, but of course she'd be spending the rest of the day with Ned and his mother. How wonderful it would be for them if Horace Lynch did decide to give her some of her mother's money. Ned would have the funds to start his own company and Emily could work at his side. The perfect match, in fact, rather like Daniel and me.

I had two strands of Dorcas's hair wrapped in my handkerchief, so I went straight to Daniel's apartment, hoping he might be there. But he wasn't.

"Called into work early, he was," Mrs. O'Shea said. "They never give that poor man a moment's peace. I tell you, Miss

Murphy, if you marry that one you won't be in for a quiet life."

"I'd find a quiet life rather boring, I suspect," I said with a smile. "And how are your children, still sick?"

"If it's not one thing, it's another," she said. "They went through chicken pox and now the doctor says it's ringworm. Still, he's given us the medicine to treat it and let's hope that will be the end of it."

I went up to his rooms and left the hairs in an envelope on his desk with a note about where they came from. Then I had the whole of an afternoon ahead of me. And a beautiful afternoon it was too — bright, warm, just the right kind of day for a stroll in the park, or even a row on the lake. Of course these activities would be no fun alone. I walked along Twenty-third until I came to Madison Square. The little park was looking lovely and I sat on a bench for a while, enjoying the sun on my face and watching children play.

I should put my work to one side today and just enjoy myself, I thought. I've concluded one case and the other — well, perhaps the other was never a crime in the first place. But I found I couldn't let it go. Too many coincidences, for one thing. Fanny falling sick right after she asked me to snoop on her wandering husband and announced plans to divorce him. Dorcas falling sick after a visit to Fanny. Honoria falling sick after a visit to Dorcas. All three could have been the flu, of course, and I would have been prepared to believe that if someone hadn't tried to run me down with that carriage, and snooped inside my house.

We could wait and see if Daniel and Ned turned up any arsenic in Dorcas's hair, or in the bottle of stomach mixture. But I'm not the kind of person who is good at waiting. What else should I be doing, I wondered. Would I learn anything from paying a visit to Mademoiselle Fifi, or to Bella? Probably not, and Daniel would say that I'd only tip off a murderer with my blunderings, but I've never been one to take wise advice. I decided that Sunday afternoon would be a perfect time to visit Mademoiselle Fifi. Theaters were dark and she'd most likely be resting.

So I walked to East Twenty-first and knocked on her door. I hadn't planned in advance what I was going to say, and this was a mistake, because when the maid opened the door I just stood there.

I decided to play it straight. "Is your mistress at home?"

She took in my funereal appearance. "If

you are from the church, you waste your time," she said in her French accent. "She will not see you."

"I'm not from the church. I have some questions about a friend of Mademoiselle's."

"Mademoiselle has many friends," the maid said.

I bet she has, I thought. "This particular friend is called Mr. Poindexter." She pretended to look blank. "And don't try to deny that she knows him. I am a detective and I have been watching the house. I saw him here."

She shrugged in that wonderfully Gallic way. "I see if Mademoiselle is awake and wishes to speak to you." And she admitted me to the house.

It was very warm inside and rather untidy, with a hat thrown on a chair in the front hall, a feather boa draped from the hat stand and a pair of high boots lying on the linoleum. Clearly the maid was not known for her housekeeping prowess. I was told to wait, overheard a rapid exchange in French, and then was admitted to what can only be described as a boudoir. Mademoiselle Fifi herself lay on a daybed, looking as if she were about to audition for La Dame aux Camélias.

"I'm sorry to disturb your rest," I said,

"but I would like to ask you a couple of questions regarding your relationship with Mr. Poindexter."

At this she leaped up, her peignoir flying open to reveal too much flesh for my taste. "That monster! Do not speak his name to me! Never again. Never."

This was a surprising turn. I took a minute to recover.

"I take it that you and Mr. Poindexter are no longer, shall we say, friendly? And that you didn't part on good terms?"

"Two years I am with him," she said, her Gallic eyes still flashing. "Two years of my life. I know he is married, but he say his wife is cold and does not love him and he is only happy when he is with me. But then last week he comes to me and says it is all over. Finished. He never want to see me again."

"Did he say why?"

She shook her head. "I think another woman, of course. Or that his wife found out about us and makes a big fuss."

"His wife is dead," I said. "She died right after he came to see you."

"Mon dieu." Her eyes opened wide with surprise, then narrowed again. "Then it is another woman. Someone suitable for him to marry, not someone like me whom he

301

could not take into polite society."

"It's possible," I said.

"Tell me who it is. I will kill her," she said with great drama. Honestly, I'd had quite enough of actresses in the past months.

"I have no idea who it might be," I said. "Have you not thought that Mr. Poindexter might be grieving for his wife and overcome with guilt?"

She shrugged again. "Possible," she said. "These Protestants always have guilt. They have no confession, you see. They have to carry it around with them."

I thought that was quite a shrewd remark. Mademoiselle Fifi was no fool.

"You are a detective?" she asked me.

I nodded.

"If you find out who the other woman is, I pay you," she said. "I pay you well."

"All right," I said, but in truth I had no intention of telling her.

I left her and walked home down Fifth Avenue, digesting what I had just learned. So Anson Poindexter broke up with her just before Fanny died. I could see Fifi being the sort of person who could poison Fanny in revenge for being abandoned, but the question was how. Someone like Fifi would never be admitted to an apartment in the

Dakota and would most certainly have been noticed.

This made me wonder whether the whole thing was cleverly orchestrated. She was, after all, an actress, and as I had found out from past experience, actresses can be horribly duplicitous. Perhaps the breakup was all part of the plan so that no suspicion would fall on her, should there be an inquiry. When the dust settled, Anson would quietly go back to her.

The other scenario would be that he had decided that a better future lay with Bella. Maybe he and she had arranged the poisoning together — he conveniently out of town, she visiting as the loyal friend and slipping some kind of poison into the water glass or whatever when nobody was looking. Again I realized that this was all a complete waste of my time. Fanny was buried and was not likely to be exhumed without the clearest of proof. The doctor had signed the death certificate. Everyone was satisfied. The police weren't about to investigate. It looked as if Anson, and possibly Bella, had pulled off the perfect crime.

So what next? Did I let it lie, put it behind me, and look for my next case? I could visit Bella, of course, but to what end? I knew she had gone to see Fanny and Dorcas. I could hardly get her to confess that she had slipped poison into either of their drinks. I probably couldn't even get her to confess that she was more than friendly with Anson.

I could also look into the death of Honoria Masters, although this would be harder, as I had never met her and had no idea where she lived. And the opera house would be dark tonight. I'd have to wait until tomorrow and see if I could entice the stage-door keeper into divulging Honoria's address.

Suddenly I felt overwhelmed and tired. I thought of Sid and Gus and their lifestyle: their exotic meals, their poetry readings and art galleries, their circle of interesting if unorthodox friends. It seemed so desirable compared to my life. For once, being Mrs. Daniel Sullivan and having time to hold tea parties and soirees also seemed desirable.

I turned into Patchin Place, my thoughts on a cup of tea, my armchair, and a good book. Maybe even a little nap. But I was just turning the key in my front door when a voice yelled, "There she is. She's home. See, I told you she'd turn up." And there was my playwright friend Ryan O'Hare bursting out of Sid and Gus's house. He was surprisingly not wearing his usual romantic poet garb, but was dressed in what seemed to be yachting attire.

"You arrived home at the perfect moment," he said. "Sid and Gus told me they hadn't seen you in days and they suspected you might have gone away, but here you are, so all is well."

"Are you about to embark on a cruise?" I asked him.

"No, my dear, I am whisking you all away for an evening of fun and debauchery aboard my friend's yacht. We're sailing up the Hudson and taking a picnic. So hurry up and change out of that awful black thing. You look like Queen Victoria mourning for Albert."

I had to laugh. "I've been paying respects at the house of a recent death."

"My dear, if I ever die, I positively forbid you to come to my funeral looking like that. I should turn in my grave, I know I should. Or in my coffin before I'm put into my grave."

Sid and Gus had now joined him, carrying a large picnic basket between them. Sid was wearing bloomers, Gus a navy outfit with nautical theme.

"You'll notice that it is Ryan who arranges a picnic and we who have to prepare the darned thing," Sid said dryly.

"Ah, but it is I who am supplying the yacht." Ryan beamed at us.

I looked at Gus and Sid.

"His new friend," Sid mouthed. "Pots of money."

"And he's divine," Ryan added. "You'll see. You'll fall madly in love with him."

"Not that that would do us any good," Gus remarked.

I laughed and ran inside to change. I felt positively energized. How long since I had laughed or had fun or gone on a picnic? My tiredness was completely forgotten. Soon we were casting off from one of the Hudson piers and sailing languidly up the Hudson on a boat that was sleek, teak, and half the size of the *Majestic.* I sat on the deck, sipping Champagne, nibbling smoked salmon sandwiches and watching the Palisades slip past me. The last time I had seen them was at Fanny's funeral. How strange life was, I thought. Someone like Fanny should have had a whole life of fun and ease and luxury to look forward to, just like the other people on this yacht, who were now dancing madly to a syncopated ragtime tune. Such a waste.

I sighed. I hated to walk away from this case without ever knowing the truth. Was it a tragic death or a clever murder? And was the death of three friends within a week no more than an unhappy coincidence? The only person who could tell me the truth was Anson Poindexter. If I had been Daniel, I could have had him brought in and grilled him. It did briefly cross my mind that I could go and interview him on some harmless pretext and see if I could trap him into some kind of confession. Then I told myself not to be so stupid. If he was a clever murderer and had killed more than once, then I'd be signing my own death warrant. Maybe I already had . . . I shivered as I thought of that black carriage coming straight at me. Would he try again if I didn't abandon this case?

I saw now why Daniel had said that criminal cases should be left to the police. They could ask questions of whomever they pleased. They could barge in, bully, intimidate, snoop around until they came to the truth. I could do none of the above. In fact if the hair samples revealed nothing, then I didn't see what else I could do.

I wondered if Fanny had told anyone else what she had told me — that she was planning to divorce her husband if her suspicions of infidelity proved to be true. Did she ever suspect she was being poisoned when she fell ill? Her mother had apparently nursed her day and night during that last week. Might Fanny have confided anything to her? If I went to speak with Fanny's mother would it do more harm than good? If I were Fanny's mother, would I want to know that my child might have been poisoned when it was now too late to save her? Yes, I would, I decided, if there was any chance of bringing her poisoner to justice. I resolved to go and see Fanny's mother in the morning, however unpleasant that encounter might prove to be.

"You're not allowed to look pensive," Ryan said, interrupting my thoughts. "In fact gloomy faces are simply not allowed on this boat. Gaiety and laughter, my dear. That's what we want to see." He held out his hand and jerked me to my feet. "Come and dance. Pierre is going to demonstrate his new phonograph."

I arrived home very late and a little tipsy to find a note from Daniel stuffed through my letter box. "Picked up hair sample. Will take it into lab tomorrow. Interesting developments to tell you about but you weren't home."

Then, of course, I felt guilty that he had been working all day when I had been having such a good time.

TWENTY-FIVE

On Monday morning I really wanted to find Daniel and learn what the new developments were that he had written about. Had the sample of stomach mixture revealed some kind of poison? He would be working, of course. I was tempted to go to police headquarters on Mulberry Street, but I didn't think he'd take kindly to this. Besides, he'd most likely be off somewhere on a case. I'd just have to wait patiently on that count.

In the meantime I had promised myself to speak with Mrs. Bradley. I was not looking forward to this, I can tell you. Again I questioned whether it was being foolish and wrong to tell a grieving mother that I suspected her daughter might have been poisoned. I decided to tread very carefully and have the sense to know when to shut up. It has never been one of my stronger traits. I realized as I set out that I didn't know exactly where the Bradleys lived. Mrs.

Bradley was hardly likely to be still camped out at her daughter's apartment, was she? But I went to the Dakota anyway and rang the doorbell at the Poindexters' apartment.

It was opened by none other than Anson, looking dashing in a maroon silk dressing gown.

"Hello," he said with a pleasant smile. "May I help you?"

Oh, now this was tempting. Daring Molly Murphy solves case by seducing murderer into giving her a confession. He looked harmless enough.

"I was wondering if your mother-in-law was still in residence here," I said.

"No, thank God," he replied. "At last I can breathe again." Then he pulled a boyish face. "Oh, dear. Not very tactful of me, was it. You're not a bosom friend of hers, are you?"

"Not at all," I said. "I was a friend of your dear departed wife's."

His face fell. "I see. Poor Fanny. Who would have thought it. She may have looked delicate but I always thought she was strong as an ox. It's quite shaken me up, I can tell you. I haven't felt like going to work ever since the funeral and I keep thinking I'm coming down with whatever that awful sickness was that took her away so quickly."

"It was very sad for all of us," I said. "You have my deepest sympathy."

He nodded. "Thank you. She was a lovely girl, wasn't she? So sweet-natured." He paused to clear his throat.

"And I understand you were away during her last moments. That must have been an awful shock for you." It was out before I could weigh the wisdom of it. But if he'd already tried to run me down once, then he obviously knew who I was. And if he hadn't tried to run me down, then who on earth had?

"Yes, I was out of town on business," he said. "I can't tell you how badly I feel about that now, but when I left she really did seem to be on the mend."

I tried desperately to think of other clever things to ask him, ways to bring Bella or Fifi into the conversation, but my brain refused to cooperate.

"Well, I'm sorry to have disturbed you," I said. "Could you possibly give me the Bradleys' address?" I tried to come up with a plausible reason for this. "I was asked to pass on condolences by an old friend of the family I met while sailing this weekend."

"It's One-eighteen East Fifty-ninth, just off the park. And you like to sail, do you?"

"Sometimes," I said. "I was with a party

on the Hudson yesterday. It was such a jolly time that I felt guilty."

"I say," he said suddenly. "I'm keeping you here on the doorstep. Where are my manners? Would you like to come in and have a cup of coffee?"

Now this really was tempting, but the words "Will you walk into my parlor, said the spider to the fly" did flash through my head. And the fact that he had opened his own front door indicated that there might be no servants in the place.

Either way, I decided that discretion was the better part of valor. "It's very kind of you, but I should go straight to the Bradleys, then I'm meeting another of Fanny's old friends for lunch. Emily Boswell, do you remember her?"

"Little Emily? Of course I do. How is she?"

"Very well, thank you. Working for her living, of course, having no family. She's working for a druggist near here."

Was I wrong or did a muscle twitch on his face? "Really?" he said. "She was always a bright girl. I'm sure she'll go far."

"It would seem so," I said. "And her young man is also very smart. He's studying to be a pharmacist."

"Really?" He stared at me for a moment.

"Well, good for her," he said. "If you see her, tell her I wish her well."

"I will indeed. Thank you for your time. I'm sorry to have troubled you."

"No trouble at all." He gave me a beaming smile.

I felt rather shaky as I rode the elevator down again. Had I been foolish to have brought up Emily and her drug connection? That news had definitely made him uneasy, I could see from his face. Then another alarming thought came to me: had I exposed her to danger by telling Anson about her?

I was across the park, hardly noticing its leafy beauty today, and found the Bradleys' house with little difficulty. Actually, house was an understatement. Mansion described it better. It was impressive, even in an area of mansions: red brick, adorned with white columns and white brick around the windows, not unlike the houses in the fancier squares of Dublin. I knocked, told the maid my business, and was admitted to a square hall with a staircase and galleries rising into the gloom. After a while there came a tap of heels on the parquet floor and Mrs. Bradley came toward me, still dressed in black, of course. I realized instantly that I should also have been wearing that color and instead I was wearing my beige business suit. Not very tactful of me.

"Miss Murphy?" She was looking at me doubtfully.

"I was a friend of Fanny's," I said. "I came with Emily Boswell to visit her when she was sick."

"Yes, of course." She nodded. "How can I help you?"

"I wondered if we could have a talk. It's of a slightly delicate nature."

She looked surprised. "Well, let's go into the music room, shall we? We're not likely to be disturbed there."

I followed her across the hall into a pretty room overlooking a back yard that was all cherry blossom and tulips. A harp and a grand piano stood in one corner. She indicated that I should take a seat and I perched myself on one of the gilt and brocade chairs.

"Now, what is this all about?" she asked.

"Mrs. Bradley, I have agonized over whether to tell you any of this, but I feel that I owe it to Fanny," I said. "Let me ask you — were you close to your daughter?"

"Very close. She was an affectionate girl."

"Then did she tell you that she was contemplating divorcing her husband?"

"Divorce Anson? Don't be ridiculous. Whatever gave you that notion, girl?"

I began to suspect this had not been a

good idea.

"I should tell you the truth, I suppose. I am a detective. I met Fanny at a gathering and she asked me to call on her. She told me she suspected that Anson was keeping a mistress and if that were true, she planned to divorce him. She hired me to find out the truth."

"Good God." Mrs. Bradley had gone very pale. "And when was this?"

"Immediately before she became ill."

She nodded. "So you never had time to do what you were hired to do?"

"Oh yes, I carried out the investigation. It became obvious that Anson had been friendly with a dancer called Mademoiselle Fifi."

Mrs. Bradley sighed. "My poor dear Fanny. We thought Anson was such a good match for her. So handsome and from such a good family. And instead we saddled her with a rogue with a wandering eye, just like her father."

I looked up in surprise. She nodded, the sort of nod of understanding that happens between women. "Oh, yes. I'm afraid Mr. Bradley used to cause me all kinds of grief. Actresses, cigar girls. He thought I never knew about them, but of course I did. Wives always do, don't they?"

"Yet you decided to stay with him?"

"I was brought up to believe in duty. I had a child and I had made my marriage vows. Besides, apart from that he was a good husband. He was generous. He's treated me well. He adored little Fanny. Of course we were both disappointed that I couldn't give him a son, but we've been a happy enough family in many ways. But Fanny was less realistic than I. A true romantic. I can see that she would not have wanted to stay with a man who didn't adore her." She looked up sharply. "You say you found out this before she fell ill?"

I nodded.

"And told Fanny what you had discovered?"

"I was never able to. By the time I had uncovered the truth, she was not allowed visitors."

She was still staring at me. She put a hand up to her bosom. "My God, you don't think . . ." I could read the rest of that sentence in her eyes.

"I don't know what to think," I said. "All I know is she hired me, then she fell sick and quickly died."

"So you do think that he might have done away with her?"

I shrugged. "It's hardly likely, is it? You

316

were with her during her last days. You saw what she ate and drank."

Mrs. Bradley shook her head violently, releasing a hairpin that went flying onto the parquet floor with a ping. "Everything she ate and drank was prepared by their cook and served by me. And frankly she could keep almost nothing down toward the end. She just sipped water, and a little broth. And there is no way — no way at all — I was with her all the time. I even slept sitting up in a chair beside her in case she needed me."

"And did her husband come into the room much?"

"He came in from time to time, but like most men he had a horror of illness. He would come over to the bed, kiss her forehead, mutter some words of encouragement, ask if he could get her anything, and then beat a hasty departure."

"If he could get her anything?" I picked up on this. "And did he get her anything?"

Mrs. Bradley shook her head. "She had lost all interest in food and drink. I had to coax a sip of water down her. And the poor man seemed quite worried. I really can't believe . . ."

"I'm sure this is a wild supposition," I said, "but it happened so quickly after she had hired me."

"I agree, it does look suspicious," she said. "But the doctor was here all the time. He would have noticed if anything was amiss. He told me he had treated so many patients this spring in which a simple influenza turned virulent and fatal."

"I may well be worrying you for nothing," I said, "but I felt it was my duty to tell you."

She eyed me for a moment. "Is that why you are here?"

"What do you mean?"

"I wondered whether this visit was to remind me that Fanny had hired you and never had a chance to pay you."

"Absolutely not." I felt my face flush angry red. "I have been looking into her death on my own time and with no thought of recompense because I have a strong sense of justice and if she had been murdered, I didn't want to see a murderer get away with his crime."

She came over to me and put a hand on my shoulder. "I'm sorry, my dear. You're upset. We all are. Fanny's death has taken a light from our lives. My husband suffers especially. His only child. I don't know if he'll ever get over it."

I rose to my feet, too. "I'm very sorry for both of you. She was a lovely young woman.

318

I grew fond of her in the short time I knew her."

"She was adored by everyone," Mrs. Bradley said. "She had so many friends. I had to keep them away from her in the end. It grieved me to do so."

"So who did come to visit her during that last week?" I asked, trying to keep my tone casual. "We met Dorcas, of course . . ."

"Poor dear Dorcas. I feel so badly that she must have contracted the influenza from her visit to my daughter."

"It does seem that way," I agreed.

"They all came — Minnie and Bella and of course sweet Alice was here all the time. She and Fanny have known each other since they were knee-high to a grasshopper. They were as close as sisters."

"Alice," I said. "If they were as close as sisters, I wonder if she told Alice of her intention to divorce her husband?"

"I have no idea," Mrs. Bradley said. "You have to understand that Fanny was extremely proud, Miss Murphy. She may not have wished to share this odious fact with anyone until she was ready to make her move." She paused and looked at me sharply. "You are sure about this Fifi person?"

"Oh yes. I visited her yesterday. She told

me that Anson and she had been friendly for two years but that he had come to break off completely with her a week ago. Just before Fanny died, in fact."

"Then his conscience did get the better of him," she said. "I knew the lad was good at heart."

I opened my mouth to say "unless he had found someone to replace her," then thought better of it.

"Do you know Alice's address?" I asked. "I think that maybe I should talk to her. I would be interested to know whether Fanny had confided in her."

"I just hope Alice has not contracted the deadly sickness," Mrs. Bradley said. "I have worried about that ever since we got the news about poor Dorcas. You see, Alice was the one person Fanny really wanted to have beside her. Such a loyal girl. She would have sat with her day and night if I'd allowed her to."

"Really?" I asked, my voice sounding sharper than I intended. "And does she live near here?"

"She does — but do you think it is prudent for you to visit her? I don't know if I want our little discussion to go beyond this room."

"I assure you I will tread with caution," I

said. "I will ask only the most discreet questions."

"I would like Fanny's memory to be treasured by her friends. I wouldn't like them to think . . ."

"I certainly would not dream of casting aspersions on her husband unless I were completely sure of my facts," I said. "That remains between you and me, and frankly I think we have no way of proving it at this stage. But I would like to know if she confided her intentions to divorce her husband to any other person. And Alice seems the most likely, doesn't she?"

"She does, but do you think she would share this knowledge with you? She and Fanny were very tight, you know."

"I am a detective," I said, "and whatever you may think, my one objective at this stage is to find out the truth. I'm sure you'd want to know that, wouldn't you?"

She stood, hesitant for a moment, then said, "Very well. Let me find my little book for you." She disappeared from the room. I stared out at the lovely garden in all its spring glory.

"Here we are," she returned with a small leather book. "She lives at Three-eighteen Fifty-first Street. Not far at all. Please give her my best. And Miss Murphy — you will watch what you say, won't you? If poor dear Anson is innocent, I would hate to think of vile rumors circulating about him."

"I will watch what I say," I said. "And I am sorry to have brought you such worry. I did agonize over whether to come to you or not."

"I'm glad you came," she said. "Although I am distressed that Fanny could not confide her husband's unfaithful behavior to her mother. I could have consoled her. Always such a proud girl . . ."

TWENTY-SIX

I found myself hurrying to Alice's house as if propelled by an unseen force. I wasn't sure if I was being driven by the need to find out that Alice was indeed alive and well, or that she had been the one confidante who sat at Fanny's bedside. Sweet, gentle Alice who would have sat at Fanny's bedside day and night if she had been allowed to . . . There have been stranger murderers before.

"Ridiculous," I said to myself. Now I was seeing suspicious motives in everyone. When I had finally finished this case it would most probably turn out to be quite simple: Anson Poindexter had a mistress. He decided to sever all ties with her because his conscience got the better of him when his wife became sick. She died. End of story. I thought of his smiling, affable face. Was that the face of a cunning murderer? If he had been guilty, wouldn't he have shown more alarm at seeing me on his doorstep? Frankly, I didn't know how murderers thought. I didn't know much of anything, in fact.

My pace slowed as I reached Alice's street. Was this really a good idea? Was I helping Fanny in any way by airing her dirty laundry? And yet I had opened the floodgates. I couldn't stop until I knew.

The establishment was humble by the standards of my recent visits — a respectable brownstone with bay trees in pots on either side of the front door. The maid who admitted me was also not quite of the quality of the last house. A trifle slovenly, in fact. It might seem that gentle Alice wasn't too good at managing servants. But I was shown into a pleasant enough sitting room up a flight of stairs and found Alice on the floor, playing with a one-year-old baby. From the blond curls and petticoats I couldn't tell whether it was a boy or a girl, and since she addressed it as Treasure I was none the wiser. On seeing me she handed it to the maid to be taken to the nursery and brushed off her skirts as she sat on the sofa. I noticed she was wearing black.

"Miss Murphy. What brings you here?" She sounded breathless and surprised.

"In the first place I was charged by Mrs. Bradley to make sure you had not taken ill. She was very worried that you had spent so much time at Fanny's bedside and might have caught the dreadful illness."

She smiled sadly. "Oh no. Hale and hearty, as you see. I always was the strong one. I didn't catch measles and mumps when Fanny did, although we played together all the time. I do hope Treasure has inherited this from me. But then my dear Arthur is also of a sound constitution. How is Mrs. Bradley faring? I worry so for her. They did adore that daughter."

"She seems to be holding up well. It is her husband she worries about."

"I can see that," Alice said. "He positively idolized Fanny. He spoiled her horribly, of course." She paused and smiled. "But who could not love Fanny? He's not the only one who feels a light has gone from their life, I can assure you. Fanny and I were as close as sisters. I feel absolutely bereft."

"I'm sure all her friends feel the same way," I said. "I've come with a rather awkward question, Mrs. Trotter. You were closer to Fanny than anybody — did she ever share any concerns with you about her husband?"

Her forehead wrinkled charmingly. "What kind of concerns, Miss Murphy?"

"I wondered if she ever mentioned to you that she suspected her husband of infidelity? Or that she was thinking of divorcing him?"

She looked shocked. "Thinking of divorcing Anson? No, whoever gave you that idea? I suppose it was Emily."

"Actually . . ." I began, then I stopped. "Emily?" I asked.

"Well, naturally she came to mind," Alice said. "Wishful thinking, you know."

"What do you mean?"

"I mean, Miss Murphy, that Emily was hopelessly smitten with Anson during her Vassar days. Worshipped the ground he trod on. Of course it was all rather awkward for Fanny. But it was obvious from the first that Anson would pick Fanny over Emily, wasn't it? Fanny had money and Anson liked to live well. Emily had nothing."

"I see." I felt as if I had been punched in the stomach.

"So I thought that maybe Emily had been spreading rumors in the hope of souring Fanny's marriage."

"So as far as you know she and Anson were happily married?"

"Oh she complained about him sometimes," she said airily. "The hours he came home. The amount he was away. Lack of attention. But then we can all find something to complain about in our husbands, can't we?"

"You were with her a lot that last week," I went on, not knowing how to put any of this now. "Was there anything about her sickness that seemed to you — well, not quite right?"

Again she frowned. "I don't quite know what you are driving at, Miss Murphy. The only thing that was not right was that Fanny got sicker and sicker whatever we did for her. Watching her slip away from us was more than a body could bear." Her expression suddenly sharpened again. "Wait? You are not suggesting that somebody — that Anson might have? No, that's too ridiculous. He was distraught. I had to comfort him."

"I really didn't mean to suggest any impropriety," I said hastily. "Emily merely suggested that the sickness didn't seem to be following the usual course of influenza and she wondered whether Fanny had been taking anything that might have further upset and weakened her."

"Emily again," Alice snapped. "It sounds to me as if she wanted to cast suspicion on Anson. Who knows, perhaps she is out to get revenge for being spurned."

"I don't think that sounds like Emily," I said. "Besides, she has a new beau now."

"She always was devious," Alice said. "I suppose it came from being on her own so much as a child."

I got to my feet. "Look, I'm sorry to have troubled you. And I'm even sorrier to have worried you in this way. Obviously nothing I have mentioned is true and Fanny's death was a tragic sickness."

I left her sitting pensively on the sofa.

I stumbled down the steps and started to walk, faster and faster, trying to keep up with my racing thoughts. It was Emily who first suggested that something wasn't right in the manner of Fanny's death. And that, coupled with what Fanny had just told me about her intention to divorce Anson, had made me equally suspicious. But I had not, for one minute, suspected Emily herself: Emily the lonely, not very beautiful child who had grown up unloved and then been thrown out into the world. Surely if anyone had become bitter and twisted it could have been she. And she was bright, too — smart enough to learn a thing or two about clever poisons.

It suddenly struck me that I had been set up. Had she made friends with me because she thought I was gullible and she wanted a gullible witness? I stopped so abruptly that a woman with her shopping bag barreled into the back of me, then took off again, muttering. Emily was Fanny's dear friend. Could Emily ever have killed Fanny just because she had married Anson? Killed her to get back at Anson? Surely this was far-fetched and went quite against the sweet Emily I had come to know. And we hadn't even been allowed in to see Fanny when she was still alive — unless Emily had come alone, earlier in Fanny's illness. Maybe Fanny had come down with a simple case of influenza and Emily had managed to administer some subtle poison or — I came to a halt again, making the crowd divide around me like a stream flowing around a rock — the stomach mixture. Emily delivered it. I had now given a sample to Daniel and he had indicated in his note that something interesting had come up.

"We're going to find out the truth about you, Emily Boswell," I muttered. Should I wait for Daniel to come and tell me what he had discovered or should I go to Emily right away? My anger and indignation swept me forward in the direction of Emily's drugstore. It was close to her lunch time. I would take her out, tell her what I had discovered about her family background, and then, while her emotions were in turmoil from that news, I would demand the truth about Fanny and Anson. I would tell her that the stomach mixture was currently being tested by the best police doctors. She would break down and tell me all . . .

I arrived breathless and with hammering heart at McPherson's drugstore. There was no sign of Emily, and Ned came around from the back room at the sound of the bell.

"Can I help you, miss?" he asked, pushing open the swing door, then recognized me. "Oh, Miss Murphy, it's you."

"Good day to you, Ned. I came to see if Emily would join me for lunch, but I see that she's not here. Is she out making deliveries again?"

"She's out sick again, I'm afraid," he said. "She sent a note that she had one of her bad headaches."

"Oh dear," I said. "I am sorry."

"And if this is going to happen with regularity, Miss Boswell will be looking for a new position," came Mr. McPherson's harsh voice from the back room.

"Come on now, sir," Ned said. "She's not often sick, you know that. And she works like a trooper when she's here."

"Poor Emily," I said. "She spent yesterday afternoon with you and your mother, didn't she? Was she well then?"

"Oh, absolutely blooming and we had a

most pleasant time together. She was her charming self and bucked poor Mother up no end."

"Your mother has not been well?" I asked.

"Frankly, Miss Murphy, she gets lonely out there in Brooklyn on her own and she broods," Ned said. "I'd bring her into the city to live with me, but my apartment's not big enough to swing a cat. She's had a hard life raising me. I only wish I could do more for her, but I'm doing all I can."

"I'm sure you are, Ned. And I'm sure your turn will come soon."

"Thank you, Miss Murphy. I very much hope so."

"I shouldn't keep you any longer," I said, conscious of Mr. McPherson listening in from the back room. "I'll go and visit Emily and see if there's anything I can do for her."

"I'd leave her be if I were you," Ned said. "When she gets one of these bad headaches then sleep is really the only cure. We've tried making various headache remedies for her but nothing seems to do the trick."

"Very well," I said. "Good-bye then."

I came out of the shop and walked a few steps, not quite sure what to do next. If Emily was suffering with one of her terrible headaches then I probably should leave her in peace, as Ned had suggested. On the other hand, it might be easier to extract a confession from her if she wasn't feeling her best. And if she turned out to be innocent, then my news about her parentage should cheer her up. I turned onto her street, went up the stairs to her room, and tapped gently on her door.

"Emily, it's Molly," I said in a soft voice through the crack in the door. "I've come to see if there's anything I can do for you."

After a while I heard slow footsteps shuffling toward the door. It opened. Emily stood there in her dressing gown, breathing heavily. One look at her told me that she was not suffering from a simple headache. I had witnessed one of these before and her face had been pale and her forehead creased in pain. Today her face was flushed, her eyes hollow.

"Molly," she said in a cracked whisper. "How good of you to come. I really feel most unwell."

"When did this start?" I asked her anxiously.

"In the middle of the night. I felt fine yesterday, as you know, because you saw me in the morning. I had a lovely time at Ned's mother's in the afternoon and then when I went to bed I felt overwhelmingly tired and headachy. I woke in the night drenched in sweat, aching all over, and I've been vomiting."

I led her back to her bed, my heart now pounding. "Lie down," I said. "Now tell me, what can I get you?"

She shook her head. "I don't feel like anything at all, thank you."

"You should take something to keep your strength up. I'll go and get some veal bones from the butcher and make you some broth. And some barley for barley water. Oh, and I can go to your drugstore and see if they can make up something for you?"

She shook her head. "It's the flu, I'm afraid. I've finally succumbed and all I can do is to ride it out."

She lay back with a sigh. I went over to her sink and dipped a washcloth in water to sponge her face. She really did look very ill. "I'm sure you could sip a little broth," I said.

She gave a tired smile. "I've only the one gas ring and a small saucepan."

"Then I'll go to a restaurant and buy some broth for you."

"You're very kind," she said in a voice that was little more than a whisper, "but I don't want to put you in danger."

"Danger?" I asked, my senses suddenly sharp again. "What kind of danger?"

"If it's the same malady that killed my friends, I don't want you to risk catching it."

"Oh, I see," I said. "Well, you don't have to worry about that. If it's the flu, then I've just had it and they say you can't catch it twice. And if it's something else, then I've already visited Fanny and Dorcas and come away safely. So lie down and I'll be back."

I ran down the stairs and back to Broadway. There I found a delicatessen where they were serving chicken soup with matzo balls, a Jewish dish I had come to enjoy when I worked in a garment factory. I persuaded them to give me a big basin of it, and left a hefty deposit for the return of the basin. Then I carried it back to Emily's room with great care.

As I walked up the stairs, I tried to harness my racing thoughts. As usual it looked as if I had got it wrong again and Emily was victim rather than killer. What if Emily was genuinely worried and suspicious about her best friend's death? What if Anson, maybe aided and abetted by Bella, had found some kind of clever poison and thought he was safe until Emily started poking around, asking questions? Emily, who was known to be a bright young woman and who worked with a druggist? Did Anson fear that she would put two and two together and decide that she had to go? In which case had I also sealed my own fate by visiting him this morning?

This is rubbish, I muttered out loud, and the words echoed through the high stairwell of the building. Anson had been charming this morning. Charming and distressed by the death of his wife. Surely such a man could not be a cold-blooded killer? Bella, on the other hand — she struck me as more the reckless and gutsy type. If she was behind this I could actually see her slipping in to visit her poor sick friend and tipping a dose of goodness knows what into the drinking glass.

I opened Emily's door and tiptoed in. She was lying with her eyes closed and there was now the smell of vomit in the room. But her eyes opened as she heard me.

"Emily," I said, "have you received any visitors at all? We went together to Dorcas's family yesterday and then you went straight to Ned's mother?"

She nodded.

"So Bella hasn't been to see you recently?"

"Bella?" She frowned. "I hardly know Bella. I've met her a couple of times at Fanny's house. Why do you want to know?"

"I'm worried that someone is trying to

poison you," I said. "You look very much the way Dorcas did last week."

"Don't say that!" She tried to sit up. "But that can't be right. I've seen nobody. I've only eaten food at that little café where I always take my lunch, or an egg I boiled myself here, or with Ned and his mother. Nobody could have slipped in here and poisoned anything. It just isn't possible."

I smoothed back her hair. "You may be right and maybe I'm over-reacting again. Perhaps it is just a nasty flu. Here, the broth is still warm. Can I feed you a little?"

She sighed. "All right. I'll try, I suppose." She attempted to sit up. I put my hand behind her head and helped her. She managed a couple of sips, then turned her head away. "I really don't feel like anything," she said. "Why don't you go? I do worry about you. Catching what I have."

"I'll be fine," I said. "Really, I'll stay if you need me."

She lay back and closed her eyes. "Molly," she asked after a while, "do you think we were right about our suppositions? Do you think that Anson killed Fanny, and then Dorcas, and now he's trying to kill me?"

"It hardly seems possible," I said. "I met him this morning and he seemed such an affable sort of man. But I understand that some murderers are extremely pleasant in their manner. And he has now achieved what he wanted, hasn't he? Fanny's money and his freedom."

"So it would seem. But if he's tried to poison me, how did he do it? He hasn't been anywhere near me and I keep my room locked when I'm out."

"A challenge, to be sure. Look, Emily, I think you should see a doctor — a good doctor — and tell him what you suspect."

"He'd think I was an hysterical female."

"I could ask Daniel for you. I know they have physicians who work with the police and he would certainly know how to test for poisons."

"But what could it be?" she asked. "The symptoms resemble nothing I can think of. The gastric upset and the flushed skin might indicate arsenic, but we know that Fanny's hair tested negative and she didn't look at all flushed in the end, did she?"

"I'll go and seek out Daniel," I said. "I'll make him listen to me and then I'll be back."

"All right." She lay back and closed her eyes. "I think I'll just sleep a little," she whispered.

I closed the door quietly behind me and tiptoed down the stairs. As I came out of that dark stairwell into the sunlight I looked down at my arm and noticed something: my light beige costume had black hairs all over it.

Twenty-Seven

I went to Daniel's residence but of course he wasn't there in the middle of the afternoon. However, I left a note for him, telling him that I'd be at home and needed to see him soon as he had a free moment. I bought some groceries on my way home. Among them were barley to make barley water for Emily and bones and vegetables to make her more soup. I put the barley and the soup on to boil and then all I could do was wait. I paced impatiently around my kitchen, down the hall, around the living room, looked out of the front window and then back again. I knew there were things I could be doing but I found it impossible to settle. For once I didn't even want Sid and Gus's company.

If Daniel doesn't come this evening, I'm going to police headquarters to root him out in the morning, I decided. And I'm calling a doctor for Emily myself. But about seven o'clock, just as it was starting to get dark, there was a knock on my front door and Daniel himself was standing there.

"Thank God," I said and flung myself into his arms.

"What is it?" he asked, holding me away from him so that he could look at my face. "What's wrong?"

"It's Emily, the girl whose family I have been investigating," I said. "She was the friend of Fanny Poindexter who died, and now she has come down with similar symptoms. I'm really afraid that she has been poisoned too."

"Hold on," Daniel said, his big hands gripping my shoulders. "Let's not jump to any conclusions, shall we?"

"But I've seen her, Daniel. She was fine yesterday and now she's very sick."

"This kind of flu will do that to you," he said. "You should know. You came down with it yourself."

"But I wasn't vomiting and I'm sure I didn't look as awful as Emily now does. And you've now had the tests administered, haven't you? You now know what killed them?"

"I do have the answer for you," he said, leading me across the room and seating me firmly in my one armchair. "My chemist friend tells me that there was arsenic in the sample of stomach mixture that you gave me."

"See, I knew it!"

"And," he continued, "that this would not be a completely unusual ingredient in such a mixture in minute amounts. The amount was minute. Not enough to harm anyone."

"Oh," I said, suddenly deflated. "And the hair sample from the other woman?"

"Also contained a trace of arsenic."

"Aha!"

"Which is also not so unusual, according to my friend. If she had taken any similar mixture, particularly one made up for her influenza . . ."

"Which she had," I agreed. "She said it tasted disgusting and she stopped taking it."

"Then the amount in the hair is quite consistent with that. It remains in the system for a long time, you know. And again he said the amount was not enough to kill anybody. So you see, my dear, sweet, over-emotional Molly, there was no poisoning. They all three caught the same disease."

"What about another poison?"

"My friend agreed that most usual poisons apart from arsenic are fairly fast-acting. The victim becomes violently ill and dies soon afterward. Of course the world is full of unusual poisons, but it would take an expert to know and to administer them. Was this husband you suspect such a man?"

"No, he's a lawyer. From a good family," I said. "I'm sure he has no such knowledge."

"There you are, then. We'll just hope that your poor friend is of a strong constitution and rides out the flu the way you did."

"But what about the hair?" I asked.

"What hair?"

"All three of them lost their hair. It came out all over their pillows. That's not normal, is it? I didn't lose any."

Daniel frowned. "I admit that is strange. It rings a bell somehow." He paused, then thumped one fist into his cupped hand. "But dash it, I can't for the life of me think what it is. Someone talking about hair falling out recently. Never mind, it will come to me."

"But in the note you left me you said you had something to tell me. I thought you'd discovered that the mixture was poisoned."

"I'm sorry to disappoint you." He came around to me and put his hands on my shoulders again, a move I found most disquieting. "No, the thing I wanted to tell you was that we've solved my arsenic case, partly thanks to you."

"To me?"

"Yes, you were the one who mentioned the green wallpaper containing arsenic."

"And they all licked wallpaper?"

He laughed. "They each lived in one room with said wallpaper."

"But surely that's not enough to kill anyone?"

"No, but it's an added factor. They had all come down with influenza, which had naturally weakened their resistance. They each bought the same patent medicine: J. D. Rowley's Flu-Stopper. It's a cheap tonic, sold on the street by a snake-oil salesman. These things are a curse, you know. Made up by people who have only a smattering of knowledge about drugs."

"And the tonic contained arsenic?"

"It did."

"But surely the police tested the tonic, didn't they?"

"They did take samples, of course. But as with any patent medicines of this nature the amounts are not carefully measured and, worse of all, the mixture was not stable. The arsenic separated out and sank to the bottom of the bottle. If it was not well shaken, the victim drank a couple of doses that were almost pure arsenic. That, when added to the amount inhaled from the wallpaper and their weakened condition, finished them off.

Simple as that."

I laughed. "Not funny for them, of course. Still I'm glad you've solved one of your cases."

"And we may be getting somewhere with our Chinese tongs," he said. "We think we've taken a young man into custody who is prepared to spill the beans if we give him safe passage across the country to San Francisco."

"And he's going to tell you how the opium comes into the country?"

"He's already done that. It's brought in by a man who poses as a missionary. Trunks of Bibles go out and the same trunks come back, packed with opium. Not the most godly of men, would you say?"

"Anything you want to know about missionaries, I'm your girl," I said. "I can give you a list of missionary headquarters and names of some missionaries who are in the local area."

"Most efficient," he said. "That would save my men some time. Although if this man is only posing as a missionary . . ."

"They can tell you the names on their books and you can check future sailings for someone who is shipping Bibles and is not a member of one of the societies."

"Smart girl." He touched the tip of my

344

nose. "Two cases solved would go down well with the new commissioner."

"And it might mean that we can actually spend some time together for once."

"And what good would that be?" he asked, playfully toying with my hair. "When I'm free you're rushing around and working, and when we are together you won't let me touch you."

"I didn't say I wouldn't let you touch me," I said, standing slowly until I was facing him. "I have no objection to a chaste kiss or two."

He laughed. "And when have you and I ever exchanged chaste kisses," he said. "And don't come the prim maid with me. You enjoy our lovemaking as much as I do."

"That's as may be," I said, "but it's going to remain chaste until we're married."

"I admire your strength of character," Daniel said. He slipped his arms around me and pulled me close to him. "You don't even weaken when I hold you like this, and then I kiss you like this . . ." His lips traced a line down my neck.

"That's not fair," I said, laughing.

He broke off, sniffing. "My, that smells good," he said. "Are you going to invite me to stay for dinner?"

"That's a broth I'm making for my friend

Emily," I said.

"Pity." His face fell.

"I do believe you only want a wife so you have someone to cook for you," I teased.

"There are other benefits of marriage, so I'm told," he said, giving me a look that made my knees go weak. But I remained resolute. "You could take me out to dinner," I said. "Seeing that I've helped you solve both your cases."

"I certainly could," he agreed. "And I know just the place."

"Nothing expensive," I reminded him.

"It's most certainly not. And it's nearby. Come on. Get your hat and coat."

Soon we were walking arm in arm across Washington Square. The trees were a mass of blossoms. The flower beds were full of spring flowers. And the children were out in force, enjoying a balmy spring evening. I watched them running with their hoops and pushing their doll carriages and thought wistfully of little Bridie and her brother Shamey, who had lived with me until their father took them to live on a farm. Much better for them, of course, but I did miss them occasionally. I let my thoughts drift to the future and imagined Daniel and me strolling through a park like this while we pushed a baby buggy . . .

"I can't tell you what a relief it is to be back at work." Daniel interrupted my reverie. "Those months under suspicion were almost the end of me. You have no idea how deeply I sank into despair. You were the only thing that kept me going."

I looked up at him and smiled. He covered my hand with his own. I felt a warm glow inside as we walked down West Tenth Street until we came to a little Italian restaurant. It had checkered tablecloths and jugs of red wine on the tables. Daniel ordered big bowls of spaghetti and I soon found that it was not possible to eat Italian food daintily and in a ladylike manner. Daniel laughed at my efforts. "We'll make a New Yorker of you yet," he said.

TWENTY-EIGHT

The next morning I took the El to the Upper West Side, precariously balancing a jug of barley water and a pot of broth. I managed to bring both of them successfully to Emily's room. She looked no worse than the day before and I heaved a sigh of relief when I saw her.

"Molly, this is so good of you," she said, lying back onto her pillows, "but I'm afraid you've gone to so much trouble for nothing. I have barely taken a sip of the broth you brought me yesterday, and I don't know what I'm going to do with all this."

"You should finish that first, so that I can take them their bowl back," I suggested. "Shall I heat some up for you?"

"I don't think I could manage it." She shuddered. "But maybe the barley water. My throat is so dry."

I sat with her while she took a few sips, then I transferred the rest of the barley water to a glass jug she had and tipped the rest of the chicken broth from the delicatessen into my jug and her saucepan. "I'd better take this back. And I'm going to see your Mr. McPherson. He might be able to make you up some medicine to take down your fever and ease your stomach. And I'm going to ask him to recommend a good doctor for you."

"But I can't afford doctors." She attempted to sit up.

"Nonsense, I'm paying. You owe me my fee, remember? Besides, I rather think that you'll soon have the money to pay for things without worrying."

"You've really found out the truth?" she looked up at me. "You know who my parents are?"

"I do indeed."

"And am I an heiress?"

"Maybe."

She reached out and grabbed my arm, her fingers digging into me. "So tell me my parents names."

"Your mother was a lovely, fun-loving young woman who married the wrong man." I paused. "Her name was Lydia."

"Like my aunt? Wait." Her eyes opened wide again. "Do you mean my aunt Lydia?"

"The very same."

"Don't tell me that Horace Lynch was my father," she said angrily. "No father ever treated his child as I was treated."

"You're right. He wasn't your father. Hence his bitterness to you and your mother."

"Then who was my father?"

"A charming and handsome Italian gardener. Your mother was a young girl at the time. She fell madly in love with him, but she was married to Horace Lynch."

"I see." She lay there, eyes closed, contemplating this. "She couldn't run off with the gardener, could she? She was stuck with Horace."

"He agreed not to turn her out onto the street, but said the baby had to go. She fought for you, Emily. He agreed that they would keep you but not as their own child."

She lay silently again, thinking, then she said, "You know it's funny, isn't it, but small children know. I said to her once, 'I wish you were my mother' and she had this funny, sad smile on her face and she said, 'No mother could love you more than I.' But she died soon after that."

I nodded.

"How did you find this out?"

"I'm a detective. I went to Lydia's birthplace and talked to people."

"Does Horace Lynch know you've found out?"

"I extracted the full story from him."

"But he still wants nothing to do with me?"

"I did point out to him that legally he is your father and things could be very embarrassing for him should this come to the courts. I also suggested that you might be quite content with a small allowance, rather than going after your mother's entire fortune."

"Molly! You didn't say that!"

"I most certainly did."

"Didn't he shout at you most horribly? He's terrifying when he's angry."

"No, I think I had shocked him into silence by that time."

She laughed. "Amazing." The laugh turned into a racking cough. When it finally subsided there were beads of sweat over her forehead.

"We must get you well again," I said. "I should go now and I'll come back with a doctor."

She touched my arm again. "Molly, do you think I'm going to die?"

"I won't let you die," I said. "If I can conquer Horace Lynch, I'm not going to let your illness win, either."

She smiled sadly, I took the china basin I had borrowed from the delicatessen then hurried down the stairs and out onto the street. I had promised Emily she wasn't going to die, but I knew that Fanny and Dorcas had had the best care and attention available and they had both died just the same. Worry clutched at the pit of my stomach. I had dropped off the basin and was just about to enter McPherson's drugstore when something in the window caught my eye. The display in the corner.

COMPLEXION CREAM FOR THE FINEST, WHITEST SKIN. AS USED BY LADIES IN PARIS.

The cream was in pretty white jars with blue lids. What's more, I had seen one of those jars recently. On Dorcas's dressing table. And I remembered the conversation at Fanny's house. She praised the cream that Ned made and told Emily she needed more of it. I stood staring for a moment, then I turned and ran back to Emily's room.

"Emily. That face cream. The jar with the blue lid." The words came out as a gasp, as I was out of breath from running up six flights of stairs.

"The one Ned makes?" she asked. "I have

one here on the shelf. Do you want to try it? It's wonderful."

I went over to the shelf above her sink and took down the small white jar. I opened it. It was full.

"Ned gave me a new one on Friday," she said. "He told me he'd improved it even more and asked me to show it to my lady friends."

"And have you used any yet?"

"Oh, yes. I used it right away."

"Emily, I know nothing about poisons," I said. "Is it possible that some element could have been added to a face cream and that a poison could be absorbed through the skin?"

She looked horrified. "But Ned gave this to me himself."

"Tell me this. I remember Fanny saying she was out of the fabulous complexion cream and asking for more. Did you take her another jar?"

"Yes, I did. Right before she —"

She tried to sit up, open-mouthed.

"Right before she fell ill," I said. "And I saw a jar on Dorcas's dressing table, too."

"But if it's possible to poison face cream, who could have done this?" she asked in a trembling voice.

"The person who made the cream would be the obvious suspect."

"Ned? My Ned? But he doesn't even know Fanny or Dorcas."

"Is it possible someone paid him to kill them?"

She looked horrified. "Ned is an ethical person. He would never stoop to that."

"Even though he needs money badly? Even though he is ambitious and a large sum of money could set him up in his own business?"

She hesitated for a second. "Never," she said. "Ned would never do that. And besides, he wouldn't want to risk harming me, would he?"

"Is it possible that someone could have tampered with the cream then?"

She frowned. "I suppose that someone could have tampered with Fanny's cream, but not with mine. Ned himself handed it to me." Then she shook her head vehemently. "You must be wrong. There is no poison in the cream."

"It is the only thing that links the three of you together," I said. "I'm taking this jar to Daniel to be tested this very minute. I hope I'm wrong, but we need to know, don't we?"

"But Ned gave it to me," she said again. "There can't be anything the matter with it."

Something occurred to me. "When we

gave those hairs to Ned to be tested, he said there was no arsenic present. But there must have been. There was arsenic in the stomach mixture Mr. McPherson made up for Fanny, so a trace would have shown up in her hair. That must mean either that Ned didn't test the hair properly or . . ."

"Or that he lied, and said there was no arsenic so that nobody pursued this." Her face was absolutely devastated. "But that can't be right, Molly. My Ned can't have wanted to kill anybody. He's gentle. He would never have . . ."

I put a hand on her shoulder. "Let's get this cream tested, then we'll know for sure. I really hope that I am wrong and that Ned has nothing to do with this."

"Yes, get it tested as quickly as possible," she said. "I won't be able to rest until I know."

I poured a fresh glass of barley water for her, then I hurried down those stairs again. Now my heart was really thumping. The obvious answer was that Ned had deliberately poisoned those face creams, but why? If he didn't know Fanny or Dorcas, the motive could only be money. Someone had bribed him to kill Fanny, and maybe Dorcas. Anson Poindexter, or even Bella. Or perhaps it was Mademoiselle Fifi, who thought at that stage that Anson might marry her if his wife was out of the way. But it seemed rather sophisticated for someone like Fifi. More likely to be Bella, who was well educated and moved in society.

I wondered if I dared pay a visit to Bella and drop hints about face cream and see her reaction — mentioning of course that I had sent a jar to my intended, a captain of police, to be tested. She was hardly likely to throttle me in her living room, was she? Then I thought about Emily. Even if Ned had been paid well to kill Fanny and Dorcas, surely he would not have agreed to harm Emily. And yet he had given her the face cream on Friday. To me this could only mean one thing . . . he wanted her out of the way as well.

Twenty-Nine

I stood irresolute at the curb, wondering what to do next. The jar of cream should go to Daniel to be tested. And Emily needed medicine and a doctor. Nothing else would matter if Emily died, but obviously a doctor would need to know what was poisoning her before he could treat her. So Daniel first. I jumped onto a streetcar as it moved off from its stop, causing the conductor to yell at me. "Danged foolish thing to do, young woman," he growled. "Don't you know you could get yourself killed that way?"

"Sorry, I'm in a hurry," I replied with a rueful smile.

I didn't think Daniel would be at home at this hour, but there was just a chance he might have the day off or have been working all night. Besides, I'd rather face Mrs. O'Shea than police headquarters. The landlady greeted me, looking somewhat distracted and disheveled. Her hair was unkempt and her apron needed changing. "Oh, Miss Murphy. I'm sorry. I must look a sight but I've been up all night with the children. The captain's not here."

"Then I'm sorry to have bothered you," I said. "And I'm sorry to hear the children are still sick."

She tried to smooth down her hair. "If it's not one thing, it's another," she said. "It's that ringworm on top of everything else that's driving them crazy. I've had to make mittens for them to stop them scratching."

At that moment the door opened and a child came running out. It was half dressed in petticoat and camisole and the amazing thing about it was that it was almost bald.

"Geraldine, whatever are you thinking," Mrs. O'Shea said in a shocked voice. "You can't let people see you like that. Get back inside this instant."

"I thought it was Captain Sullivan," Geraldine said with a pout. "He promised he'd bring me some of that sour candy."

"Children!" Mrs. O'Shea shook her head as she pushed Geraldine back into the room and closed the door.

"What's happened to her hair?" I asked, staring at the closed door almost as if I could see through it.

"It's the ringworm medicine. It makes their hair fall out. The doctor says it will grow back again just fine."

"What's in the medicine that has that effect?" I asked.

"I wouldn't know, my dear. It's what the doctor prescribed for them. I had it made up at the pharmacy on the corner of Broadway."

"Thank you, Mrs. O'Shea." I beamed at her.

"You're welcome, I'm sure," she said, looking at me oddly.

I hurried along Twenty-third to Broadway and into the pharmacy there. "You made up a ringworm medicine for the O'Shea children," I said, realizing that the words were coming out in a torrent. "What was in it?"

The druggist stared at me as if I was a crazy person.

"My dear young woman, I could not possibly discuss a patient's prescription with you."

"But it's very important," I said. "A matter of life and death, in fact."

"Really?" He looked almost amused.

"I have a friend whom I suspect is being poisoned," I said. "I need to know what there is in the medicine you made up to counteract ringworm that would make the hair fall out."

"That, young lady, would be in the inclusion of thallium."

"And is thallium a poison?"

"Deadly. It can kill in relatively small doses. We have to make sure when we handle it that we wear gloves and a mask. It can be absorbed through the skin and inhaled too, you know."

I looked around the dispensary. "Do you happen to have a telephone?"

"I do not. I have no interest in these newfangled ideas," he said, and indicated that he was going back to his work.

"Do you happen to know who might have a telephone near here? One that I could use for a matter of great urgency?"

"As I said, I have no interest in these ridiculous contraptions. Now, if you will excuse me, I have orders waiting to be filled." And he went back to his work.

I felt angry, frustrated, and so tense that I might explode any minute. I now knew that thallium was the ingredient that made hair fall out and that it was a deadly poison. I wondered how hard it would be to detect whether thallium had been added to that face cream. I jumped back on the Broadway trolley and rode it, fuming with impatience as it stopped at the corner of every city block, all the way down Broadway, until I was at police headquarters.

"I need to speak to Captain Sullivan. It's very urgent," I told the constable who was manning the front desk.

"I'm sorry, miss, but the captain is out on a case. Can I see what other detectives are here at the moment?"

"No. That won't do at all," I said. "If you can find me some paper and a pen, I'll write the captain a note."

"Is this to report some kind of crime?" he asked. "Or is the note of a personal nature?" His smirk implied that young women were prone to chase after Captain Sullivan. I thought about setting him straight on this, but instead I kept strictly to business.

"A crime." I gave him a cold stare. "A case of poisoning."

He went and produced a sheet of paper and an inkwell. I wrote,

Daniel. The poison was thallium. This jar of cream needs to be tested immediately. Emily Boswell is very sick. I'm summoning a doctor but he may not know how to treat a poison. If you know of a poisons expert, please send him immediately to Emily.

And I wrote down her address. "Please come yourself as soon as you can," I added. Then I handed the note and the jar of cream to the policeman at the desk. "Captain Sullivan is to see these the moment he comes back. Will you keep them down here or take them up to his office?"

He looked rather surprised at the forceful way I was speaking, also that I knew where his office was. "I'll take them to his office, miss. Don't worry. I'll see he gets them."

When I came out of police headquarters, I was unsure what to do next. Find a doctor for Emily, I supposed. Would any doctor believe me if I told him she was suffering from thallium poisoning, and would he have any idea how to treat it if he did believe me? I took the El this time, knowing it to be quicker than the trolley. As I watched the second-floor windows of the buildings pass us by, some only a few feet away, I tried to make sense of everything that had happened. Someone must have bribed Ned to poison that face cream. But why kill Dorcas? And what about the opera singer Honoria? How did she come into this?

Then I thought I saw what might have happened. The poisoned face cream could have been intended only for Fanny. But Fanny had sung its praises to her friends.

What if she had passed along the jar to Dorcas? And what if Dorcas had let her friend Honoria try it when she came to visit? It seemed more likely than somebody deliberately killing Dorcas and Honoria, didn't it?

Fifi, Bella, Anson. I toyed with each of the names. How did they discover Ned, assuming that Ned had added the poison to the face creams he made. Anson might have had contact with McPherson's drugstore, because Fanny liked the stomach mixture they made up. And Bella learned about it from Fanny. But what would induce Anson or Bella to think that Ned could be bribed to kill someone and that he would not go to the police? Unless . . .

Unless Ned were not being paid to kill Fanny. What if he had his own reason for wanting her dead? I couldn't think what this could be, apart from a paranoid hatred of rich women. Was it possible that he was systematically killing off rich women because they had everything he had lacked growing up? It seemed rather improbable. Suddenly I thought of the first time I had been to McPherson's drugstore. Emily had been to visit the older woman who worked with Emily behind the counter. She had become sick and died from very similar symptoms. Had she tried the face cream?

Was it possible that Ned was not the good pharmacist he imagined himself to be and had created a mixture containing lethal elements? I knew that some face preparations contained arsenic. Maybe Ned had thought that thallium would be a good addition, and I had just heard from Daniel that a badly made tonic had been responsible for killing people. But then Emily had used the cream previously and suffered no ill effects. Just this current batch then.

The closely packed buildings gave way to a more genteel landscape. Out of the window I glimpsed Columbus Circle and the elegant area around the southern entrance to the park. Carriages were passing here, fashionable folk were strolling. Watching them made me think of that one particular black carriage. Who had tried to run me down? Not Ned. He would have no access to such a vehicle, and besides, it had proved rather easy to kill with a simple jar of face cream. Perhaps the carriage had been a mere accident after all, the result of a bad coachman and a great hurry and nothing to do with someone wanting me out of the way.

A good motive, that was what I needed. I toyed with the idea of Ned loving Fanny from afar — but knowing he didn't come from the right background to ask her to marry him. But from conversation it seemed that he only knew Fanny as Emily's rich friend. And if he loved her secretly, would he want to kill her?

Then, as the train slowed for the Seventy-third Street station and I stood to disembark, the germ of an idea started to grow in my brain. I considered Ned's hard life, growing up in extreme poverty as an illegitimate child without a father. And I thought of Mrs. Bradley and her husband's roving eye . . . actresses, cigar girls, she had said. Could it be possible? I had to see Mrs. Bradley and find out for myself.

So instead of going straight to Emily, I crossed the park to the Bradleys' mansion. Mrs. Bradley had been about to go out and was fixing an enormous hat to her head with several lethal-looking pins.

"Miss Murphy!" She looked startled.

"I'm sorry to trouble you yet again, Mrs. Bradley," I said, "but I have to ask you an important question."

"Very well."

"Not here." I looked around the vast front hall with all the doors opening from it. "It's of a rather private nature."

"Very well," she said again, looking both startled and annoyed now. "But I do have an appointment for which I cannot be late."

"This will only take a minute."

She ushered me through the nearest door into a cavernous drawing room and shut the door behind us.

"Well?"

"This may seem like an impertinent question," I said, "and I would never have dreamed of asking it unless I thought it might unmask your daughter's killer. You mentioned that your husband had a roving eye. To your knowledge did he ever father an illegitimate child?"

"What a preposterous thing to say. Absolutely not!" She spat out the words.

I said nothing, but continued to look at her. I saw her face twitch uncomfortably.

"The answer is that I really don't know," she said.

There was another long pause and I saw her expression change.

"You've remembered something," I prompted.

"There was one young man, a few months ago," she said hesitantly. "He came to see my husband. I never knew what it was about but I assumed he might have been asking for a loan, or a job. Anyway, I heard raised voices. The study door opened and the young man stalked out with my husband hot on his heels. 'And don't let me ever see your face again,' my husband shouted after him. His face was almost purple with anger. I'd completely forgotten about it."

"And what did this young man look like?" I asked.

"Personable. Well turned out. Dark hair. A good-looking boy, in fact. I was a little surprised that Mr. Bradley had been so rude to him."

"Thank you." I beamed at her. I turned to go. She grabbed my arm.

"Miss Murphy — my husband is not an easy man. I would advise caution about approaching him with this. He may not wish to discuss it with a stranger."

"Of course not," I said. "If your suspicions are true, then I can find my confirmation somewhere else."

She was still holding onto the fabric of my coat. "Miss Murphy. You think this young man may have killed our daughter?"

"I think it's highly possible."

"And he may have been her half brother? But that's monstrous, absolutely monstrous."

"It is indeed," I said. "Of course I may still be wrong, but I'll know by the end of this day."

THIRTY

I left her and crossed back to the Upper West Side. I was rather tired by the time I came to Emily's neighborhood. Even for one like myself, used to tramping the wild west coast of Ireland, I had been doing an awful lot of walking recently, and most of it at a great pace. It occurred to me that Emily should probably be in a hospital, where she could be properly cared for, but it would take a doctor's recommendation to send her there. It also came to me that I should pay a quick visit to McPherson's to let Mr. McPherson know of Emily's current condition and to watch Ned's reaction. I knew this was a somewhat risky move, but Ned would be safely at work all day and by nightfall perhaps that jar of cream would have been analyzed and Ned Tate might find himself behind bars.

I have to admit it was with some trepidation that I pushed open the door of McPherson's and heard the bell jangle. It came to me, a little too late, that maybe Mr. McPherson might also be in on the whole scheme and that I might be walking into a trap. Before I could pursue these thoughts, Ned himself came around the counter, looking dapper and chirpy as always.

"Miss Murphy. My, we are seeing a lot of you recently, aren't we? What can I do for you today?"

"It's about Emily," I said, loudly enough for Mr. McPherson, in the back room, to look up. "I've just visited her. She's very sick. It's a lot more than a mere headache. I think she has contracted that awful flu. I wondered if Mr. McPherson could recommend a doctor around here."

"I'm sorry to hear that," Ned said. "If it's the flu, there isn't much anyone can do for her. Believe me, we've had people pestering us all spring, asking for something to cure the influenza, and of course we can't give them anything. Just liquids and keeping down the fever. We can make up a powder for that. Mr. McPherson has quite a good one, don't you, sir."

The druggist himself now came out through the swing door. "Emily's got the flu, you say?"

"I can't think what else it could be," I

369

went on, trying not to look too obviously at Ned. "She's running a high fever, she's vomiting, and can't keep any food or drink down, and her breathing sounds terrible."

"Sounds like she might have contracted pneumonia, too," Mr. McPherson said. "I could make up my preparation to bring down the fever and send young Ned round with it —"

I almost squeaked out the word "No!" but I bit my tongue.

"But, frankly, if she's not keeping anything down, it will only irritate the stomach even more," he finished.

"I really think a doctor should take a look at her," I said. "I believe she should be in a hospital where they can give her constant care."

"There's not much a doctor could do, except charge her a hefty bill," Ned said quickly. "Like Mr. McPherson says, it's only a question of fluids, sleep, and the body fighting it off. It's almost my lunchtime. Why don't I go and visit her? That would cheer her up."

"No!" This time I almost shouted it. "She wouldn't want you to see her looking the way she does," I added hastily. "Women have their pride, you know, and she looks terrible."

"Yes, my boy. You stay away," Mr. McPherson said. I wondered why he was being so considerate for once until he added, "I don't want you coming down with it. I've already lost two assistants."

"I'm going to be staying with her and nursing her," I said, "but I would like a doctor to see her, just to make sure I'm doing everything right. I'm happy to pay for the doctor myself if need be."

"You can call on Doctor Hoffman if you've a mind to," Mr. McPherson said. "His office is on the corner of Amsterdam and Seventy-fourth. He's a good man and won't charge an arm and a leg."

"Thank you, sir," I said.

"And now let us get back to our work," McPherson snapped, reverting to his usual unpleasant personality. Then he added as an afterthought, "Give our best to Miss Boswell."

"Yes, please do," Ned said. He gave me a syrupy smile.

I was glad to be outside in the fresh air again, safely away from Ned. What I had interpreted as charm before now seemed to have sinister undertones. I went straight to Dr. Hoffman's and was told that the doctor would not be able to make a house call until he had finished his afternoon consultations.

I left the address and went back to Emily's room. She was sleeping as I let myself in but she stirred as she heard me and regarded me with a hollow-eyed stare.

"Molly, you're back," she whispered.

"I am," I said. "Here, let me get you some more to drink."

I held the glass to her cracked lips for her to take some sips and then I sponged her face and neck with a cool washcloth. "I've a Doctor Hoffman coming to see you later," I said. "And I hope that by then Daniel will have had that cream analyzed."

"Doctor Hoffman," she repeated.

"And I have to leave you now for a little while," I said. "I need Ned's mother's address."

"Ned's mother?"

I nodded. "I have to pay a call on her."

She frowned. "I know it's Hicks Street in Brooklyn, but I'm not sure of the number. It's a white frame house, just down the block from a laundry. It looks rather run-down and she has the ground-floor flat at the back."

I tucked her in, made sure she had everything she needed, and then prepared to leave again. "If I were you, I wouldn't open the door to anyone until I come back," I said. "I should have enough time to get to

Brooklyn and back before the doctor arrives."

I didn't tell her that Ned had been awfully keen to come to visit her and luckily had not been allowed to do so. I'd make sure I was here when his workday was over.

It took what seemed like an eternity to ride the train all the way down the length of Manhattan and then the trolley across the bridge, but at last I was standing outside the dilapidated wooden house. I opened the front door and went down a long, dark passage to the door at the back. I tapped and a face peered out. "Yes?" she demanded in the darkness. "I don't know you. What do you want?"

"Are you Ned Tate's mother?"

"What if I am?"

"I'm a friend of his and I wanted to ask you a couple of questions," I said.

"All right, come in then." She gave me a half smile. "He was here on Sunday with his lady friend, you know. Always comes to visit me on Sundays, like clockwork. Such a good boy, he is. So faithful to his poor mother."

We had entered a dreadful, dingy apartment. It was dark, it smelled of drains and boiled cabbage, and it was furnished in the most threadbare manner. It was hard to picture the fastidious Ned growing up here. As my eyes accustomed themselves to the darkness I was able to study Ned's mother. She looked like an old, old woman. Her front teeth were missing, her face was sunken, her hair was gray, and yet she couldn't have been more than fifty at the most.

"Would you like a cup of coffee, honey?" she asked.

"No, thank you, I can't stay long," I said. "I came to see you because I need to set something straight. It's about Ned's father."

"What about him?"

As I looked around the room my eyes fastened on a photograph on the mantelpiece — a lovely young woman in a scanty costume. She was holding a tray of cigars and smiling coyly. And beside it a picture of a handsome, dark-eyed child, looking angelic in lace petticoats and holding a dove.

"Did you tell Ned who his father was?" I asked.

"Not in so many words," she said, then she winked. "Between us women, I was never rightly sure which one his father was, if you get my meaning."

"So you never told Ned that his father's name was Bradley?"

"Oh, that's what he's been telling you, has

he?" She gave me the coy look that I recognized from the photograph. "Well, I might have hinted. He was a strange child, you know. Born with big ideas. He kept pestering me to tell him about his father and the longer I kept quiet the grander his ideas became. Then one day I took him to Central Park for a treat and this open carriage passed us. What's more, the toff in the carriage was looking straight at us and I could tell that he recognized me. Well, I recognized him too, right enough. He'd been one of my customers and I'd sold him more than cigars, if you get my meaning. Well, like I said, my Ned always was a sharp little thing. He noticed that Mr. Bradley looking at us, so he got it into his head that that was his father. I didn't want to disillusion him. Could have been, of course." She gave me a knowing, toothless grin. "Has he been spouting off about his father, then? Always did like to talk big, my Ned. I said to him, you want to watch that. Pride comes before a fall."

"Did the Bradleys have a little girl in the carriage with them?"

"They did. A lovely little thing she was. Like a little angel. I think Ned was smitten with her too."

I pictured the little boy, watching that

passing carriage in Central Park and then coming back to this hellhole, and felt a momentary pang of sympathy for Ned Tate. Then of course I remembered Emily, who lay dying, and any scrap of sympathy vanished.

"Thank you, Mrs. Tate, you've been very helpful," I said. I reached into my purse to give her money, but her defiant, proud stare stopped me.

"Nothing to thank me for, honey," she said in her scratchy voice. "What did you want to know all this for?"

"For his sweetheart, Emily," I said, not wanting to hurt her with the truth. "She was curious about Ned's father and he would never speak of him."

"Oh, I see. Well, she would be, wouldn't she, if she's thinking of marrying him. I told him, boy, you could do a lot worse than this one. Got a good head on her shoulders, she has, and anyone can see she's a lady."

I thought of Ned, bringing Emily home as his sweetheart when he had already given her the preparation that was going to kill her. And I looked at this broken wreck of a woman who had obviously done everything she could to make sure her son was raised with an education and prospects. It would break her heart when she learned the truth.

Thirty-One

I fussed and fumed as my transportation crawled back to the Upper East Side, driven by my anger and a sense of urgency. Was there a cure for thallium poisoning? Would the doctor believe me and would he know how to treat her if he did? And would Daniel have received my message yet? I now realized we were dealing with a cold-blooded and ruthless killer who was even prepared to kill the girl he professed to love. I hoped that Emily's door had a strong lock on it and that we could hold out until Daniel got there. I ran all the way from the El station. I was gasping for breath by the time I had climbed all those flights of stairs. I went to tap on Emily's door and it swung silently open. The room was in complete darkness with the heavy drapes drawn. I could make out the figure of a man bending low over the bed.

"Oh, Doctor," I said breathlessly, "I'm

sorry, I wanted to be here when you arrived but —"

The man started at the sound of my voice and straightened up. Then I saw that it wasn't a strange doctor at all. It was Ned. In a flash I also saw the pillow he had been holding over Emily's face. I rushed at the bed, and the pillow fell to the floor. Emily gave a mighty gasp and started coughing.

"You — you animal!" I screamed at him. "You pretended to love her and you do this? You couldn't even wait for her to die slowly." I lifted Emily's head and gave her a sip of water. "You're going to be all right," I said. "Lie still."

"Molly, he — he," she started to say.

"I know. I know everything."

Ned had backed away from me and was now standing by the door. At first I thought he was going to make a run for it, but then I watched him turn the key in the lock and give me a triumphant smile. "You're right," he said. "I couldn't believe it when I found out that her best friend was my own half sister. How perfect a chance. But Emily was too smart for her own good. No good ever comes of educating women. She should have kept her nose out of my business. And so should you. Now you've sealed your own fate."

I actually laughed. "Don't be stupid," I said. "Emily might be lying sick in bed and easy to smother, but in case you hadn't noticed, I'm a strong, healthy woman. And what's more, a doctor is due here any second, and my young man, Captain Sullivan of the New York police, has been testing that face cream and will be here any moment as well."

"No problem," Ned said, reaching into his pocket. "It will only take me a moment to get rid of you." I was half expecting a gun, and I heaved a sigh of relief when I saw instead that he had brought out a small glass bottle. He opened it and a sweet, sickly smell filled the room. Suddenly I knew what that smell was. It was chloroform. As I watched, fascinated like a rabbit confronted by a snake, he reached into the other pocket and produced a gauze pad.

"And where do you think you'd go if you kill us?" I demanded. "They're going to find you soon enough. They already know you put the poison in the cream and that you killed Fanny Poindexter. You can't get away, you know."

"Yes, I can. I will." But there was a hint of desperation in his voice. "There are ships leaving New York every hour. With my knowledge and experience they'd take me on as a ship's doctor, no questions asked. And I'll spend a few years in the Orient, or even on the West Coast, then come back with a new name and a new look when the hue and cry has died down."

"You'd leave your mother to face the music?" I said, trying to appear calm and in control. "Hasn't she suffered enough for you?"

"I did this for her," he said angrily. "In revenge for what that brute made her go through. I went to my father. I thought he might see how well I'd turned out and recognize me as his son. But he chased me away. He told me if I ever came near him again he'd call the police. So I paid him back."

"Only he wasn't your father," I said.

"What do you mean?" His dark eyes flashed with anger. "Of course he was."

"I've just been to see your mother. She said you'd latched on to the idea of Mr. Bradley as your father and she hadn't had the heart to disillusion you."

"No," he said. "That's rubbish." But I heard the hesitancy in his voice.

"It's true. She never really knew who your father was. It could have been any of the men who paid her for the pleasure."

His face twisted into a snarling rage. "You

dirty vile little —"

He flung himself at me. I brought up my arm suddenly to defend myself and the bottle went flying. Drops of chloroform splashed over both of us. My head started singing as the vapors got to me. Ned was now trying to get his hands around my throat, but the vapors must have been affecting him too because he staggered. We went down together. He was now panting like a wild beast as he tried to pin me down. I fought him off with all my strength even as the world around me started fading to blackness. Then a figure loomed over us, there was a loud thump, a groan, and Ned slumped across me.

Emily stood there, breathing heavily, holding a cast-iron frying pan. "I didn't know whether I'd have the strength to do it," she said, gasping. Then she sank to her knees beside us.

At that moment there came a loud knocking at the door. I crawled across to open it. The doctor had arrived with Daniel, two police constables, and hospital workers hot on his heels.

"What the deuce?" the doctor demanded as Daniel pushed past him into the room.

"Are you all right?" he demanded.

I nodded as he helped me to my feet.

"That's the man you want," I said. "He admitted to killing Fanny Poindexter. He was trying to kill us too."

"And obviously was no match for you," Daniel said dryly, kicking at the prostrate form on the carpet.

"That was Emily. She hit him with the frying pan," I said.

The hospital workers were already lifting her up to the nearest chair. "We've come to take you to the hospital, miss," one of them said.

"Would somebody explain to me what is going on here?" the doctor asked.

An hour or so later Emily was safely in a hospital bed, being treated with Prussian blue and charcoal, which we were told were the only effective countermeasures against thallium. Since she had had the thallium in her system for three days now, her chances were not good, but at least she was getting the best care possible.

Daniel and I left her sleeping quietly. On the way home I insisted on stopping at Mr. Horace Lynch's house and telling him that Emily was in the hospital and might not survive. After that it was up to him to decide whether to visit her or not.

"Another case concluded," I said. We were

382

sitting side by side in the darkness of a hansom cab. For some reason I had just begun to feel shaky, as one often does after the danger is safely past, and I nestled close to Daniel, feeling the comforting warmth of his presence.

"The same for me," Daniel said. "Another case concluded, thanks, in part, to you."

"Me? What did I do?"

"You gave me the names of the missionary societies. We apprehended a certain Mr. Hatcher as he was about to sail for Shanghai. He was carrying trunks full of Bibles, but the trunks contained traces of the opium he had brought back in them. A nice little trade, don't you think? Under the umbrella of the missionary society, he was making himself rich supplying the Chinese opium dens of New York City."

"Mr. Hatcher," I said. "But I met him. I gave you his name."

"You did indeed." He slipped an arm around my shoulders. "And you know what else? Our Mr. Hatcher was quite aware who you were. He knew someone was asking questions around the missionary societies, and he discovered your connection to me and was convinced that I had sent you to spy on him. He decided to frighten you off."

"By trying to run me down with his carriage?"

"Precisely. Nasty piece of work, if you ask me."

"And he must also have broken into my house."

"He or one of his Chinese henchmen, if he had one who could read English."

I shuddered.

"Don't worry. He's now safely behind bars and the opium trade will have to find another way to smuggle in the goods."

"How about that," I said. "I never took to him from the start. Too annoyingly effusive and much too nosy."

"Well that was an eventful day," Daniel said as we entered the calm of my little house. "Another of your nine lives gone, I fear." He took off his hat and pulled out a chair at the kitchen table. "I wish you would stop living like this, Molly. I have enough worry in my life without wondering if you are going to find yourself in yet another dangerous situation every day. Being a detective is no job for a woman."

"Oh," I said frostily. "And who was it detected thallium poisoning when a doctor swore it was pneumonia? Who was it found the motive and cornered the murderer? And who helped you solve your two big cases?"

"I am not saying that your ability is any less than a man's," he said. "It is just that you are not built to take such risks and abuse. Any able man could overpower you."

"Maybe if women could wear sensible bloomers and not these ridiculous tight clothes I'd be able to hold my own," I retorted.

"You are not to go around wearing bloomers." He took my hand. "Molly, I want you to give up this life," he said. "I love you. I don't want to be weeping over your body."

"You'd do that? You'd weep over me?"

"Of course I would," he said. "I've loved you since I first set eyes on you on Ellis Island. Even though I thought you were married to another man, I still loved you. I don't want to lose you. In fact, I want you to marry me."

Then, to my intense astonishment, he got down on one knee. "Molly, this is not the time or the place that I had planned for this to happen, but seeing what we've just been through, it seems appropriate. Molly Murphy, will you marry me?"

Although I had seen it coming for ages, although we'd had what people called "an understanding" for a while, I was still speechless.

"You do love me, don't you?" he asked when I said nothing.

"Yes, yes I do. And I do want to marry you, but only . . ."

"Only what?" I felt the pressure on my hand tighten.

"Only if you'll let me be myself and not want to keep me shut up in a cage, stuck home all day like the good little wife."

He chuckled. "I think it would take some pretty stout chains and bars to keep you anywhere you didn't want to be."

I looked up as there was a sharp knock at my front door. I broke away to answer it. Sid and Gus stood there. "We're off to a planning meeting for the next suffragist rally," Sid said. "We wondered if you wanted to come with us. We're planning a march on the state capitol in Albany and we're going to chain ourselves to the railings until the state legislature gives us the right to vote."

"Sid has written a ripping piece and she's sending it to the *Times* and the *Herald,*" Gus said. "She wants to show it to you. And I've designed us a banner. You have to see it. Sid thinks it's most eye-catching." She broke off and eyed me. "What's the matter, is something wrong?"

"I'm sorry." I started to laugh. "But Daniel was just in the middle of proposing to me."

"And have you answered him yet?" Sid demanded.

I looked back at Daniel, who was regarding me with interest.

"Not yet," I said.

"Well, for God's sake get back in there and do it," Sid commanded.

I turned back to Daniel. "Daniel, I accept," I said.

"About time," Gus turned to nod to Sid. "We couldn't take much more of the tension, could we, Gus? So I suppose we can't count on your support anymore for our rallies, and you won't be coming along tonight?"

"Not tonight." I looked back at my kitchen. "Tonight I think we need to be alone, although I don't see why you think you can't count on me in future."

I thought I heard a heavy sigh from the kitchen.

POSTSCRIPT

Emily did recover, although she has residual numbness and tingling in her feet and hands that may last for years. But, as she said, she is luckier than her friends to have survived at all. And Horace Lynch did visit her in the hospital. Who knows what might come of that?

Ned Tate is in jail awaiting trial for the murder of four women. It seemed that he killed the counter assistant, Mrs. Hartmann, merely to try out his preparation on her and to see how much thallium was needed. A cold and heartless young man indeed.

As for me, I had better start getting used to the idea of being Mrs. Daniel Sullivan. I think I might even like it.

ABOUT THE AUTHOR

Rhys Bowen's novels have received a remarkable number of awards, including the Anthony, Agatha, and Macavity Awards as well as the Bruce Alexander Historical Award and the Herodotus Award. She is also the author of the Royal Spyness series and the Edgar Award–nominated Constable Evan Evans mysteries. Born in England, she now lives in San Rafael, California, with her husband. Visit her online at www.Rhys Bowen.com.